A PRAYER FOR DAWN

A PRAYER FOR DAWN

NATHAN SINGER

Published by Bleak House Books, an imprint of Diversity Incorporated
P.O. Box 8573
Madison, WI 53708
www.bleakhousebooks.com

ISBN 1-932557-04-0
Library of Congress Control Number: 2004100859

Jacket design: Peter Streicher www.shushudesign.com
Cover photograph: Roxy Erickson www.roxyerickson.com
Author photograph: Kurt Brueggmann
Book design: Kristyn Kalnes and Jennifer Green

Printed in the United States of America by McNaughton & Gunn.

For everyone who is lost in the storm.

SECTION ONE

THIS IS TRULY A GLORIOUS AGE. EVERY JOY,
EVERY SORROW, EVERY WONDER, EVERY TERROR,
EVERY DESIRE IS A MERE CLICK AWAY.

So click away. Or click it away.

IT WAS EARLY TUESDAY morning when Alain Childress painted the walls with his own blood. Wincing as he popped another wrist vein, Alain reached to fill a fresh pan. *Slop it on. Don't be stingy. Drip drip drip right over the doorway.* His efficiency reeked of salt and cigarettes and gunpowder. Outside his window, red and blue rollers spun wildly as sirens whined.

"You fuggin' pigs," he muttered. "You murdered me."

Alain loaded his .45 and pointed it at the door. Then he waited. Waited for them to charge in. To barge in. Larger than life. Cowboys in blue.

"Fuggin' pigs. I was sick. I needed help. And you murdered me! Come on through that door. You built the monster now face the monster. I'm a walking living fucking BIOHAZARD!"

Twelve blocks away, little Dawn, eight years old, slept quietly in her bed. Oblivious to it all.

click

OKAY, HI. This is Dawn here. Um, okay, let's see. I'm supposed to tell you about myself. I guess. Okay, if you didn't already know, I'm eight and a half—almost nine, I'm white, um, I'm in the third grade, and I really like soccer. And MTV, but not M2 because M2 plays all those loud videos with the ugly boys in them and it doesn't have TRL. Oh, and my favorite food is cottage cheese. I'm not really sure what my last name is because I'm…because my parents are divorced and my mom doesn't like it when I use Daddy's name but I do anyway on papers at school because the principal told me I have to. I live with Mommy most of the time, but I stay with Daddy every other weekend and over the summer for a month. Mommy has a house and I have my own room here. That's where I am right now (twelve blocks away from that sick Childress guy with the paintbrush. People think I'm blivyus to everything, but I'm not. I hear stuff. You'll see what I mean). At Daddy's apartment I sleep on the couch, but that's okay. I like having my own room at Mommy's, but sometimes our electricity gets cut off. And sometimes the phone too. That's usually during the time when Mommy doesn't have a boyfriend. You can bet your life, if we lose power, Mommy will have a new boyfriend by the end of the day and we'll have power again.

Daddy's never had a girlfriend as far as I can tell. Daddy's an artist. He draws comic books and he paints. And that's pretty much all he does. And he sometimes works at BP. I like staying with Daddy because we do a lot of cool stuff together like go to the park and rent movies. We eat a ton of mac n' cheese. That's cool.

I love my mom, but her boyfriends are usually a bunch of loads. Some of them are okay, I guess. Here's a list of things I like and things that I think suck royal.

I LIKE
1. Soccer.
2. Cottage cheese.
3. Horses. And kittens.
4. Boys with freckles. (except Chris Herbert at school. Yuck.)
5. Carson Daly.

SUCK ROYAL
1. Chris Herbert.
2. Losing power.
3. Math. And History.
4. Cole slaw.
5. Having to listen to the noises coming out of Mommy's bedroom.

This is a list of things I don't give a rip about.

I DON'T GIVE A RIP ABOUT
1. Mommy's boyfriends.
2. Parsley.
3. That "o" at the beginning of opossum.

4. Social Services.
5. Chris Herbert.

Mommy has one main boyfriend who comes and goes. His name is Flemming Brackage. Isn't that the most wackest name you ever heard? Practically everybody in the universe calls him Brackster or The Brackster. Mommy calls him Brack. I call him Phlegm. I know it's a cheap shot, but can you blame me?

The one time Social Services made me not allowed to see Daddy for a while was when Mommy and Phlegm first got together. I guess Phlegm and Daddy knew each other before. Phlegm is an agent of some sort and he was gonna manage or represent Daddy but it didn't work out (Phlegm thinks he represents Daddy to me, but he doesn't). They must have had a fight and Daddy did a painting or a cartoon of Phlegm and Phlegm got really mad because it got published. I never saw the picture but I've heard it's pretty disgusting. Or funny. Depends on who you ask. I'm not allowed to see any of Daddy's work. Daddy says when I'm grown up he'll show them to me and we'll talk about it but not now because I'm too young. Whatever. Daddy said he was sorry to Phlegm, but Phlegm called him a Chickenhawk and Mommy said Daddy was a Freak. I didn't cry, but I almost did and then I did a little. But then I stopped. And I didn't cry anymore except just a little bit.

I like to make this face:
00
)

Because it's not happy and it's not sad. That's how I feel a lot of times.

The reason Phlegm is the worst boyfriend in my life is because he's never gone for good.

I overheard Mommy tell one of her girl friends that he, ugh, that he "sets her" you-know-what "on fire." Her "special area." I guess she didn't mean that he REALLY does, but that she likes what he does to it. Ugh. Any night he's over I know I can look forward to, "Oh yes! Brack! Put it in! Put it inside me! Ohh right there it's so good!" Blah blah blah. Makes me wanna barf all over myself. Then the other night she was screaming like "Oh Brack! I want it in my—" you know. She wanted it, up her, you know, in her bottom. Ugh!!!

I wanna go live with Daddy. He never has anyone sleep over. He's an artist. Sometimes he works at BP.

click

CAROLINE POWELL shuddered as images of Guatemalan cocoa fields bullied through her mind. Little, golden-skinned children forced into slave labor. Peasant fieldhands maimed and disfigured. Terminated. Exterminated. U.S. corporate jackals slobbering over blood-soaked profits oceans away from plantation hell. Wracked with guilt, she went ahead and ordered her double shot espresso mocha latte to go. She'd make it right later. Salve her conscience with a fat donation...tax-deductible, but, of course, that's immaterial.

"Always live better than your clients," said Benjamin Sonnenberg—the most brilliant publicist to ever grace this continent or any other. "Always live better than your clients." *No problem, Benji,* Caroline thought bitterly as she drove her rented 2000 Dodge Intrepid from the airport parking lot, sipping joylessly at her latte and not-really listening to *All Things Considered* on NPR. "Always live better than your clients." Caroline's best client was currently serving one-to-three for domestic violence at the medium-security penitentiary in Chillicothe, Ohio. *Just keep lowering the bar, Caroline.*

Pulling into the pen's gated parking lot, she chucked her empty cup and most of her dignity into the back seat, and grabbed her note file, her planner, all pertinent documents. This was her only meeting today, but damn it, she was still a professional.

Since Caroline's expulsion from Geffen paradise, renegade writer/publisher/agent/spouse-abuser Joey Spitfire had been her cash cow, sad as that may be. Joey sold. Sold like hell. Even behind bars, he moved product. He *was* product. That helped.

> *J. Spitfire (real name ?) born 1968 Vermont*
> *1). In 1990, along with three buddies, Joey started a little punk and*
> *rockabilly 'zine called Psychobilly Freakout! It caught a following fairly*
> *quickly, and Joey's editorial column "The Spitfire Grill" began to devel-*
> *op a cult all its own. Disgruntled young white males, for the most part.*
> *Gradually, as underground music news became less of a Freakout! focus,*
> *Joey's politically incorrect rants began to dominate the magazine. And*
> *cause quite the commotion. Liberal panties twisted across the continen-*
> *tal U.S. and, eventually, most of Western Europe [that's a good line. Use*
> *that somewhere]. Today Psychobilly Freakout! is one of the most popular*
> *(and notorious) alternative rags on the market. Damn good press (but*
> *watch your back and your purse).*

PR for Joey Spitfire. Like taking the day off, Caroline thought as she flipped through her notes and looked around the prison wait-ing room. *It's anti-PR.* These days Caroline's clients didn't really R to the P. What an angle. *Circus barker. Side show. Doing my job doing my job doing my job. I'm slumming. Sluuuuummmmming.*

Visiting an inmate is a bit like being a prisoner yourself. Shut-up-get-in-line-take-a-number-sit-down-shut-up-waitwaitwait-waitwait. Wait in the waiting room with no room to wait. And *this* lot here…Caroline hated to judge or feel superior, but come on now! Nothing but teenage white trash bimbos and their babies. Ba-bies wandering around in nothing but soggy diapers. Screaming. Caterwauling. Sucking on bottles with RC Cola in them. Babies. Little coffee-colored babies (not that that matters, of course).

After four thousand years, a bored, crackly, disembodied voice finally called Caroline's number.

"How are they treating you in here, Joey?"

Caroline kinda-sorta-maybe-but-not-really had a *thing* for Joey Spitfire. He was nothing an educated, professional, 37-year-old woman should want. But that's how it goes sometimes. She *liked* him. His pouty lips. His pointy mutton-chops. His pompous pompadour. His ridiculously dated '50s rock 'n roll swagger. She dug it all. Sometimes she'd study that ever-present bulge in his pants, and then...*oh, can't think about that.* After meeting with Joey, she always resolved to make it okay by touching her husband that night. But she never did. Some guilt is livewithable.

"Like a fucking prince, Caroline," said Joey, in a jittery *faux*-Memphis drawl. "That's how I'm living. Hell yeah. And you? You're lookin' awful fetching today. If it wasn't for this goddamn Plexiglas...just kidding. I know you're happily married. Me too, can'tcha tell? Hey, congratulate me! I've been officially baptized! Read all about it in this week's column."

> *J. Spitfire*
> *2). It is a crime to conduct a business or profession from within a correctional institution. Due to states aping "The Mumia Rule" started in Pennsylvania, "conducting the business or profession of journalism" usually carries a pretty stiff penalty if the perp is caught (which he always is). Joey had worked out a deal with a guard—Burt Kridell [get the guard's home address] so that his columns could be smuggled out every week in exchange for certain favors (a clean smack connection—use info if Joey is threatened). All was cruising smoothly until Joey's PF! co-publishers, Sponge, Bishop, and Dogjaw (see "magazine" file), were banned from the visitor's list for trying to pass through to Joey an angel food cake with a file in it. (These three are not as dumb as they seem. Get everything in writing).*

"Okay, here's the deal, Joey," Caroline said, pulling her contract. "I am now the only person on your visit list, besides your wife...who will probably not be stopping by. My fee for collecting your weekly 'Grill' is an additional ten percent on top of my standard flat. Your cut of the net profit from the magazine will be funneled into some account of which I have no knowledge. You'll have to discuss that with those sub-mongoloid partners of yours, although I don't know how you could go about doing that."

Caroline instantly felt guilty for saying "sub-mongoloid," unsure as to whether it was a racial slur or not. Perhaps there is a Mongoloid Anti-Defamation League Of The United States somewhere (M.A.D.L.O.T.U.S. Mad lotus?). She'd have to check on that. Maybe cut them a donation check.

"Yer killing me, Caroline." Joey sang. "But I just can't say 'no' to a gal so fine."

Caroline rolled her eyes.

"And you sure look cute in your little orange jump suit, Joey."

Cute is not a good look in Chillicothe.

click

"911. WHAT IS YOUR EMERGENCY?"

"Hello? Oh please! You've got to send someone over immediately! My neighbor down the hall is screaming about pigs! And he's firing his gun! And screaming about murdering pigs! Please you've got to send—"

duuuuuuuuuuuuuuuuuuuuuuuuuuuuuuuurrrrrrrrrrrrrrrrrrrrrrrrrrrr rrrrrrrrrrrrrrrrrrrr...........................

"Hello? Ma'am? Are you there?"

click

THE SPITFIRE GRILL

by Joey Spitfire

Howdy, kids! Well, in case you've been lying unconscious in a pool of your own piss and vomit for the past four months, you'd know that my darling wife, famed low-rent porn starlet Clover Honey (star of such cinematic gems as Bit O' Honey, Nut On Honey, and the sequel Honey Deux), has pressed DV on me and I'm paying my debt in Chilly Cothy. Yes, the same woman who has stabbed me with a serrated steak knife on twenty-seven non-consecutive occasions had da noive to call the po-po on yours truly for slapping her and pushing her against a wall. That's women for ya. And the judge took her side! That's the law for ya. So here I am surrounded by inked-up spics, niggaboos of all shapes and sizes, and motherfuckers who didn't know they were fags until they saw me in the shower. Who says my life ain't full?

Which brings me to the porpoise of this week's column. I've been prison baptized, gentle reader! Joey Spitfire is officially a block wench. Always said I was punk rock. Never thought I'd be a "punk."

See, I had this cell mate named Ping-Ja-King-Wu-Fung-Boing-Doing-some shit. Big fat-ass chink, yeah? Well, he'd been threatening me for weeks with this 'n that and so I said, "Look, Slanty, get any ideas and I'll choke ya with yer chode, if that little yellow nub could even gag you, bitch!" Well, tear my rectum and call me Charlotte if he didn't give the ole college try. Held my arm behind my back, slammed my precious face into the wall, drooped me knickers and had a go. Oi! Took me right back to Catholic summer camp. And all that stuff about Oriental guys having tiny tackles? Bullshit. Sumbitch full-on punctured my lungs. I got even, though. Sort of. Cacked him in his slit-eye with a razor blade. Screamed just like a baby, by gum.

So why am I telling you all this? Hmmmm. Cuz it's funny. Right? Right? Men getting raped is funny. Folks joke about it all the time. It's funny. Woman gets raped and it's a grand tragedy. Fella gets raped and it's knee-slappin' fun for the whole family. Hey, I'm here to entertain you people. I've been cramping and can't eat OOOH THAT'S TOO RICH! I've got cold sweats and night terrors TEEHEETEEHEE! I've been puking for four days HAHAHAHA! I can't sit down without open-

ing the stitches in my— WOOHOOHAAH! Can't stop
hemorrhaging out of my asshole HAHAHA!!! STOPIT!!!
YOU'RE FUCKIN' KILLING ME!!!!!!!!!!!!

gabba gabba hey,

JS

"Screw you, Joey-boy," Caroline said aloud to the written text.
"*Innocent* women get raped all the time. Only men who get raped
are scumbag convicts." Not very bleeding heart, but who was listening to her anyway.

She opened a letter that Joey had included with the hardcopy.
It read:

> *Caroline,*
>
> *I know things have been hard for you since your Cali
> connection went ass-up. When I heard you were doing
> PR for that German Hip-Hop label, I thought to myself,
> "Now there's a brilliant player being forced from the
> game too early." I mean to say, as Kraut Rap goes, Glok
> 'N Spiel featuring DJ Uberdope is not the worst there is,
> but hardly worthy a PR agent of your calibre. Which is
> why I have a prop for you. I've been in contact with a
> lot of underground talent in my years with Psychobilly
> Freakout!, and what I've realized is that the only thing
> separating these artists from the big candynosed Hollow-
> wood whores is decent management and exposure. I
> think I can handle the former, if you'll just serve as my
> pub agent. We'll be partners. Equal percentage. To test
> me out, I would like for you to get in contact with a
> cartoonist/painter named Jeff Mican—the single most
> bad-ass young talent out there. Scout's Honor. See for
> yourself on page 24 of PF! Issue #17. His work's a little
> loud, and may offend your delicate libber sensibilities.
> You might not be able to handle it, and if not, I'll take
> him elsewhere. I'm telling you tho' baby, he's gonna make
> somebody really rich someday. Might as well be us. Check*

it out. Think about it. Ask your husband's opinion and
be subservient to his wishes.
Spilling over with lust,

JS
Inmate # 250624

Caroline crumpled up the letter and went off to take a long, herbal bath. To spite her husband, she masturbated quickly, fantasizing about no one at all, and came so lightly that her orgasm barely registered.

After a mud mask, dermal scrub, and a self-pedicure, she went to her file cabinet and pulled out *PF!* # 17. The front cover screamed, "It's a PSYCHOBILLY FREAKOUT, that's what it is!" and featured two large-breasted, barefoot, teeny moppets licking lollipops in the back of an El Camino.

The cover contents read:

"EL CAMINOS—
DO THEY PISS YOU OFF OR
ARE THEY WICKED COOL?"

"OUR ONGOING COURT BATTLE
WITH THE REVEREND HORTON HEAT—
AND A REVIEW OF HIS LATEST DISC!"

"CRANK—IS IT THE NEW HEROIN?"

"WIN A DATE WITH LULA AND PEGGY
SUE, THIS WEEK'S COVER DEBS!!!"

"JOEY SPITFIRE TAKES ON
THE JEW-RUN MEDIA."

Caroline sighed in pained disgust and flipped gloomily to page 24. Jeff Mican. *Who? Whothefuckever.*

But there on page 24...*oh my God!* Caroline fell pale and very ill. On page 24, a crude, almost childlike charcoal one-panel glared malevolently back at her. A bit of visual molestation that she would have blissfully skipped had she not been looking for it. But seeing this now...this...artwork, this drawing...this horror...this abomination...this crime against humanity rendered in Xerox gray, Caroline dropped to the floor, doubled over on her knees, and dry-heaved into her bedroom carpet. Retching. Crying. Holding her head trying to shake away that image. *How could such a simple...all the blood....it's just a cartoon...just a ohh...*

"Caroline? Sweetheart?" called her husband Chet from the downstairs rumpus room. "Caroline? Are you okay, dear?"

"I, th-think," Caroline gasped, still clutching her convulsing stomach, "I think we got a...a goldmine."

Caroline looked up Jeff Mican's website. It was blank white with black 12-point type in Times New Roman:

JEFF MICAN'S HOMEPAGE
this site is still under construction
last updated 03/06/1998

And that was it. *Christ almighty.*

After waiting on the phone for 25 minutes while *PF!* Deputy Managing Editor "Banana Sponge" McTill rummaged through his office for Jeff Mican's phone number, Caroline dialed up the creator of page 24's sick-inducing masterpiece. He answered on the first half-ring.

"Hullo?"

It was a flat, congested sort of voice. Not necessarily one that a person would equate with a criminal pervert...but who knows.

"Jeff Mican? This is Caroline Powell."

"Oh hi, Caroline! I received a letter from Chillicothe Correctional that said you were going to contact me. Thank you for calling! Wow. So you're a publicist, huh?"

"That's right, Jeff. I saw your work in *Freakout!* #17. That's some, uh, powerful stuff."

"Ha ha. Well, gee, thanks. Yeah, you should have seen the hate mail I got from that one. A few people said they actually threw up when they saw it. I'm not quite sure how to take that, ha ha ha."

"Well, they must've been real wimps, Jeff. Your work...although definitely much more *extreme*...in a way kind of reminds me of H.R. Giger."

"Who?"

"I think you've got a lot of talent. A lot of talent. And, with the right exposure, you could really go places."

"Awesome!"

"Yes. So I understand that Joey Spitfire is your *agent*?"

"Well, yeah, I guess. I mean, he is in prison and all that. I'm not really sure what an agent does, to tell you the truth. Come to think of it, I'm not sure what a publicist does either. No offense."

"My job, Jeff, is to let the world know you exist. I say, 'Hey, turkeys! Look over here! You're missing out on something great over here!' That's what I do."

"Awesome!"

"Yes it is, Jeff. It is awesome. Okay. First thing's first. Your website."

"I have a website?"

"Worst goddamn thing I've ever seen. I've got a guy building you a new one right now. We're going to need to put some of your artwork on there. Send him something striking, but not too offensive, you know?"

"Well, I don't think *any* of my work—"

"Okay, second. We need to get you some exhibits where you live. It's good to build up local support, even if it's just in cult circles. This 513 area code...that's not what I *think* it—"

"It's Cincinnati."

"Oh God no!"

"Yeah, well, I used to live in Pinellas County in Florida, but I caught a bit of static out there. Folks are real hung-up on community values in those parts and I was, well, not well liked. In fact, they tried to make me a suspect when those kids got killed at the University of Florida. I wanna say…1990? Just 'cause of my drawings. Assistant State Attorney Baggish really was after my behind. So I moved. I've only been here a short while and don't know a whole lot about the place, but I think things will go much more smoothly now that I'm in Cincinnati, don't you, Caroline? Caroline? Hullo?"

click

HARLAN DANIELS was into body art, dig? But he didn't dig pain, can you dig that? Pain hurts. He bought Novocaine wholesale. In bulk. Tattoos, piercings, brandings, you name it, Harlan had it. Loved 'em. Put 'em on other folks. But before too long, whip scars became his bag. Whip scars, ya dig?

Harlan was squatting in San Fran with these two tagger runaways when somebody from a bookstore in Haight got him hip to this collection of photos from the antebellum South. There was one picture that just went, "Bam!" right? It was of the back flesh of this old black slave. Owner beat him real hardcore and his skin was whipped and ripped to ribbons. It was real sad and all, but it was far out too. That afternoon Harlan scored a bullwhip and an assload of painkillers. Some for himself, and some for, well… the kids. Gotta look out for the kids.

Harlan dealt, but he didn't push, right? He wasn't a capitalist. He was Robin Hood. Fed the hungry as it were. Get ya anything you need, clean and uncut, and he would charge you what he paid for it. He might even offer you a reduced rate on a whip scar if he was feeling it. Yeah, man. For junkies across the nation, Harlan was the Smack Messiah. He even tried to wean crackheads off the rock by feeding them pure Peruvian. And when he wasn't sliding a phat deal to poor addicts, he was scamming his rich clients left and right, up and down, breakfast, lunch, and dinner. I know, cuz he dealt coke to my dad, and my dad is one rich cocksucker…figuratively speaking. Who am I? Well, I actually do...never mind who I am. Fuck off. Uh, okay...there's already been a "Deep Throat?" Well, you can just call me "Gag Reflex." Anyway. Yeah. Real top-floor cat all around, that Harlan. Damn shame what happened to him in Chillicothe.

click

THE SPITFIRE GRILL

by Joey Spitfire

Howdy, kids! I'm feeling a little rundown right now, on account of I had to fight three guys at once in the laundry room earlier this morning. Let's just say it was a tie and leave it at that.

Number forty-seven said to number three:/ 'You're the cutest jailbird I ever did see/ I sure would be delighted with your company,/ come on and do the Jail House rock with me.'—I never fully appreciated the meaning of that song until recently...

Well anyhoo, what should I rant *aboot* today, then? How about this: A lot of sensitive bleeding-hearts are all up in arms about putting retards who are convicted of murder to death. Hello? Did I miss something? Obviously, I don't have a problem with executing these drooling tools. Most of the fucks who are pulling the switch are goddamn morons as well. Idiots murdering idiots, and thus leaving more swimming room in the gene pool for the rest of us. Perfectly Darwinian I'd say, dear chap.

Speaking of retards, you ever meet somebody who seemed like they had Downs Syndrome, but it turns out they didn't and they were just fucked-up looking? Isn't that weird? Don't you feel misled?

This is my favorite Death Row story right now—it goes like this: There was this old-ass guy, like 60 or so, waiting to be electrocuted in Cincinnati, Ohio [where my kick-ass artist client Jeff Mican lives and he has a show coming up in September at the Contemporary Arts Center in presentable downtown Cincinnati—there's your plug for the day, Jeff!]. He'd been clogging up the courts for decades trying to scam out on death. Finally the old coot runs out of appeals, and the time is nigh. For his last meal, he drank three full pots of coffee, and ate seven, count 'em 7, three-ways from Skyline Chili*. Sweet Jesus and baby Jesus, when they sent them 30,000 volts through that old bastard he went off like a biological weapon! It took three weeks to get the chamber fully scrubbed out, and from what I've heard, you can still smell it all down the mile. One guard was actually killed in the blast and another died trying to mop up electrified body fluid. That old feller is my hero of all time! May he rot in pieces. Many little teeny pieces.

Here's another bit of chicken soup for the scumbag's soul; Seems there's this broad serial killer in California. What she does is she answers personal ads of dudes who are into that erotic-asphyxiation crap. She hooks up with them, does them, then she does them in, and then she jets. She was finally caught, and managed to argue down from 1st degree murder to manslaughter, claiming that they were getting it on, and it got out of control, and he accidentally choked himself to death while he was choking the proverbial poultry. Now get this; she then argued them down to a FINE! Seems she convinced the court that, although yeah, she did have sex with the deceased, he was already dead when she met him. Necrophilia, being a misdemeanor in California, ain't no jailable offense—as well it shouldn't be. Congratulations, Ms. Necro-nympho! Way to buck the system, sista.

Well, that's all for now. Be sure to club a baby harp seal sometime today. It's your duty.

Three cheers for Captain Spaulding,
JS

p.s. A lot of you pathetic, dateless losers have been writing me whining that I don't talk enough anymore about Clover and her astounding career in professional pornography. Obviously you all know more about it than I do at this point, but I'll do my best. Being as it is Sunday (as I write this), it's no doubt a pretty light load for Ms. Honey today. She probably took a maximum of three huge, black cocks and was napping by noon. All I can say to that is; what a coinky-dink.

p.p.s. For those of you cheapskate thieving bastards who read the online edition, don't bother sending me e-mails. I won't be able to read them. I'M IN PRISON! Okay. That's all. Have a good one. Gabba gabba hey.

p.p.p.s I built this prison. I built this prison on rock n'roll...

*Spaghetti, cheese, Cincinnati chili—ground beef, tomato paste, cinnamon. Truly rancid.

click

"HEY, CAROLINE!"

"How are you doing, Jeff? Excited about your show? Cincinnati CAC. Damn, I'm good. All due props to Joey Spitfire as well."

As Caroline entered Jeff Mican's squalid apartment, it really hit home for her how artists suffer in American society. There is just no value put on creative expression in a market-driven economy. There is no *culture* in a pop-culture culture. She vowed to write a check to the Enjoy the Arts Foundation as soon as this meeting was completed.

"Oh, sure, I'm excited. It's been a while since I've had a showing. And I've never had one in the Midwest, so yeah, it's new."

"Jeff, did you, by any chance, vote in the last local election?"

"Nope."

"Does the name 'Sheriff Lester Simmons' mean anything to you at all?"

"Nope. Why do you ask?"

"Okay, then. Let's get started. You have your samples?"

Jeff showed Caroline the pieces he had planned to exhibit, and a few alternates. *Okay lessee ...botched back-alley abortions...a sobbing Indian girl stuffing sand in her vagina...oh, here's a nice one, "Raped With a Crowbar," wonderful...*As Caroline paged through the portfolio, Jeff busied himself in the kitchenette preparing tea and fixing dinner for his daughter. *Hmmm ...Three Kings molesting baby Jesus, Oh, come on!..."Virgin Mary Whore of Jerusalem," oh, I guess this is a series...*Caroline didn't know what to think. How could this guy, this simple, sweet, kinda cute, kinda goofy, average guy...how could he? Where did it come from?

"Dawn, sweetheart!" Jeff called, "It's time for dinner!"

From out of the bedroom came the most adorable little elf Caroline had ever seen. Curly amber locks, emerald eyes, Caroline's heart melted on sight.

"Hon, say 'hullo' to Miss Caroline."

Dawn extended her hand to Caroline. They shook fingertips.

"Hello, Miss Caroline."

"Hello, Dawn. It's nice to meet you."

Dawn blushed and took her macaroni and cheese back into the bedroom with her. She came back out for a glass of milk and a bowl of cottage cheese, then retired once again.

"Girl sure loves her dairy," Jeff said to no one in particular. Caroline nodded, smiling. Before too long, Dawn returned to the living room to join them for dessert. Hydrox cookies. The three talked for hours, careful to avoid the topic of Jeff's divorce and Caroline's dismissal from Geffen Records (due to "The Nirvana

Incident," legend has it). Caroline looked briefly through some of Jeff's old sketches.

"Daddy, can I see the sketchbook?"

"Sweetie, you know the rules about the pictures. When you're older we'll look at them together, okay? Nice try, though, sneaky-girl."

"I think your daddy's right about that rule, Dawn."

Dawn took to Caroline immediately. Much to her surprise. Children often found Caroline standoffish. But she braided Dawn's hair, and she let Dawn paint her toenails sparkly aqua, and it was sort of like a little party. Finally, when it was well past Dawn's bedtime, she was shuffled off to sleep in Jeff's room. She kissed them both goodnight.

"She's really something, Jeff. Bright. Beautiful. You must be so proud of her."

Jeff beamed his response. Caroline smiled contentedly. This was the first *quality* client meeting she'd had since back in *the days*. And it was the first quality evening she had spent with other honest-to-goodness *human beings* since as long as she could remember.

Then all of the sudden, Caroline was overcome with a terrible feeling. She grabbed Jeff's sketchbook and flipped quickly through the drawings. *Something about the girl…Something about that girl… There it is!…Oh dear god…ohhh dear god…*In a piece titled "Suffer The Children," a large, muscular male figure with massive genitals and no head was portrayed viciously penetrating a crying little girl. The child, in no uncertain terms, was Jeff's daughter. Dawn. Caroline's stomach filled with a violent sickness, the same as when first she saw Jeff's work in *Psychobilly Freakout!* issue #17 on page 24, *but so much worse. So so much worse.*

"Jeff!" She choked, "Oh dear God, what the hell is the matter with you!!!"

Jeff looked at Caroline blankly, having absolutely no idea what was wrong. Caroline ripped out the offending picture and shoved it in his face accusingly. He shrugged, still thoroughly baffled.

"Suffer The Children," he said meekly.

"That's your *daughter!*" Caroline spat, her eyes burning with tears. "You horrible fuck! That's your daughter!"

"Caroline," Jeff whispered, humiliated and confused, "Please keep your voice down. My daughter is trying to sleep."

"She should be taken away from you!" Caroline cried. "I had my doubts about you, Jeff. God, I'm such a fucking idiot. Why should I risk what's left of my pathetic career hyping you to the fucking press? Fucking *chickenhawk*. I did my research, you know. After that 'incident' in Florida, Child Services did take her away for a while. Why, huh? Can you tell me?"

Jeff lowered his head. What Caroline was implying was more than he could handle.

"You th...you think I would hurt my child. Oh my. Caroline...that thing at the University of Florida happened three years before Dawn was born. You need to double-check your sources. The reason...the reason Child Ser—Do you know a guy, an agent, by the name of Flemming Brackage?"

"Heard of 'im. So what?"

"Well, he was set to be *my* agent. He was, actually, for about a week. Then he started having sex with my wife. Still does to this day, on and off. We had a row, and I drew this three-panel of him in a dress sucking off a man with no arms. In a public restroom. The armless man was a caricature of Florida Assistant State Attorney Stuart Baggish. It was published in an indie rag called *Metal Thrashing Madd* that doesn't even exist anymore. It didn't hurt his career one bit—either one of their's—but Flemming tried to take me to court, and he convinced Child Services that I was doing something wrong because I've used Dawn as a model since she was a baby. Boy, he's a real jerk, I'll tell you what. But I've never touched my little girl, and I never, ever, ever, EVER would. I use her as a model because I need a model sometimes, and I feel safer using her than someone else's baby. It's as simple as that."

"It's just...I think it's obscene, Jeff. That's what I think."

"You know what I think is obscene, Caroline? That right now, what's happening for pretend in my drawing is happening for real somewhere. That's obscene."

"You can't yell 'fire' in a crowded theater, Jeff."

"But the theater is on fire, Caroline."

click

HI, EVERYONE. It's Dawn again. Well, the writer wants me to talk a little about—huh? The WRITER. Yeah. The omni-*something*. The omni-Max. Anyway. The writer wants me to talk a little about Daddy's life as an artist.

Okay, so not to say bad things, because I know Daddy has a lot of talent because people are always saying he does, but he's sure not raking in the big bucks. Daddy does have an agent, but the guy is in prison right now for beating up his wife. Sometimes these three really stupid, smelly guys stop by the apartment to give Daddy a check. Royalties they're called I think. The guys all have funny names like "Banana Sponge" and "Dogmouth" or something like that. Daddy tells me that his getting royalties for reprints of a magazine is "unprecedented." I guess that's good. That's why "Dogface" or whoever brings him a check. That pretty much says all you need to know about Daddy's career.

He has some other kind of agent too. I'm not sure what she does, but I think her job is to call newspapers and tell them what Daddy is up to. Seems like a pretty gosh darn easy job to me. I could do that. I like that lady, though. Miss Caroline is her name. She's really, really pretty. And nice too. She let me paint her toenails with blue sparkles. But I hope she doesn't become Daddy's girlfriend. I like being able to sleep sometimes, for Pete's sake.

I thought of something good about when Mommy is hooked up with Phlegm. Phlegm (who is still married to his wife, I thought I should mention) has a son named Dalton. Dalton is really kind to me and I like him a lot for a friend. He's got freckles, which I like, but he's chubby. Also, he's an eff-aye-double gee-oh-tee. At least that's what he says. He taught me my new favorite word, although I'm not supposed to say it around anybody but him. The word is—cocksucker. Doesn't that sound great? Say it with me. COCK-SUCKER. Dalton says all the best people are truly cocksuckers but you don't wanna call them that. All the really awful people are *called* "cocksuckers," but they don't really suck you-know-what. I know, I don't understand it either. It's probably a teenage thing. You should talk to Dalton. He knows a lot.

click

it either. It's probably a teenage thing. You should talk to Dalton. He knows a lot.

You should probably double click.

click click

YEAH, SO HEY what's up, right? When *the writer* first came to me, I wasn't gonna use my name with this thing, but I guess Dawn Mican narc'd me out. Oh well. That's cool. She's a good little chick anyway. Plus, the pseudonym "Gag Reflex" totally sucks, dig? So what do you want to know? I'm fifteen, I'm an only child, I'm queer, what's *your* excuse? My dad fucks Dawn's mom and my mom pops a lot of pills. And snorts all my dad's coke, the greedy cunt. We have a housekeeper. My dad fucks the house-keeper. My mom also fucks the housekeeper. My dad doesn't know mom fucks the housekeeper and mom doesn't know dad does be-cause she's fucking stupid. Sometimes guests come over and some-times they fuck the housekeeper too. My dad is a big-time talent agent. You name somebody big and fancy, and dad's probably had his dick in their cookie jar. Oh, by the way, the housekeeper is writ-ing a tell-all, and that book is gonna bury all those people—mom and dad especially. That's gonna rule!

Don't tell Dawn I'm telling you this, but that lady she likes? Miss Caroline? Well, she came over one time and fucked the housekeeper too. Or she tried to. I guess the housekeeper was fucking *her* and she didn't like it. All I heard was her crying saying, "Stop! Stop! I'm sorry. I can't do this. It's not right!" And she ran away crying. She ran off and left her shoes here. So I took them. I'm wearing them right now. They fit real well and they look bitchy on me.

Coincidence? What coincidence? Come on, folks, it's not that hard. Okay, it works out like this: Caroline Powell does PR for Joey Spitfire. Well, Joey Spitfire knows fucking *everybody*. His drug connection is (*was*) this scar freak Harlan Daniels. Oh, you read about him? Yeah, I know. I fucking wrote it. Anyway, Harlan dealt me pot and dad coke for about three years. Dawn's father Jeff (whose artwork is fucking hardcore!), his agent is Joey Spitfire. Jeff's agent used to be, yep, my dad. That's, uh, that didn't last too long. By the way, when Joey Spitfire first went to the pokey, he hooked Harlan up with more clients than you can imagine. Prison is a drug dealer's paradise. Well, this guard, Burt Kridell, was buying junk from Harlan and he got busted with it. Covering his own fat ass, dude set Harlan up for a sting. That's how Harlan got killed in Chillicothe, can you dig it? Harlan would have gotten away, but he had so much metal hanging off his skin, it was weighing him down. Plus, he had ink and 3rd degree burns and decorative open wounds all over his body healing at the time. That impeded his movement and totally jacked up his escape, right? Damn shame. He was top floor, that guy. They say no one was able to identify his body at all. They just assumed that it was he.

You know who else bought smack from Harlan? Alain Childress. You heard of him?

click

"WHAT DO YOU WANT me to say, Caroline?"

Joey looked like he'd been in an industrial dryer full of rocks set to "damp dry cycle." His lips were busted, his eyes were blackened, his wrist was in a cast. He looked like a...rape victim. Upon seeing him, Caroline chuckled lightly to herself. Hopefully he didn't see it. She'd send a check to the local Rape Crisis Center as soon as she was finished here.

"I don't know, Joey. I guess I want you to remind me why I agreed to take up this venture with you. Have you seen his *artwork*? It's depraved! I've sold the public a hell of a lot of snake oil in my time, Joey. You of all people know that. But there is no way in hell I can put a positive spin on this stuff. We'll all be crucified. We'll be drawn and quartered on Cincinnati's Fountain Square!"

"It's not possible to back out of it now, Ms. Powell. Every issue of *PF!* that features Jeff's work has been reissued, and they are selling out daily. Hourly in some places. Selling faster than Bishop can print them. Whatever you wrote for that press packet worked like a fucking voodoo hex. You're just as involved as I am. Cincinnati needs a Jeff Mican. Cincinnati needs a goddamn enema."

"He drew a picture of his own daughter being raped by a headless man!"

"Oh, Cecil?"

"What?"

"Cecil. That's what that headless figure is called. All muscles and powerhouse cock? Yeah. Cecil. He represents our id-driven male-dominated society. He is the embodiment of repression that women suffer throughout the world and have suffered throughout history. As a feminist, I thought sure you'd at least be hip to *that* aspect of his work."

"But Dawn—"

"Sweet girl, isn't she? We need to protect the Dawns of the world from Cecil. And it's not just women either. Or children. It's the defenseless, the timid, the passive. At least, that's what Jeff would say. I don't give two bits of mule shit about any of that."

Caroline bit her bottom lip and looked away pensively.

"Well…I'm not saying I'm backing out, Joey. But there's a lot about this that leaves a bad taste in my mouth."

"Man, some jokes just write themselves."

"What's that supposed to mean?"

"Nothing. Any word from the home office?"

"Yeah. Sponge wanted me to tell you that *Pleasure Dome Productions* called. They said you are to desist writing about Clover Honey in any of your columns, lest you face serious litigation. And this time they are not bluffing."

"Oops."

click

THE SPITFIRE GRILL

by Joey Spitfire

Howdy, kids! I give up. I was going to write a column about the idiocy of slave reparations, and why all politicians, Democrat and Republican alike, need to be hanged from the lampposts by their internal organs. But instead, I'm gonna write about porn.

Since so many of you have written in asking about my dear wife Clover, I figger'd I send this one out to y'all and be done with it.

To answer your number one question, "What wuz yer sex life like, Joey?" Let me reply to that with this: the shoemaker's family runs around in their socks. The master chef's family starves to death. Are ya hearing me?

Question number the second: "Hey Joey, howz come ya was banned from every porn flick locale in the continental US?" I'm surprised that so many of you even knew that happened. You jizzlobbers really do your research. Technically, I'm not allowed to discuss the particulars of that incident, but since I'm in prison anyway...

Some years ago, when Clover and I first were wed, I came to her shoots every day. No big deal; fucking is her job. She didn't sweat my magazine, I didn't sweat her fucking. Easy piecy Japanesey. Sometimes I even helped carry lighting equipment and whatnot.

Anyhoo, one day she gets offered one of those "World's Biggest Gangbang" videos, you see? As most of you know I'm sure, really high-level porno chicks don't do those kinds of "world record" videos. They're not one bit sexy. It's just an endurance challenge. But good exposure, I suppose.

So they sent out this call in a bunch of spooge magazines for amateurs who didn't have anything better to do that day to come to this warehouse and fuck Clover Honey on video. So something like 2,000 lame-ass gobs show up on shooting day. Each one got three minutes of fuck time. If they cum, great. If they don't, NEXT! It was tedious, boring work. My job that day was to make sure Clover had plenty of water to drink and ice packs to put on her crotch to keep the swelling down. Seeing all those sorry hams lined up with their dinks hanging out, wearing nothing but socks and t-shirts, kept my attention on just about anything else. I spent most of the day gabbing with some gofer. In the background, I could hear Clover going through the motions like, "Oo baby yeah that's it," and so forth.

At some point I noticed all the gobs were getting for-real excited. Little rods at 11:00. Then they all start chanting, "Go go go go go!" I look over, and this guy, strapping young buck that he was, is really going to town on Clover. And she's genuinely loving it. Believe me, I can tell. She was sweating and whimpering, her skin was getting blotchy, not like when the rest of those guys were doing *their* thing. The gobs kept chanting and they started going faster and faster and finally everybody cheers and Clover arches her back and squeals. The place goes ballistic. The director's actually bawling he's so happy to have gotten it on tape. Afterwards, Clover and Big Johnny Sausageboy lie there holding each other and just basking in the glow. Then she *kissed* him. Dude was offered a contract that very minute.

He never got a chance to honor that contract.

"Say, bro, can I talk to you fer a sec? Come on into this trailer."

He didn't know me from Adam. Probably thought I was there to offer him a better deal or some shit. Poor guy. I've heard, in the years that have passed, and with medical technology and physical therapy improving by leaps and bounds, he's now able to hold a small rubber ball in his hand. But he's still not able to shit without the bag.

The studio, already skittish about negative press, bought homeboy off and I was blacklisted throughout the entire "legitimate" porn world. To this day, I am banned from all sets. Fine with me. Clover ended up not making or breaking the gangbang record. Because so many of those pudwhaps couldn't resist sticking their fingers in her ass, she ended up getting an infection and had to be rushed to the hospital. How did she feel about what I had done? She said, in a way, it was kind of romantic. Then she stabbed me with a serrated steak knife.

So what does the future hold for our beloved heroine? Psssst...here's something neither she nor anybody else in the biz wants you to know. Clover Honey's days in pornography are numbered. Why? You see it's like this; there's a funny little disease of the nervous system wherein the brain and spinal cord degenerate and decay. The victim almost always ends up paralyzed. It's called multiple sclerosis, kiddies. Maybe you've heard of it. Hey, ain't that what *you* look for in jerkin' material? The next time you're yanking and

spanking to one of Clover Honey's video treasures, try
to picture in your mind what she's going to look like in
a couple of years. Hey, it gets me hard.

We're a happy family,

JS

p.s. On a somber note, I'd like to ask for a moment
of silence for former inmate, and my good friend,
Alain Childress. RIP, brother. Rest in peace and find
your piece of the sky.

click

ALAIN CHILDRESS WAS A FULL-ON JUNKIE.
Had been since he ran away from home at fourteen. Smack sick
was his constant reality. It wasn't the smack that made him sick,
though. It wasn't so much the smack at all. It was the *bonus prizes*.

Baby laxative. Bug powders. Anything white that dissolves in
water. See, most heroin dealers don't really care too greatly for the
well being of their customers. It's a harsh reality. The wondrous
benefit of an illegal capitalist system is the absolute infallible holi-
ness of The Almighty Profit Margin (hallelujah!). So stretch your
product however thin you like! There will always be a demand.
The consumer simply can't live without it.

Alain was a very weak boy and weakness will not be toler-
ated. His sickness fed his habit, his habit fed his sickness, somebody somewhere got *muy rico*. Until he was busted for possession
in Ohio. Ohio. In Ohio. Under the lifeless, hopeless haze, Alain
was sentenced to ten for possession of narcotics. A light sentence by
some comparisons.

Sending a junkie to prison is kind of like sending a pederast to
kindergarten. However, although junk was plentiful, it's hard for a
160-pound addict to defend himself in lockdown. Especially when

spiders are crawling out of his pores and his stomach is trying to se-
cede from the Union. Alain's nickname quickly became "Holland."
As in the Holland Tunnel.

Thanks to a white-trash wife beater named Joey Spitfire, Holland, or rather Alain, was finally able to secure a clean connection.
The cleanest connection of his life. Heroin flowed in whenever he
needed it, and it was pure, and clean, and good. His liaison was a
junkie guard— perfect for in-house protection. Life for Alain was
finally a-ok. Few find ultimate serenity in Chillicothe Correctional, but hey. All shapes and sizes.

But then, carriages turn back into pumpkins, horses turn to
mice, and prison guards turn back into rat finks. Alain's savior on
the outside was brought down in a spray of machine gun fire, not
two miles from the prison walls. Alain returned to grabbing his
ankles and shooting up generic household products. And getting
sicker. And sicker. And sick beyond bad junk. He was full-on full
blown. Full blown. AIDS.

During a routine transfer from lockdown to hospital, Alain
made a break. And broke. He holed up in his old apartment, still
unoccupied. His neighbors didn't ask questions. Some warned him
when the boys in blue were coming a-knocking. And they did from
time to time. And he'd be gone like a rumor on the wind.

Mostly he stewed. And smoked. And shot and snorted. They'd
come eventually. Take him back. And he was dying. He was dying.
Dying. If they were going to come and take him away, then, it was
going to be a bloodbath.

"I wasn't hurting anyone but me!" he muttered to himself.
"And they killed me for it. Tortured and killed me. For hurting
me."

The cutting started with a fingertip. Into a plastic bag. Into
the fridge. *A little more today, then. Fill a few bottles. Seal them up
tight.* Every bit of his place would be covered with infected fluid.
If they open fire, he would open fire. Would they risk infection for

one dying junkie? If Alain knew pigs like he thought he knew pigs, the answer was "yep."

Finally, he simply grew weary of the wait. He woke up in the morning, screamed at the top of his lungs, and fired his .45 right through the efficiency window.

"Fuggin' pigs! Murdering pigs! I'll murder the pigs! Welcome to the slaughterhouse!"

And then he started decorating.

It was early Tuesday morning when Alain Childress painted the walls with his own blood. Wincing as he popped another wrist vein, Alain reached to fill a fresh pan. *Slop it on. Don't be stingy. Drip drip drip right over the doorway.* His efficiency reeked of salt and cigarettes and gunpowder. Outside his window, red and blue rollers spun wildly as sirens whined.

"You fuggin' pigs," he muttered. "You murdered me."

Alain loaded his .45 and pointed it at the door. Then he waited. Waited for them to charge in. To barge in. Larger than life. Cowboys in blue.

"Fuggin' pigs. I was sick. I needed help. And you murdered me! Come on through that door. You built the monster now face the monster. I'm a walking living fucking BIOHAZARD!"

Stalemate. The first officers through the door did not expect to find what they did. And they were just as trapped as Alain. Blood dripped from the ceiling right onto their shoulders. So much as a paper cut would put them at serious terminal risk. And Alain Childress, dying and dying with nothing to lose, had his fully loaded .45 pointed right at them. Even if they all shot at once, he'd still manage to squeeze off a few rounds.

"Welcome to the slaughterhouse."

"Mr. Childress, put the weapon down. We don't want to have to take you out."

"Really? I don't mind killing *you* one bit."

"This is your last chance! Put the weapon on the floor, now!"

"Why did you do this to me? You fuggin' destroyed me for no reason!"

"It's the law. That's our job."

Explosions of gunfire could be heard from blocks away. Bullets tore through fuse boxes and severed phone lines. The perp was taken down. The good guys won. Sure, hair was a little mussed, but overall it was a job well done. Several officers went home to their husbands and wives glowing with pride in their hearts. And plague in their bloodstreams.

click

MESSAGE TO JOEY SPITFIRE:

Your wife committed suicide last night. Left a note. Said it was all your fault. Hope you're happy. Have a nice day.

click

"WHAT DO YOU THINK is the best thing in life?" Dalton Brackage asked Dawn.

"Hmmm…I guess I would have to say soccer," Dawn answered. "What do you think is the best thing in life, Dalton?"

"Revenge."

Dawn and Dalton sat in Dalton's bedroom playing PlayStation 2 for most of the afternoon. Dawn always felt uncomfortable being at the Brackage house. Mainly since the reason she was there was because her mother was down the hall in the master bedroom with Dalton's father. Dawn always worried that Mrs. Brackage would come home. But she seldom did.

"Hey, Dawn, did you end up kissing that Chris Herbert kid like you said you were going to?"

Dawn shook her head and took a bite of her cheese and Cheez Whiz sandwich.

"Nah. I wanted to at first, but then I decided to just be friends with him. He gave me this note that said 'Do you like me? Circle yes no just friends.' I wrote in 'Maybe,' but then later at recess we were gonna kiss, but I said 'Let's just be friends' and he said, 'Okay, but we still gotta get married when we get to 8th grade,' and I said 'okay.'"

"Well, good for you, kid. That's outta sight. I'm glad you decided to save yourself. And congratulations on your engagement."

Dawn giggled and punched Dalton on the arm. She then quickly became somber and still.

"Dalton, there's a lot I don't know."

"Yeah, join the club, right?"

"But, I mean, what's it all about? What's gonna happen?"

"The world's gonna fuckin' end, dig? That's what's gonna happen. It's all going down the tubes. We're all gonna get ebola or cancer or be sprayed with Agent Orange or flaming gasoline jelly. And those of us who won't, will catch some other disease or be killed in a plane or a car crash. People will turn on each other like starving dogs in a reservoir, killing for rotted rat meat. We'll all mutate and drag our superfluous limbs about writhing in agony, moaning in church about how merciful God is and we must count our blessings and be humble and obedient. I tell ya what, Dawn, if I ever catch the big fag disease, the virus, The Syndrome, I'm gonna jack off into the holy water."

"Oh...I kinda wish I'da kissed Chris Herbert now."

The two kids turned instinctively to the wall as they heard Dawn's mother squealing from down the hallway.

"Dalton, everybody says I'm too young to know anything. But I'm not. You're the only person who's ever...who tells the truth. Daddy does too...but he's still Daddy, y'know?"

Dalton exhaled a deep, thoughtful sigh.

"I believe it was Nietzche who said—"

"*Nitchy?*"

Dalton laughed and put his arms around Dawn, squeezing her tightly.

"Never mind. I'm sorry, Dawn. That was nonsense. *Nietzche.* I'm an idiot sometimes. Really…the only thing I've figured out about adult life is that it's one big *self-delusion marathon.* People waking up every morning, 365 days a year with only one goal. To bullshit themselves for another day. That little party down the hall? Your mom and my dad? Nothing but fantasy, can you dig it? Fantasy. *Life is thrilling, and exciting, and worthwhile.* Fantasy."

Dalton set his game controller on the floor.

"Let me show you something—and for the record, I don't think you're old enough to see this stuff, but I also don't think it's my job to shield you from anything."

He reached under his bed and retrieved a cardboard box. Inside it—over one hundred magazines. Magazines. Pornographic.

"Stole these from my uncle. Loser knows who took 'em, but who's he gonna tell, yeah? Avoid the German and the Japanese stuff. Those people are ill."

Dawn paged through one after another. She was horribly embarrassed, and more than a bit confused, but she was bound and determined to experience. Dalton picked up an issue of a magazine called *Studbowl.* Nothing but men inside.

"This one's my favorite. See what these two guys are doing? I did that one time, speaking of revenge."

"So that's…'cocksucking,' huh?" Dawn asked, her face bright crimson.

"Yep."

"How is that revenge?"

click

DALTON'S STORY:

So yeah, I'm in Biology class with all the fuckin' white ballcaps, right? The fuckin' mooks. The jocks. And they're having quite a bit of fun with me, calling me "fatgirl" and "queerbait" and

all that, like I'm fuckin' ashamed or something. I don't give a rancid rat's ass, ya dig? So a couple weeks ago, Duncan Holmes, he's
like quarterback or something, comes up to me. "Hey, Dalton," he
says, "I hope you didn't take all that the guys were saying too hard.
They're just, ya know, playing around." And I'm like, "Yo, cat, I
don't care what anybody says, can you dig that? Cuz I'm riding my
own wave, right? And you all can lick my balls." He just laughed,
and asked me if I felt like coming to his house after school to hang
out and maybe *schmoke* a little bud and I'm like, "Whatever."

So we go back to his house, it's even bigger than mine, ya dig?
And three other guys from the team are there too. A halfback, a
tight end, and a wide receiver. At first I was nervous, you know,
sweating the bucket of pig's blood on my spotlight dance, right?
But everything was mellow. We burned a few joints, and then we
all went swimming in the pool. I didn't really know what was happening, but before too long, me and Duncan are making out like
crazy. The others were laughing and whooping it up, and before
too long I was making out with all four of them! It was nutz. The
tight end dared me, like double dared me, to go down on Duncan
in front of them. So I did. Fuck it. Got him off like a pro. Then I
did each one of them. We were so high, it was just far out. Out of
control. Duncan went and got a bunch of his mom's make-up and
clothes and a wig and I got all dressed up and went down on all of
them again, and we were just laughing and taking Polaroids and
getting stoned.

I kept the photos...can you dig it?

I knew none of those guys would speak to me at school the
next day, and I was right. I saw Duncan in the hall with his girlfriend Nicole and a few other people. I walked past and nodded,
and he was like "wussup?" like he didn't know me. Then later on,
he was all creeping up on me on the sly like, "Hey, man. You don't
still have those pictures do you? Cuz it would be completely un-

cool if those got out, right? I have a football scholarship waiting on me and my future and my girl and *bleh bleh bleh bleh…*" I'm like, "Don't even sweat it. I burned the photos."

Yeah, sure.

I'm gonna bury those fucking guys. Deep. With their asses sticking out of the ground so the world can take turns on 'em, right? I'm gonna fucking bury them. And everybody else who fucks me over. Bank on it, yo.

click back

"YOU'RE SO ANGRY, Dalton," Dawn said.

"Naw, I'm cool."

Dawn picked up a magazine called *Chicken Little.* Dalton snatched it out of her hand.

"Not that one, Dawn. You can look at anything else, but I can't let you look at that."

"Those were little kid—"

"Yeah. I know. The only reason I keep that one is so, when I'm old enough, I'm gonna hunt down the people who made that magazine, and I'm gonna slash their throats. Here, look at this."

Dalton opened a different magazine to its centerfold. He displayed it for Dawn.

"She's really pretty," Dawn said. "She's pretty, but she's sad. She's trying to cover it up, but I can tell that she's sad. Girls are in tuition. I'm really in it, so I can tell."

Dalton grinned.

"I'd say that *tuition* you're in is mighty strong, Dawn. Do you know who this is?"

Dawn shrugged.

"Her name is Clover Honey. You heard of her?"

She shrugged again.

"You're right," said Dalton, "She was sad. She must have been sad, because she killed herself a couple of nights ago. She put her husband's gun in her mouth and blew off the back of her own head, right? That's kinda unusual for a woman to commit suicide in such a messy way. Women usually like to leave a good-looking corpse. Why? I have no idea. Why do you think she was sad, Dawn? Was it because she had to take off her clothes to make money?"

"Nah. It wasn't that. It was something else. I can see it in her eyes. If I was gonna kill myself, I think I'd take sleeping pills or jump off a bridge...but that would be pretty scary. How would you want to go, Dalton?"

"I'd wanna be catapulted into a tree shredder, then put in different parcels and mailed to all the people I hate."

click

"YOU'VE REALLY screwed up this time, Joey."

As Caroline fumed at him through the Plexiglas, Joey sat, nearly comatose.

"The press is going nuts over your wife's suicide. I'm trying to play up your grief, and still keep some interest in Jeff's upcoming show. How are we supposed to raise awareness about Cincinnati when you're hogging up the front page driving your wife to off herself? Mighty selfish of you, Joey. Mighty selfish. Do you want our company to be a success, or do you wanna live out your little Sid Vicious fantasy forever? Cuz if this is how it's gonna be, then to hell with it. I can do this on my own. Take Jeff with me. Build up a REAL client base. I'm sure I can do what you do twice as well as you do, you got me? Chill out with the monkeyshines, or you can consider our partnership kaput, and you can write your little rants in prison until the end of time. But I'm doing something."

Joey stared blankly past her. He looked defeated and lost. Hair flat against the top of his head. Pompadour no longer pompous. Caroline felt bad, and made a mental note to write a donation check to The Richard Pryor Foundation for M.S. Research. First she had to find out if there was such a thing.

"So, Joey, uh…how have you been since you, you know, you heard?"

"What did the note say?" he whispered faintly.

"Uh…it wasn't much of a note, really. She just kind of wrote on the wall. In blue lipstick."

"What did the wall say?"

"It said, 'Is this what you wanted, Joey?' That's it."

Joey slumped forward. He looked as though he may topple over.

"I loved her so much."

"I know you did, Joe."

"I loved her so much."

"I know."

"I loved her so much."

"Yes."

"I loved her so much."

"Okay."

click

DON'T DO THAT BIG DARK LETTER THING on my parts, okay? Use something pretty *like this*. Yeah. Cool. That way, when people see that pretty writing, they'll know it's me, *Dawn Mican (aka Dawn Salk)*.

click

"THIS IS A COLLECT CALL from Chillicothe Correctional Facility. Caller, say your name—*Joey*. If you accept this call, do not use three way or call waiting or you will be disconnected. To refuse this call, please hang up now. To accept this call, dial 1 now."

beep

"Caroline?"

"Hey, Joey. What's goin' on?"

"Not much. Just wanted to see if you've read The Grill yet."

"Nope. Just got home. I'll read it after my bath, mud mask, and pedicure."

"Oh. Okay. Caroline?"

"Yeah, Joe?"

"Why don't you love your husband?"

Caroline sighed. This was not the call she really needed at the moment.

"Why do you ask?"

"If you're not attracted to him, why'd you marry him?"

"I don't know. I guess I was at one point."

"Has he ever *satisfied* you?"

"No, actually not."

"Has any man?"

"Not really."

"Has any woman ever satisfied you?"

"You called me collect from prison to ask me this shit? Well… not that it's any of your business, but no. No woman has ever satisfied me either. Any man ever *satisfy you*, Joey?"

"I was never not in love with her. Never."

"Then why'd you hit her?"

"I'll see ya, Caroline."

"Wait, Joey. I was just wondering…Did your wife really have M.S.?"

"Does it matter? Yes. Yes she did. I may be a lot of things, Caroline, but I'm not a liar."

"Well, you'll always have that."

click

THE SPITFIRE GRILL

by Joey Spitfire

Hey kids, here it is. The column you've been waiting for. Yessir, this is the one where I answer all your questions and lay the ultimate truth smackdown. This is the one where I let the world know that I take tragedy on the chin, and keep right on laughing.

Fuck off. Fuck you. You want to know what I've been doing for the past week? Sitting in my cell rocking back and forth praying to any supernatural force that will listen to tell me that it's all been a dream and I can wake up now. But the sun never rises, and I can't wake up.

I've got a story for you. It's about my momma. See, my momma, was very, let's say *free with her affections*. Or to put it another way, she was a spunk-guzzling mattress-back. Lots and lots of dudes had my momma. She was also real Catholic, and didn't believe in abortion or birth control. So needless to say, I've got a ton of sibs. But momma had this thing. It was goofy. She thought that every single life on earth was sacred. That God, whoever it is, made each of us special and precious. She called it *our song*. Everybody has their very own song, and it is unique to them. That's what my momma thought. Crazy bitch, huh? She would see one of us just waking up in our crib, and she would say to each of us, "Hiyee, babee! With him's very own song." She never got tired of saying that.

We never got tired of hearing it.

This is where it gets bad: I still hear that in my head. Sometimes I say it to myself. "Hiyee, babee! With him's very own song." I say that to myself every time the state puts someone to death. Or the cops kill someone. Or someone kills a cop. Or someone's dying. I say it to myself. Or Momma says it. Somewhere, wherever she is, she's saying it. "Hiyee, babee! With her's very own song." With her's very own song. Hiyee, babee! With her's very own song.

I'm sorry, Clover. I wish I would have said it when I had the chance.

As I write this, it is now September 7th, 2001. By the time most of you read this, it will be September the 10th, 2001. You should remember this date, because this is the last Spitfire Grill I'm ever gonna write. I've lost my "fire." My fire is out. Just call me "Spit." That's pretty punk rock. Here's something that ain't too punk rock at all, but I'm gonna say it anyway: just try to love each other tonight. Even for just one night. You never know what's gonna happen tomorrow. You never know.

Best wishes,
Joey
inmate #250624

click

JOEY SPITFIRE NEVER saw the world burn. He never saw the planes crash into the World Trade Center. He missed the anthrax. He never saw bombs drop on Afghanistan and *everywhere else*. He never saw the influx of smallpox-ridden petty crooks into the penitentiaries. He never saw the internment camps. The detention. The interviews. The tribunals. He never saw an absolutely necessary absolutely unwinable war. A war without end. He lived in a world of meaningless piffle. Cool world. Cold world. The world of empty irony. He died with that world. A meaningless death.

On the evening of September 10th, Joey and his pod were watching tv as normal. Local news announced that a pregnant Cincinnati girl was found dead, buried on the side of the road.

"Hiyee, babee," Joey whispered to himself. *"With her's very own song."*

Her boyfriend, the father of her unborn child, confessed to the murder. Joey's fellow inmates laughed and cracked wise. At the same time, Cincinnati police were under investigation for the suffocation death of a suspected drug dealer. They had piled on top of him until he was crushed to death. Allegedly. Local black ministers waged a protest against police brutality. News footage showed angry black youths hurling bottles at police in riot gear, who were shooting rubber bullets and "beanbags." The inmates said nothing.

"Hiyee, babee, with him's very own song."

After lights out—"Come on, Joey boy, let's speed this along"— Joey was lead outside to a wagon. Idling. For him. He knew why. Between the drugs, the fights, the media exposure, the *Spitfire Grill*, and the dirt he had on the guards, his presence at that institution had become too much to tolerate. He was being transferred. Relatively routine. Transfer. He had been transferred within Chillicothe from the "barracks" style quarters of minimum security to the medium security cells almost immediately upon his arrival some months ago. Now he was being relocated. But where? Close security? Maximum? Where? Ohio State Pen? Mansfield?

Lucasville. SOCF. 1724 State Route 728.

Burt Kridell and a guard named Stickle delivered him. Three SOCF guards were there to receive him. Joey did not struggle.

"Whoo boy," said one Lucasville guard to Joey Spitfire, "We've been waiting on you, son."

Joey looked him in the eye.

"Hiyee, babee, with him's very own song."

"He's been saying that the whole goddamn way here," said Burt Kridell. "Good luck shuttin' him up."

As the wagon pulled away, Joey Spitfire was stripped naked right there in the lot. Lead inside on a waist chain. Naked.

All were silent as he was chucked into his new cell. Three cons awoke and eyed him like cougars on a wounded elk. They looked to each other, then back to him. One finally spoke.

"Nothing personal, bitch."

And so it began.

Joey's teeth were smashed into the bars of the cell, and he was bent over like a clothespin. One man entered him from behind, one in front. *I could castrate them both right now,* Joey thought as he felt the now-familiar sensation of his insides locking. *I could castrate all three of them. Rip their cocks asunder. Kiss them as they bleed to death.*

But he didn't.

"Hiyee, babee," Joey said, gagging and wincing, "With him's very own song." After 45 minutes, round one finally ended. He was then dragged to the next cell. More and more cell doors opened. Not a guard to be found. Cons came in twos and threes and fours and kept on coming. Five. And kept on coming. Seven. Some would beat him. Some would curse at him. Some would laugh. Some would try to be tender and kiss his ears, and whisper sweetly, laying on the sugar. Ten. Thirteen. Sometimes blood is a lubricant. Nineteen. Hours went by. Twenty six. Hours went by. Thirty three. Would there never be daylight?

In his delusion, Joey thought that maybe the rising sun would bring this to an end. So he tried to will the sun to rise. Forty-four. He was pissed upon. Forty-nine. Shat upon. Vomited upon. Fifty-two. Bloody. Soaking. Drenched. Dragged to a new floor.

Joey squinted through swollen eyes to Golgotha. He saw Jesus of Nazareth throwing a mad roundhouse. The son of man buried his holy fist deep into the chest of a Burly Centurion, pulling from within his beating heart, and swallowed it whole. Christ gnashed his bloody teeth and napalm rained down upon the wailing Philistines. Jesus was not taking to the hill without a fight, so neither would Joey Spitfire.

Joey managed to break three noses and pull one man's eye from its socket before the mass fell upon his naked frame in a blood-maddened frenzy. By daybreak, bits of Joey Spitfire could be found strewn about. Guards finally entered the cell block surveying the scene. Expectations surpassed. They were going to need a high-powered hose.

Bye-bye, baby. With him's very own song.

click

CAROLINE POWELL, like everyone else in the developed world, watched *the footage* over and over and over and over all day. Planes. Buildings. Carnage. Suicide. Tears. She stayed home on September 11th, furiously writing donation checks. Red Cross. Fireman's Relief Fund. Families of the Victims. Horrible. Tragic. Devastating. Caroline felt *nothing*. She tried to force herself to cry or to be overwhelmed, but it never came. So she kept writing. Check after check.

"Caroline? Sweetheart?" her husband Chet called from the downstairs rumpus room. "Caroline? You okay, dear?"

"I think so."

Ring, Ring.

"Hello?"

"Hullo, Caroline?"

"Hi, Jeff."

"I guess you're watching it, huh? It's a tragedy."

"It sure is."

"Did you hear about Joey?" Jeff asked. "I guess that's a tragedy too. I don't really know. It's hard to qualify anything anymore."

"I know what you mean."

"I thought I should tell you. I'm changing my show. I think there's enough blood and guts right now."

"I know what you mean."

Jeff was asked to identify Joey's body. He and the *Psychobilly Freakout!* committee. Caroline was glad she didn't have to. She'd always kinda-sorta-maybe-but-not-really had a *thing* for Joey Spitfire. She wanted to remember him the way she remembered him.

"Caroline? Joey wasn't…intact when they found him. He was kind of all over the place."

"I know what you mean."

"In light of recent events, I guess it doesn't matter, doesn't compare to, well you know…but still…"

"I know what you mean."

click

I can't believe it, but Daddy actually showed me some of his art today! It is so good! I think he's been really shook up by this whole terrorist thing. I have been too, but I'm not sure I fully understand it. I asked Dalton what it was all about and he said, "This is it, ya dig? We are all going to die. Two spoiled, privileged rich kids are gonna kill us all." I guess he meant President Bush and that Binloden guy. Dalton should know. He's a spoiled rich kid himself.

Some kindergartner came up to me and told me that the planes were coming to knock down our houses. He was really scared, you could tell, so I told him that the grown-ups were going to take care of everything and he didn't have to be scared. I lied to him I think. Right after that, the principal came on the PA and sent us all home but he didn't say why.

Anyway, Daddy has a big show coming up at some art gallery in downtown Cincinnati. He was worried that the stuff he planned to show was going to upset people, so instead he did this tribute to the victims in New York and DC. It's beautiful. All in these pretty pastel charcoals. It shows the towers, standing and then falling, but it also shows all these people of different races hugging and stuff. It made me cry a little bit and Daddy gave me a hugantic hug and said it's good to cry. Daddy said in a way this horrible thing could be good in the long run because maybe people will remember what's important and not fool around with all this "malarkey" and "balderdash." Daddy says goofy jazz like that all the time, because he knows it makes me laugh.

Another part of Daddy's show is this piece called "Pal Joey." Just a little tribute to his agent, who got murdered in jail. He was ripped apart. I'm not supposed to know about it, but Dalton told me. There is also a section that is a mem...it's a memor...that is in memory of this Joey-guy's wife who killed herself. When Daddy showed me the picture, I had to pretend like I didn't know who the lady was. There's an awful lot of death. I almost think we should break them down into Big death, Medium death, and Little death. Dalton says get ready for lots of all three. "Just keep digging graves," he said. "Just keep on digging."

click

THE FOUR OF THEM barely spoke as they pawed through Joey Spitfire's personal belongings. Caroline Powell. Angus "Banana Sponge" McTill. Owen Bishop. Eric Dodger— aka "Dogjaw." Joey didn't keep much of value in his cell. A black comb. A pair of sunglasses priced at $1.26. A tin of hair gel. Two issues of *Easy Rider Magazine*. One issue of *Outlaw Biker Tattoo*. One dubbed cassette of Link Wray. One dubbed cassette of Chet Atkins. No tape player. Four blue ink pens. And about 400 pages of written material—poems, rants, experimental gibberish, half completed and barely started columns. Here is a sample:

I Wish BY JOEY SPITFIRE

I wish I was a rabbit so I could run away
I wish I was a bird with wings to fly
I wish I was a rabbit with wings so I
could be shot from the sky
and mounted and put on display.
I wish I were a snake, then I'd sing out loud!
About love, and joy, and kissing.
I'd sing from my soul, 'til I'm bashed with a pole
cuz all THEY ever heard was hissing.

I wish I were a hog wallowing in mud
waiting to be lead to the slaughter.
I'd be ground into slop and then fed to me Pop
who with me he never really could bot'er.
I suppose that me hooves would be fed to the wolves

and me ears would be sewn into silk purses,
And the rest of me tripe would be stuffed in a pipe
and smoked by registered nurses.

I wish I was a rabbit so I could run away
I wish I was a bird with wings to fly
I wish I was a rabbit with wings so I
could be shot from the sky
and mounted and put on display.

Nonsense Verse #12 BY JOEY SPITFIRE

Smakdabb in tat midlen,
Heil peh ruke und rallen tah satis fuy maa soluh, ya.
Hahm leven tahbeh duyun. Tyuh fass fer loof,
Un Oy hain gutah notten tuh levefer.

Grill BY JS

Howdy, Kids [need intro—second paragraph]. If Robin
Hood were alive today, he'd steal from the rich and give to the
poor. The poor would immediately run out and buy alcohol
and firearms, thereby returning all of said money to its owners.
The poor would then proceed to get liquored up and shoot one
another faster than you can say "community service." Robin Hood
would be offered a six-figure corporate contract [insert bit about
welfare and teenage mothers].

Clover, My Honey BY JOEY SPITFIRE

If Clover came over
to the white cliffs of Dover
I'd probably shove her,
but just 'cause I love her.

Our Dog BY JOEY SPITFIRE

WE have a dog. A Chihuahua named "Wetback."
Whenever WE have a fight, I move out and I take Wetback
    with me.

A week later, and it never fails, SHE will call.

"I miss the dog," SHE says. "Can I come visit the dog?"

So SHE comes to visit the dog.

"I love you so much," SHE says to the dog. "And I miss you, sweetie."

"Please, come home with me," SHE says to the dog.

"I miss you and I love you so much."

SHE says to the dog.

A Sestina (for my Twitchy Lovely) by Joey Spitfire

Kissing thin cinnamon twitching lips
to keep tongues from being swallowed
is my devotion to my heart, my love
to my spastic fantastic
my exotic erotic quixotic cystic-fibrotic.
Holding your tiny body close
as you gag and spit...
Lover, lovely, love to love you too.
A cough and caressing
and a coffin for us both
my one, my only, my joy.

Hannol ba terezneh gosthem hedrenya
Hak blen entah ba snevnah katameljey

Savhadda kren hagh sckrem ba hak megheknal
Ghenuus kranna kuiblact kranna scagkuumat
Zhok kranna ba hagh muu rambun ibernmed
Hazth teyvel splackka vizth scatapp yorvevtep.

Shiver at my touch, do you my sweet
and shake as your nerves unravel
"I'll love you 'til there's no light
left in the sun," I whisper in the moonglow
"and then I'll love you still."

CRUUUCK! HAAAK! you reply, my turtledove.
CUT CUNT!! And then you're sick with desire
And your desire sticks, lingering, seeping.

> *Vizth heayey fadda kranna channek hagh yorvevtep*
> *Muuna grapeh splackka vizth hembret hedrenya*
> *Fetzed yint vuukan hak ba muuna lought ibernmed*
> *Gallewet scatapp rambun ba kuiblact kranna katameljey*
> *Zhok kranna hannol sckrem ba hak scagkuumat*
> *Entah ba hedrekketel fetzed megheknal.*

If I can sing no lullaby that'll soothe,
If no poetry drips dulcet from MY tongue,
perhaps in yours, my dearest one, it will.
A sonnet then, my darling?
Or a ghazal like the Persians wrote?
Nay, nay, a SESTINA!
With repeating fragments
for a love undying
Even for my dying lovely.

> *Hak kren ghenuus kranna megheknal*
> *Savhadda ba snevnah rambun yorvevtep*
> *Muu sckrem hazth teyvel kuiblact kranna scagkuumat*
> *Yint vuukan channek hak ba hedrenya*
> *Hembret gallewet hannol sckrem katameljey*
> *Muuna ba hedrekketel ibernmed.*

I will compose this sestina in your words
for your fair ears, my queen.
Sob no more in your anguish.
VUUKAN!! Hak, hak, hack...baaa
muuuuhhhNAA!!!!!
I know, precious one. I know.

Splackka vizth yint rambun ba muuna ibernmed
Kuiblact kranna zhok granna ba hak megheknal
Fetzed yint ghenuus kranna katameljey
Kren savhadda hannol ba snevnah yorvevtep
Vuukan ba rambun muu sckrem hedrenya
Gallewet zhok granna hak ba scagkuumat.

Gargling gorgeous spastic fantastic.
Erotic exotic quixotic ebolic.
The blood in your vomit is
from a heart overflowing.
I feel it as well
feel it swell…
Holding your tiny body
as you shiver and spit.

Hannol hazth vuukan adderef scagkuumat
Ghenuus kranna sckrem ba fetzed ibernmed
Yint ba muuna kuiblact kranna hedrenya
Vuukan splackka ba muuna megheknal
Scatapp adderef hak ba sckrem yorvevtep
Zhok kranna hak muuna ba snevnah katameljey.

Lover, lovely, love to love you too—
HAAAACK!!!
A cough and caressing
and a coffin for us both…

Preghelm tachim ba vuukan katameljey
Yint muu adderef hak fetzed scagkuumat
Snevnah ba muuna sckrem lought yorvevtep
Zesheer nik heyite adderef ibernmed
Kuiblact kranna ba hak megheknal
Splackka ba scatapp zesheer nik hedrenya.

Shake no more today, mon fleur,
and I'll lay you down for your rest
as I kiss thin cinnamon twitching lips
(to keep tongues from being swallowed)
one last time in the moonglow.

> *Zhok kranna ba hedrenya muuna katameljey*
> *Adderef hak megheknal zesheer nik scagkuumat*
> *Heyite sckem ba hak ibernmed lought yorvevtep*

"I'll love you 'til there's no light left in the sun,"
I whisper, "and then HAAACK! CUT CUNT!!
I'll love you, love you, love you still."

"I don't think Joey quite had a grasp of what M.S. is," said
Sponge.

"Sponge—" Bishop tried to interrupt.

"No, man, I'm serious. What is this, fuckin' goddamn hi-fi
sci-fi? I mean, Clover didn't fuckin' have the ebola virus, for fuck-
sake. She didn't have tourettes. She didn't have cystic fuckin' fibro-
sis. What the hell is this shit he's written here? I'm telling you…
peekin' into the mind of Joey Spitfire. Where angels fear to tread
upon hallowed ground."

"Well," Dogjaw interjected. "I will hand it to him. That mess
on the right side of the page? It really is a sestina if you look at it.
It's all gibberjabber, but it's…actually…"

Everyone stared at him blankly.

"What? Hey, I was an English major, right? How do you think
I ended up robbing liquor stores?"

"Caroline," Bishop said turning away from his compatriots,
"What do you think we should do? I mean, should we try to publish this shit? Or is that too morbid?"

"Don't be such a pussy, Bishop," Caroline replied. "Of course
you should publish it. How could you even think of NOT publish-

ing it? Joey Spitfire's final love letters, of sorts, to his beloved wife Clover Honey."

"Yeah, people will eat that with a knife and fork!" Sponge interjected.

"Of course, I minored in modern dance..." said Dogjaw

"Yeah," Bishop answered, "But would Joey want us to?"

"If Joey didn't want it published," said Caroline "he wouldn't have written it."

Caroline, Dogjaw, and Sponge all nodded in collective consent. Bishop frowned at the three of them, bemused. He held up another manuscript that Joey had written. It went like this:

fuckyoufuckyoufuckyoualldiediediediediediediediediediediedie diediediefuckyoufuckyoufuckyoualldIdon'tcareIdon'tcareIdon't carefuckyoufuckyoufuckyoufuckyoualldiediediediefuckyoufuckoffdiedie diediediefuckofffuckofffuckofffuckofffuckofffuckofffuckofffuckoffdie diediedie

for twelve pages.

"We should publish that too," said Sponge.

"*True at First Light,*" Dogjaw said.

A deadening pause the size of an eighteen-wheeler drove through their conversation.

"*True at First Light*", Dogjaw repeated. "In the 1990s, Patrick Hemingway, son of famed novelist Ernest Hemingway published, posthumously, an 850 page piece that his dad had been working on around the time of his demise. It was, is, called *True at First Light.* People were pissed as hell. Of course, young Patrick did change a few things in the work, but still..."

"You just compared Joey Spitfire to Ernest Hemingway," said Bishop.

"And I'd do it again."

click

SMACK DAB in the middle,
I'll be rock 'n rollin' to satisfy my soul. Yeah.
I'm livin' to be dyin'. Too fast for love.
And I ain't got nothin' to live for.

click

HAD HE LIVED to see it, Joey Spitfire would have said
"Sweet Jesus and baby Jesus!" Jeff Mican, malignant tumor on the
neck of the Art World, too sick even for most in the underground,
opened at the Contemporary Arts Center in Bumblefuck, Ohio (or
Cincinnati as at least eight people still call it) to *staggering enthusiasm*.
Critics from all over the country packed onto buses (still afraid to fly)
and poured into town for the show.

> "Brilliant!"

> "Raw and real and gorgeously human."

> "In such dark and murky times, Jeff Mican
> is a shining beacon of light."

> "An American artist if ever there was one."

> "The cynical depravity of modern art
> is finally dead.
> Thank God for Jeff Mican."

Crowds packed the CAC, sobbing and embracing one another.
Perfect strangers. Strangers. Perfect. Signing Jeff's guest-book with
four and five paged "letters" thanking him for his tribute to the
victims of September the 11th. Purging their sorrow over lost loved
ones and lost innocence. A simple statement of universal love in a
time of trial and hate. Pretty pastel charcoal. A simple statement.
An interviewer asked Jeff:
    "What are you trying to say with this exhibit?"
    "We matter," was his reply.
    "Big death and little death," Dawn said.
    "We all matter, sugargirl," said her daddy.

People who had never heard of Joey Spitfire and Clover Honey, and people who *had* and thought them *trash*, now bowed their heads in reverence when in proximity to Jeff Mican's shrines to them. Violent redneck scumbag convict? Sleazy diseasy porno slut? Star crossed lovers. Young. Beautiful. Tragic. Holy. Scrubbed clean of their sins by art and death.

click

CAROLINE POWELL said to Owen Bishop, "Way back in the day, before Nirvana broke, you know the band Nirvana, back before they broke, I thought they were just 'okay.' Pretty good group, but not great. I didn't really want to hype them. Then they just blew up. Bigger than Jesus. Who knew? After Kurt Cobain was mur—I mean killed himself, I fought hard with the label over how to handle his death from a PR standpoint. So they dismissed me. Then they ran with it. Milked that poor sap's corpse. Well, this is *my* opportunity. I'm going straight to the top. Between Jeff and Joey…I won't ever have to slum again. This time I'll get my chance—"

"—To exploit a man's death?" asked Bishop. No malice. A simple observation.

"I'll finally get my chance to do it all *right*. I'll show them. Bastards. Cast me out like some bad dog. Fuckers. I'll get even this time."

"Careful, Caroline. You're starting to sound a little like Joey."

"Joey's dead, Bishop. *But I'll be Joey* when I need to be."

Always live better than your clients, said Benjamin Sonnenberg, the greatest publicist to ever grace this continent or any other. *Always live better than your clients.* Caroline's best client was in separate pieces six feet underground. But she was *flying high. Flyyyyyyy-ing.*

click

HEY YO, so congratulate me, right? Cuz it's outta sight. My dumbshit mother finally grew a brain and filed for divorce. Laina and The Brackster—separated at last. Maybe I can just collect my inheritance now and hit the open road, ya dig? Maybe they can both kiss my fat, white ass.

Too bad for Dawn, though. I guess she's gonna be stuck with "Phlegm" for quite a while now. Guess he really IS gonna *represent daddy*. Joking. Joking. Bad joke. I tried to say that to Dawn one time, but I don't think she understood me. I'm an idiot sometimes.

One time, when Dawn's mom had a placebo boyfriend while she waited for my dad to come back, the boyfriend looked at Dawn (she was like seven at the time), smacked his lips, and said, "Hot damn, she's gonna be a little tart when she's ripe."

I oughta find that dude and kill him. At least my dad wouldn't do something like that.

I think. I hope.

Hey, you know what? I've given you my story. As much as I have so far. And there you go watching me, watching all of us, and you get to sit back and be all *omniscient* and shit. I want a piece of *your* story, ya dig? Give me something. Give me some…anything. Give me some process, okay? Something from your past. Nope. Forget about *your audience*. Just tell me.

Okay…then whisper it to me. Yeah, anything, but something good. First kiss, yeah, oooh, that's cool. I dig that, right? Uh huh. So you were a runaway, huh? What do you mean "sort of?" Okay…go ahead. Right. Gotcha. First kiss. Cheap flea-bag motel, right. Late at night. With a teenage black whore. *Yeah…that's nice.* That's far out. So…did she blow your mind?

click

CAROLINE POWELL, for the first time in a thousand years, was as horny as a caged jackrabbit. Maybe it was Jeff's successful show, and her opening fast-track. Maybe it was Joey Spitfire's death. But she had to have it. Right now. No one but her husband Chet was available. He'd have to do.

"Caroline? Sweetheart?" asked Chet. "Caroline? Are you okay, dear?"

click

I'm happy, and I'm not so happy. Daddy's show went awesomely. People loved his artwork, and somebody said it helped "fassillutait healing." Cool. All sorts of folks, folks with money I guess, want Daddy to come to their city with his artwork. He's been offered jobs to draw for people. That's great for a bunch of reasons. He told me that someday soon hopefully he's gonna buy a house and I can have my own room. I asked him if I can have a couch in my room and he said sure.

The drag of it all is, Phlegm and Mommy are probably gonna get married now. They ran off to Florida together to celebrate their engagement. Back in two weeks. Ugh. I mean, it's not so bad when you think of some of Mommy's other boyfriends, but I don't know. Dalton's happy that his mom and dad are getting divorced. Good for him. Now he's gonna be my brother. Or "big sis" as he likes to say.

Sometimes I wish I could just disappear. I mean, it's not like I don't want to be alive. That's not what I mean. I just wish I could disappear sometimes. Or at least I wish I could, you know, skip parts. Of my life. Skip ahead. Or maybe even skip back. Skipping back could be good too. Go back and fix whatever stuff you messed up. Or skip over all the messed up stuff in the first place. But I'd really just like to disappear.

Miss Caroline stayed over the other night at Daddy's…but not like that. None of that moany-groany business. Just regular business. I was pretending to be asleep in Daddy's room and they were arguing out in the living room. Not fighting, but definitely having words. Miss Caroline said, "You have an audience now, Jeff. You've got to consider your audience." Daddy said he doesn't have an audience, and even if he did, he didn't care. He had to draw what HE wanted, and to heck with everybody else. Finally I fell asleep, but I woke up around 3:30 in the morning. Miss Caroline was asleep on the couch. Her toes were still painted sparkly blue! She must have re-painted them with the same color polish I use. I looked at her sleeping for a long time. She's even prettier when she's asleep. Her face is calmer and she makes little sounds like a baby kitten.

Daddy was passed out all propped up against the fridge. He was drawing in the kitchenette, and must have fallen asleep. I sneaked a peak at the picture he was drawing. It was…well, um…I don't really want to talk about it. But I didn't feel very good after I looked. I kinda understand now why Daddy won't let me see them. I still don't feel very good. I think there are some things Daddy isn't telling me about his life. I went and looked at Miss Caroline sleeping on the couch and then I felt a little better.

click

JEFF MICAN HAD offers so sweet they dripped honey all down his coffee table. L.A. called. Begged. Pleaded. They thought he was the perfect distraction to sell to a ravaged public. Everything was off-limits now. Movies. Theatre. Music. Not happening. Visual art was all that remained. Pure and simple in its simplistic purity. Jeff could be *the man*. Rockwell for a new millennium. Jeff did like the idea of making people happy with his art. Hadn't really considered it before.

But he had so much old work left over that simply would not fit into the new paradigm. This was art his agent/publicist Caroline

Powell wanted kept under wraps for a while. Release it years later on the downswing. Jeff hated that idea. So it was time for one last foray into the land of *guerrilla publishing*.

Jeff collected forty of his most gruesome pieces, Xeroxed 500, stapled them together, and hit the Cincinnati streets. First stop: University Village. Then, he had to go Xerox 500 more. He headed down Vine St., through Over-The-Rhine, into downtown.

For the most part, this slapdash trifle of a 'zine leaned toward the puerile. Tedious spurts of violence and mutilation and terror. That wouldn't have been such a problem if the front cover didn't feature a burning American flag and a cartoon of President George W. Bush executing a crying little Arabic girl in a Texas electric chair. "Please, Mr. President," read the caption at bottom, "Please don't kill me!" The girl in the electric chair? Dawn. A swarthy little Dawn. But clearly Dawn. Cecil also made a few revolting, headless appearances. Among other pieces— "Suffer the Children."

Did this fall into the hands of moral crusader and county sheriff Lester Q. Simmons? Yes, it did. Did he appreciate the artwork? No, he did not. Was Jeff Mican arrested? Yes, he certainly was. And was the law on his side? Nope.

click

"YOU KNOW, JEFF, when Joey Spitfire passed away, I honestly thought my days of holding client meetings separated by bullet-proof Plexiglas had finally come to an end."

"Sorry, Caroline."

"I spoke with your lawyer. She said that you have nothing to worry about."

"Awesome!"

"Yes. She's full of shit, Jeff. At the risk of coming across nega-tive…you are so utterly fucked."

Jeff nodded, but he didn't seem too concerned. *God, who is this guy?* Caroline thought. *Is anybody at home?* She looked down at her "Jeff notes."

Jeff Mican born 1971 Tampa, Florida. Agent—Joey Spitfire [see "Joey Spitfire"]. "Single most bad-ass young artist out there."

She didn't really have any Jeff notes.

"Jeff, in 1996 an anti-child pornography law was put into place—"

"Child pornography!?!"

"I'm sure your lawyer will explain it to you, but in a nutshell, it says that any image depicting sexual activity involving a person who *appears* to be under eighteen, is obscene and illegal. Your work definitely qualifies."

"But they're just *drawings*! And bad ones at that! That's a horrible, corrupt law!"

"Maybe it is, maybe it isn't. Not my place to say. I'm not exactly crying on my pillow worrying about the fate of your average pedophile, if you get what I'm saying. What I *am* saying, is that Hamilton County is certainly going to use this against you. I'll do my best to paint you in the press as a victim, but don't expect much local support. Except maybe from the acne ridden losers who collect *Psychobilly Freakout!*"

"You'd be amazed how many convicts read *PF!*"

"No I wouldn't."

"I guess I…I guess I'm just not that politically minded, Caroline."

"Then why, dear god in heaven, why did you have to put that shit with President Bush on the front cover?"

"Cuz he's a thief, and a murderer, and an imbecile."

"Jeff, goddamn it, do you realize how popular he is!? Especially around here. We are at war, for godsake! People are terrified! They're gonna follow whoever is in charge, and anyone who doesn't fall into line is going to be crucified! That reads: you. I mean, Jesus, did you even vote in the presidential election?"

"I certainly did. I voted Green."

"Nader?"

"Nope. Jello Biafra."

"You voted for Jello Biafra? What planet are you from, Jeff!?! And how could you know enough about Jello to vote for him and not know H.R. Giger?"

"You're ranting, Caroline—"

"H.R. Giger did the jacket art for the Dead Kennedys record *Frankenchrist*. It spawned a huge obscenity trial. Similar to what you are facing right now, although, not to be negative, but you are *more fucked*."

"Who in heck are The Dead Kennedys?" *beep* "Rats. Caroline, our time is up. They're going to shut off the phone. Just talk into the ear piece, and I'll still be able to hear you."

"Like I said, Jeff, I'll do my best. But Cincinnatians despise people like you. And the whole country is Cincinnati now. One big scared, skittish, *Cincinnati*. We were so close to legit, Jeff. We were so, so close. Almost there. You're killing me, Jeff. You know, after Joey Spitfire passed away, I honestly thought my days of holding client meetings separated by bullet-proof Plexiglas had finally come to an end."

"Sorry, Caroline."

click

I PUT THE CHROME *to they dome, then send 'em on home! TAGOW!!!*

click

THERE WAS SPLASHBACK that Jeff Mican had not considered. His renegade 'zine was being bootlegged by the thousands. "Free Jeff Mican!" websites began to sprout up all over the Internet. But, not a single one was really dedicated to freeing Jeff Mican. They existed only for their message boards. Some people loved the 'zine. Some people thought Jeff needed to be executed for his lack of patriotism. And there was splashback that Jeff had not considered.

"Seen the rag? Young chick in it. Crazzzy shit."

"Never thought I'd get a hard-on from a drawing LOL."

"I agree. I'd break her little hips if she was real :-)."

"Heard she is real! And 2 young, so back off you pervs LOLROTF."

"Think the headless guy is real? LOLROTMFF!"

"His name is Cedric."

"Wrong ☹. Cecil."

"I like his cock. Gets me wet ☺ "

"Hey, is there a chick here?"

"No."

"It's like genius. Although I don't like when he did all that shit against President Bush."

"President Bush is GOD."

"Ever hear the joke about the ten dead babies in a garbage can? hahahaha."

"Thank god for little girls..."

"JM is god."

"Could fuck her. Will fuck her."

click

"Could fuck her. Will fuck her."

click click

"Could fuck her. Will fuck her."

CLICK CLICK CLICK CLICK

SO YEAH, I got a copy of the infamous rag, ya dig? Man. I don't know. I mean, I love Jeff Mican and all, but that brother is siiiiiiiick. I don't think he shoulda been thrown in jail, but...I'm kinda worried about Dawn. She's been crying like mad cuz she's scared about her dad being in lockdown, right? Especially after what happened to Joey Spitfire. She keeps talking about running away. Wants me to run away with her. Can't do it. Visions of Alain Childress dance in my head, sugar plum.

Former LA Police Chief Darryl Gates once said that all drug users in America should be lined up and shot. His reasoning was; America's at war with drugs, so all druggies are wartime traitors. Can you dig that? Wartime traitors. I hadn't heard that term since Gates said it. I've been hearing it a lot lately. Jeff better watch his back.

Dawn's staying with her grandma 'til her mom gets back from Florida tomorrow. Dawn's mom's all pissy cuz they had to cut their trip short. She sent an e-mail to the house saying Jeff is an impotent jack-ass and he's not allowed to see Dawn, even if he makes bail. He ain't making bail, right? It's fucking high.

Dawn's grandma doesn't have the Internet. Thank god. I asked my mom if Dawn could stay here, and she said "That little hussy is not setting foot in my house ever again." Bitch!

Speaking of the Internet; I've been reading what you fux are writing about Dawn on your rotten little chat lists. Fuck you! Remember the rhyme, "Old enough to bleed, old enough to breed?" Well, she ain't old enough to bleed, right! So leave her the hell alone! I'll kill every single one of you! Bank on it, yo! I'm starting up a new business— Castration Inc. Bank on it.

click

No, stay away from me! Ever since I first talked to you, there's been nothing but bad! Get out of my room! I don't want strangers in grandma's room. Yes, you are a stranger! No, no, no, you are not my friend! Get away! No, I won't give you a hug! GET AWAY FROM ME! I'm running away! I'm running away from everybody!!! I'm going to disappear!

click

Thrash Ghetto Radio by Daddy Molotov

Just look around/ and hit the ground. You know what's going down? They're gonna beat on my ass/ and broadcast/ in surround sound. And I don't understand/ What's the plan?/ Is it the Klan/ who wanna grind up my bones into crack for the rich man?/ And cry/ spy/ sky high/ lie/ die/ Why?/ We'll do anything for our fucking piece of the pie. So don't sit back and relax/ Taste the blade of the ax/ face the facts/ pay the tax/ and listen to your bone cracks.

But whatcha say now? Guess a fair trial ain't your style. Riding the high mile. Let another child die as you lie and beguile. Wage a war on crime/ war on drugs/ war on my time/ war on the youth/ war for the colorless/ bloodless/ war on nevertheless/ cuz one less nigger is one less you'll figure for next year's census. Can we get a consensus? War on those who chose to stand opposed to all the bullshit wars you wage on the poor/ How bout a war on the spics/ the gooks/ the spooks/ the wets/ the reds/ the chinks/ would you think it un-American how he can take the stand that he hates his own land? This nigga would/ would/ would if he could move away/ but there's nowhere to stay/ nowhere to escape the States and its cold hard erection/ raping continents inconsequential and spread American infection. Love it or leave it?/ Would you believe it?/ Or hardly conceive of it/ that it's down to one/ with nowhere to run from the land of the slaves. And every potential savior is bleeding in lock down for disruptive behavior. Let the Christian middle-class hup-two fast!/ to wage a war on the fags/ and all us creating unrest by burning your flags. Keep ideas suppressed/ and the rest well dressed/ and preach all possible gospel against freedom of thought/ sold and bought/ let it rot/ and once we're all caught/ praise God for one more agitator shot!

B-b-b-b-back again to bruise and bash/ bringing yo'
boys a badly needed backlash/ Ya sitting in your million
dollar cesspool of blood soaked profits/ well you can just
drop it/ and maybe just then we'll stop it/ but a rage of
this age is just a turn of the page/ got a tiny bit of love for
the French guillotine/ and what's it all mean when you're
keepin it clean/ if you gotta, call it treason/ but we got a
reason/ to open season/ on ya'll/ watch ya fall/ aristoc-
racide/ you got no place to hide/ you treat a man like a
lab rat/ you gonna see where it ends at/ taste the gat/ rat-
tat-tat/ cutting slack to the fat backs/ while taking flack
for some bad crack/ you can only rape so many times before the rape is returned/ feel the churn/ and watch it all
burn/ burn/ burn it all down/ let the fires fry brighter in
each American town/ let's stand on the same ground/ on
smoldering ash/ everything that's paid for gone in a flash/
down go the prison walls/ down all the prisons fall/ as I'm
hopin' to break open/ the cuffs on my wrist/ And some may
try to take my hand this time/ But you'll have to pry with a
crowbar to unclench my fist!

click

RING RING
   "Hello?"
   "Miss Caroline?"
   "Dawn? Is that you?"
   "Uh huh. Could you come pick me up?
   "Dawn, sweetie, it's 10:00 at night."
   "I know. Could you come pick me up?"
   "Honey, I'm a publicist. I'm not a baby-sitter."
   "I know. Could you come pick me up?"
   "What do you want me to do?"
   "Come pick me up."
   "Dawn, have you been reading stuff on the web?"

"Uh uh. I haven't. So can you?"

"I don't really think—"

"Please?"

Caroline sighed.

"Okay."

click

DAWN THOUGHT the Powell residence was very cool. And she said as much repeatedly.

"Thank you, Dawn. That's a nice thing to say. This is really just our autumn house. We've been living here temporarily, trying to get your father in good shape for his...never mind."

"Where is your mister?"

"I don't know. He's been gone for a couple of days now."

"Do you miss him?"

Caroline smiled. She went to the kitchen to make some cocoa. Dawn sat on the floor of the rumpus room and took out her drawing paper and markers. So many of her drawings were variations on the same theme. Non-committal faces. Must have drawn twenty of them at least. Non-committal faces. Faces. Non-committal.

Caroline shuddered as she thought about what Dawn's grandma had told her before they left. She said people, men, had been calling on the phone all night breathing into the receiver. Asking for "the girl." They didn't want to speak with her. They wanted *her*. Dawn's grandma told them all to kiss her scaly, wrinkled ass, *dirty old white trash broad, God bless her,* but she was scared. Called the police. Police circled the house a few times, then went on their merry way. Did Dawn know about the calls? Her grandma didn't think so. Grandma tried to catch every one. *Everyone is sexualizing that little girl,* Caroline thought to herself. *Even people who aren't trying to. Like me. We may be even worse. Going overboard. She's just a baby. Goddamn you, Jeff. She's just a baby.*

Caroline brought Dawn a hot cocoa with extra marshmallows. The marshmallows were shaped like stars. The stars were pink. The pink stars made the cocoa pink. The pink cocoa made Dawn laugh. *She's just a baby.*

"Miss Caroline? What were you doing when I called you?"

"Oh...nothing much of anything, really." As a favor to the *PF!* committee, Caroline had been reading over ad copy sent from *Pleasure Dome Productions.* PDP were pimping Clover Honey's final video release *Honey Sssuckle*, and with Joey Spitfire safely underground, they wanted to advertise in the back pages of *Psychobilly Freakout!*

"Miss Caroline? Do you have caller ID?"

"Sure do. We've got call block as well. And a direct line to the police, and four panic buttons."

Dawn smiled relieved.

"So...nobody's gonna call for me here, right?"

A knot suddenly popped into Caroline's throat.

"Why do you...? Have...people been calling you, sweetie?"

"Nobody's gonna call for me here, right?!" Dawn burst into tears. "People think Daddy is gonna hurt me. But he never, ever, EVER would! But people call on the...*sob*...call on the phone! And *they*...! Why can't it...*sob*...can't, can't it be morning? I just want the night to be.... *sob*...to be over!"

Dawn sat on the floor sobbing and pulling at her hair. Caroline felt helpless. She didn't know what to do with children.

"Miss...*sob*...Miss Caroline?"

"What is it, sweetheart?"

"Could I hug you, please?"

Caroline wrapped her arms around Dawn as tightly as she could. Caroline was not an experienced hugger. But she did her best.

"Dawn. It's okay. It's okay. How can I make you feel better? What can I do? Should we, I don't know, say a prayer or something?"

"A prayer to...*sob*...to who?"

"God?"

"God is a COCKSUCKER!"

"Oh, Dawn, sweetheart, you should never say that!"

"Why?"

Caroline sighed and looked at the floor.

"Because...Because God...um..."

Dawn sniffed.

"Miss Caroline? Can I...kiss you?"

Caroline became tense.

"Dawn, I don't know if—"

Dawn kissed Caroline lightly on the lips. Caroline relaxed. Felt a little embarrassed for thinking...*no, of course not. She's just a baby.*

No sooner did Caroline think that, when Dawn touched Caroline's left breast and slid her little tongue into Caroline's mouth. Caroline's eyes bulged in horror. She pushed the little girl away and recoiled onto the couch.

"Oh, Dawn! You can't ever, ever do that! Don't ever do that again!"

"Why? I like you. I want to make you feel good."

"Dawn, no! You can't!"

"But I know how. I've seen it done. I can do it."

"It's wrong!"

"Why?"

"Dawn...I could go to jail, and—"

"But you didn't do anything, Miss Caroline. I did. Will I go to jail?"

"Of course not, but—"

"You could say I lured you."

Caroline gasped and put her hand over her mouth. She shut her eyes tightly and shook her head.

"Dawn, no, that is very, very wrong! You can't lure anybody! *You cannot.* Did somebody say that to you? Did somebody try to tell you that you lured them?! Because you didn't, okay? Okay?! You didn't!"

Dawn rubbed her eyes and shrugged.

"I'm sorry, Miss Caroline. I didn't want to make you upset. I just want to make you happy."

Caroline's eyes welled with tears.

"You don't...have to do anything to make me happy. Just be you. Just be *little*. Okay?"

Dawn nodded.

"Miss Caroline? I really want this night to be over. Maybe we *should* say a prayer. But not to God."

"Well, who should we pray to?"

"The sun. Let's pray to the sun, okay?"

"Okay. We'll pray to the sun. We'll ask him to rise real soon."

INTERMISSION

JEFF MICAN'S stay at The Hamilton County Justice Center was not altogether unpleasant. All things considered, it was not terribly unpleasant in the least. He was not yet aware of the ruckus he had caused out in post-September 11th America. He was blissfully ignorant of the fact that his eight-year-old daughter had become an object of lust for cyber-geeks and pedophilic fanboys nationwide. His status in certain circles as an "outlaw artist" to be championed and celebrated had not as yet registered in his comprehension. Little did he know as well, that there were many folks currently plotting his demise in a rabid, desperate, pro-American fervor (or if they weren't seeking his immediate death *per se*, at least, they thought, he should be beaten senseless with Louisville Sluggers before being shipped off to Afghanistan to join Al-Qaeda so we can cluster-bomb his ass like an unwashed camel jockey. Or he should be horsewhipped in public and sent to scrub out the Port-O-Sans at Ground Zero. Or at the very least, for the unforgivable crime of speaking ill of our beloved president GWB, he should be transferred to a prison in Fort Worth, Texas, where they know how to handle commie perverts like him). In fact, all things considered, he was having a splendid time at County. He was even a touch disappointed upon receiving word that his bond had been paid.

Sponge, Bishop, and Dogjaw were there to pick him up in Sponge's brand new Dodge Ram. Sponge had only that morning finished airbrushing a flaming skull on the hood, and installing mud flaps containing mirrored silhouettes of naked women. Jeff whistled his approval of this superior road machine before jumping into the truck bed with Bishop. Over the blasting wind, Jeff shouted, "I met a fella on the inside you guys might wanna maybe contact for a piece in *Psychobilly Freakout!* He's a writer and a big fan and he's serving time for statutory rape! I figured you guys would really like him!"

The fella in question was one D'antre Philips. Prior to his arrest, D'antre had worked on an assembly line at a Liquid Container factory in Mason, Ohio. And he was a part-time MC in a local hip-hop outfit called Da Bomb Droppas. His stage name was *Daddy Molotov*.

The day he met Jeff Mican, D'antre was laying down a phat rhyme. It went like this:

Get in line right behind the white light/ the ties/ the lies/ the hollowed eyes/ the mama cries/ Do nothing while the vulture feeds (what?)/ and smile 'til yo' face bleeds (what?)/ But I'm a superhero/ supercharger/ blowin' up and gettin' larger/ Wannabe, want to be down wit' me? Testify, brutha! I'm gonna be gonna be higher than a satellite/ down in the dark creepin' like a rat 'til light/building up my battle might/ haulin' my ambition (what?)/ callin' my intuition (what?)/ It's goin' down, right? It's goin' down. So let's rock this joint/ and spark this joint/ then Fuck this joint!/ cuz we straight on point/ I'm warmin' ya ladies up like the sticky green kind/ I'm an empirical lyrical miracle and I'm blowing yo' mind/ Cuz this is non-stop body rockin'/ non-stop clock is tockin'/ body tremblin'/ boots are knockin' BOOM BOOM BOOM—

D'antre stopped short when he saw Jeff Mican sketching in a yellow spiral notebook. He recognized Jeff immediately (and was actually in possession of the two most recent issues of *Psychobilly Freakout!—The Joey Spitfire Tribute,* and *The Free Jeff Mican! Issue*).

"Jeff Mican,…Well I'll be a goddamn muthafucka. Man, it's good to meet you, dawg. I gotta say I like your style. It's off the hook, knahmean? I ain't never saw no shit like that before. First time I seen it, I ain't gonna lie, I straight puked like a bitch."

"Yeah, I get that a lot," laughed Jeff.

"So what you drawing there?"

Jeff held up his current sketch. It depicted Dawn riding across a barren plain on a dark, spotted horse. Her hair sailed in the wind, as she held up her little left fist in a power salute. Since September 11th, Jeff had made it a point to *draw for Dawn*. At least some of the time. After seeing how thrilled she was with his work, he tried to create one piece every week—only for her to enjoy. This was of particular importance now, being in lock down. Importance. Particular. As much for Jeff as for Dawn.

D'antre Philips looked at Jeff cockeyed, surprised at the relative "wholesomeness" of the sketch. He squinted, studying the piece—searching in the background for exploding bunny rabbits or a mongoose with a syringe in its neck getting buggered with a crucifix by Attorney General John Ashcroft. Seeing nothing of the kind, D'antre shrugged, nodded, and smiled.

"I feel you, man. I feel you. I got a little girl myself, probably about your girl's age. It tears me up when I can't see her, ya heard? But what can you do? Bad enough I only got to see her once a week, but now, goddamn…I shouldn't even be up in this piece, knahmean? Straight played, dawg. 'Member that. I got played like a sucka. Sheeeeeeit, some blond trick tells me she 18 then shows up at my door wearing nothing but a belly-button ring and a red Christmas bow over her *sumpin'-sumpin',* I ain't tryin' to ask for no ID, ya heard? Now the chick writing me a letter a day saying 'Oh, I love you, D! You gotta marry me once you out! Daddy doesn't even hate you no more!'"

The two men laughed. Talked. Talked about their daughters. Talked about their ex-wives. D'antre's baby's mama was a Covington stripper named Tijuana Smalls. And it was revealed (further proof of the world being ever more diminutive) that TJ Smalls and D'antre Philips were familiar with none other than the late Clover Honey. They knew her. *With great intimacy.* Or TJ did at any rate.

"See, it went down like this," D'antre explained, "Seems somebody got the notion to shoot a spank flick in Kentucky. And they needed a big star to give clout, knamsayin'? So they knew somebody who knew somebody who knew some otha muthafucka who brung in the Honey girl—your homeboy Spitfire's ball 'n chain, ha ha ha. Well, the last scene of the picture was this crazy-ass orgy, and they needed people, you know, in the background up in there. Not to do no fuckin', but just to wiggle and shake they nekkid booties and fake it like a Prince video, ya heard? So alla these strippers from Kentucky got brought in to work the periphery. TJ was one of them…"

D'antre stopped to wipe his brow. Jeff sketched D'antre in his yellow notebook. D'antre stood and paced as he talked. Pausing with great drama and mopping his forehead like a Baptist preacher.

"Now see…TJ, she just got a way with folk. She got it. She wins people over. That's why she stay at that big ole house in Newport and I got my little rat hole in Over-The-Rhine. Anyway, TJ come home one night, this is when we was still together, but not on good terms, ya heard? TJ come home and she got the girl with her. 'D,' she say, 'This is my new *friend*—Clover Honey.' Without another word spoken, the two of them go into the bedroom, *MY* bedroom, knahmean …and lock the door! At first I don't hear nothing but talking and giggling. Then it gets to be only giggling. Then, they ain't giggling no more. And then before I can say boo, fuckin' pictures falling off the walls and shit and neighbors all screaming talking bout 'Keep it down!' and alla that. Hours and hours go by and they in there squealing and breakin' shit, and it ain't like I can jut *not notice* or nothing! It was kinda like being in Hell, my brotha…if your idea of Hell is being nauseous and jealous and humiliated and distracted and cuckolded and blue-balled all at the same time. I know *mine* is, goddamn it!"

Jeff laughed and nodded, waving a hand over his head.

"Tell it!"

"Jeff, I ain't bullshittin'. I couldn't get no sleep for nothing. This went on night after night. Close to a month…bout *KILT'ED* my ass and that's no lie."

"Did you just say *cuckolded*?" Jeff asked.

D'antre nodded and paused for a breath. "And that's no lie…but then…then one day, Clover Honey just up and moved away. And we ain't never saw her since. Not in person. On video, sure, but not in flesh. TJ don't talk about it. Actually she cried for months afterward. Then, nothing. Like it never happened. I didn't blame TJ, though. I never did. I see why people got nuts over that girl Clover Honey."

D'antre crouched down to Jeff's level. He looked around and leaned in closely toward Jeff.

"You know what she had that made her special?"

Jeff shook his head. "Her fondness for steak knives?" he asked with a grin.

D'antre laughed. "I ain't playin' with that, ya heard?"

"I only met her a few times," said Jeff, "And I'm really not into pornography…"

"Ahh, but see I'm not either," said D'antre. His voice and speech suddenly clear. Crystal. Clear. As if his earlier speech had been an act. A performance. "I'm not either, Jeff. That's the *thing*. It was something *special* about *her*. She made you *forget*. She made you forget all the garbage. Made you forget that everything IS garbage. She made you forget about whatever scars you had…acquired…accumulated…"

D'antre looked over to examine the slapdash portrait of himself on Jeff's sketchpad. He smiled in appreciation, then looked away thoughtfully.

"TJ had been molested by her uncle when she was little. Clover made it go away. TJ had been manhandled this way and that way doing private bachelor parties and whatnot. Clover made it all go away. She was completely…she was *untouched*. And she made everything else seem untouched while she was there. That girl Clover had probably been fucked inside out every day since she was 17…but you'd never know it. She never got *sour*. She never spoiled. Even though she was supposedly sick, you'd never guess. Bet nobody would have *ever* known. She would have just disappeared one day. She was special like that. She didn't get ruined by experience. I know we men are not supposed to say this, but you know I'm right, Jeff. You know I'm right. Experience ruins women. Uses them up. 'Til they're useless. Experience will make a woman suffer. Make her rougher. Make you love her less. But Clover, she…had a force field…or something. I think that's how Joey Spitfire killed her. That's how he finally ended up killing her. He ripped down her shield…and she couldn't handle being naked."

click

Could I ask you a question? What's that? Oh. Okay. Well, um, I'm back at grandma's house. Mommy and Phlegm are back in town, but they needed time alone to talk. Guess what they're talking about. I'll give you three guesses and the first two don't count.

Daddy's out of jail until his court date. He has to be in court on December 10th. It's now November 11th, two months since "it" happened. We're at war. Today is also my birthday. Mommy and Phlegm bought me a bunch of presents. I got an X-Box and three new Barbies.

So this is what nine feels like, huh?

I wouldn't kill myself, but if I did, this is the list of ways I might want to do it:

WAYS I COULD KILL MYSELF

1. Eat every pill in grandma's medicine cabinet.
2. Jump out a window (too scary AND messy).
3. Shoot myself with Phlegm's gun (pretty messy).
4. Stick my head in grandma's gas oven (too hot).
5. Get shot out of a cannon into a tree shredder (Dalton's idea).

Daddy is forbidden from coming near any kids. Court said so I guess. He has to stay like four miles away from anybody under 18. That includes me too. That includes me too. What can you do?

That includes me too. We're at war. So this is what nine feel like, huh?

I'm looking at the pictures Daddy drew for me when he was in the pokey. I wonder why they call it "the pokey." Is it cuz they poke you in there? The pictures Daddy drew are awesome. I think they're awesome, but you know...

I've been drawing a lot too. I'm getting way better I think. Course, I'm not quite sure why I'm doing this. I definitely don't want to grow up to be like Daddy.

I'm sorry I yelled at you the other night.

Huh? My question? Oh, my question is— Did you ever love somebody and they didn't love you back?

I'm running away tonight. Far.

Here's something that doesn't have anything to do with anything else: Dalton got his revenge. And now he has a girlfriend too.

click

ALL RIGHT, SEE, I DON'T have a girlfriend, ya dig? I do not. Fuck all that shit.

click

DUNCANSAQWERE.COM was the name of Dalton Brackage's website. Revenge. All the pictures of his rendezvous with Duncan Holmes and his football cronies were there for the whole school to see. And with the wig and skirt, you couldn't even tell that it was Dalton administering the blowjobs. Could have been any pasty, chubby, white boy. And Duncan and his boys weren't talking. At all. In fact, *no one was talking.*

High school was a somber place the morning after Dalton posted the photos. He was a nervous wreck, but no one seemed to know he was the one who'd done it. Or sent every student, teacher, administrator, security guard, and alumnus an anonymous e-mail with the hotlink.

Dalton saw Duncan in the hallway. *Holy Christ! I can't believe he showed up!* Dalton thought to himself. *If I were him, I'd be at home right now stuffing myself into a tree shredder.* Dalton shut his eyes and braced himself for the beating of a lifetime …but it never came. Duncan was as bug-eyed and blank as a half-inflated blow-up doll.

Dalton thought he might possibly escape this whole affair unscathed, until Duncan's girlfriend Nicole approached him after seventh bell.

"Wanna come home with me after school?" she asked.

Dalton wasn't sure why he got into Nicole's car at the end of the day. Guilt? Morbid curiosity? They drove in thick silence for ten minutes before Nicole popped a CD into the player and a Nicorette into her mouth. The speed limit: 55. Nicole's speed: 48.

"So...this the new Tori Amos?"

"Yeah. You like Tori, Dalton?"

"Yeah, sure. That song 'Raining Blood?' That's, uh, originally by Slayer."

"Huh?"

"Never mind."

"I wish I was Tori Amos."

More silence. In lieu of conversation, Dalton tried to watch Nicole out of the corner of his left eye. She popped another Nicorette. And then another. It was early November, and Nicole was in pink flip-flops and silver rhinestone jeans and a pink cut-off tee that read "Princess" across the chest. Her nails were all pink. Her lips were pink. Everything about Nicole screamed PINK! She even smelled like pink bubblegum.

Nicole had to punch in a code to gain access to her own driveway. (As wealthy as they were, the Brackage's driveway had no buzzer. Perhaps it was the relative seclusion of their estate. Perhaps a coke addled Brackster was paranoid about late-night buzzer amnesia. Heaven knows he set off the house alarm many a hazy morning).

Nicole's father was a lobbyist for Phillip-Morris. Her mother owned a travel agency. And it showed. In the house. Less a house, really, than some sort of fantastic fairy tale castle. Dalton had seen plenty like it, *but not in Ohio.* Sprawling acres, tennis courts, three swimming pools, and a subservient Cuban on every floor. Except the floor that contained Nicole's bedroom. Esmerelda was given the rest of the day off.

What the fuckin' hell am I doin' here? What does she want from me?

Nicole clearly had something to discuss, but she wasn't feeling chatty just yet. She kicked off her flip-flops and knelt down to peruse her CD selection. After centuries of careful deliberation, she finally dropped in a disc.

Hmmm…more Tori Amos.

The album? *Under The Pink.* Nicole danced barefoot across her leopard skin rug to the strains of "Cornflake Girl." Dalton sat down nervously on a lime green bean bag chair. Watching her. Like a skittish suburbanite watches waltzing derelicts.

"So what are you thinking, Dalton?"

"About what?"

"Everything. Life. School. The war. All of it."

"It's okay, I guess."

Nicole turned to look at herself in a large vanity mirror. "I hate my forehead," she said. She pulled off her pink cut-off "Princess" tee and tossed it into the corner. Ivory silk bra. Laced frills. Dalton began to sweat ice water. His fists and teeth clenched in dread. Nicole grabbed her perfectly toned midsection and pinched at her tight skin. "I'm so fat," she whined. Dalton rolled his eyes and pulled his shirt just up over his belly.

"You don't know from fat, chick," he said. "I know fat, can ya dig it?"

Nicole turned back to look, and pouted out her bottom lip.

"Awww…you just a widdew piggy, hmmm?" she simpered.

Dalton pulled down his shirt again. "Whatever," he said.

Nicole spun into a dance, unbuttoning her jeans. She fell backward onto her bed and peeled them off, kicking them into the corner. She rolled over to completely display her ivory silk panties. *Oh god please no…*Dalton thought. *Why?!*

"Come sit on the bed with me, Dalton," she cooed, patting her mattress.

"Look, Nicole, I don't know what you think is—"

"Oh…you're gay?" she said sarcastically.

"I...don't like that word, right?" he sighed. "I'm not so much gay as 'not straight,' ya dig? And everything that *goes with that*, yo."

"So you're *queer*, huh? Do you spell that q-w-e-r-e?"

Goddamn. Here it is.

"Tell me, Dalton. Why *did* you spell it like that?"

"Other way was already taken," Dalton mumbled into his chest. He turned away, sitting on the corner of the bed.

"I'm cold." Nicole said softly.

"You're almost naked."

Nicole wrapped her bare feet around Dalton's neck. He tensed up like granite. She giggled.

"Do my feet feel cold to you, Dalton?"

"Whatever."

Somewhere else in Hell, someone is being eaten by rats. A little further down the way, a giant carrot peeler skins a man alive. In Dalton's room in Hell, the prettiest girl at school presses her soft, cold, bubblegum-scented flesh against his neck. *Please let this be over soon.* Nicole suddenly burst into tears and screamed at the top of her lungs—"FUUUUUUUCKKKKK!!"

She flipped over and buried her face in a hot-pink, heart-shaped pillow. Sobbing. Cursing. Her screaming and groaning rendered all the more horrid by the muffle. Dalton was at a loss. Completely. Lost. He stood up and considered making a break for it, but images of slamming drawbridges, armed Cuban houseboys, and fag-munching Dobermans flooded into his mind. He quickly sat again. She looked up at him fiercely. Tear-drenched bloodshot eyes burning lava.

"Just tell me...did you...*sob*...swallow him...*huhhh*...swallow his cum?" she growled.

Dalton nodded.

"Did you let him shoot it all over your face and your chest and your tits and your thighs and on your toes and the bottoms of your feet and the backs of your knees?!?! Did he cum all over your back and in your hair and up your ass and inside your pussy, you little fucking TRAMP-SLUT-WHORE!?!?!"

Nicole screamed again and threw a Betty Boop alarm clock at Dalton's head. He did not duck, and it crashed against the wall, missing him by a yard. She crumpled in defeat.

"Ohhh…why, *sob,* why couldn't he just *huhhh…*I just wasn't ready yet! I just wasn't, *sob,* ready. Is that so fucking…*huhhhh…* Why couldn't he just wait?!?"

"I…don't…have a pussy, yo." Dalton mumbled quietly.

Nicole's eyes flashed pure evil. Tear-drenched bloodshot eyes brightening with Hellfire. She bared her perfect teeth in a sickly grin.

"You got a peeeenis, Dalton?" she sang. "I wanna see it."

"Whatever."

"Let me see your peeenis, Dalton. Pretty please? Just one little look-see. I won't touch it if you don't want me to."

"Whatever, ya dig?"

"Come ooooon. I'll pay you. Five dollars. Twenty. Fifty. I'll write you a check for *anything you want* if you'll just let me look at your penis. I'll even write in, 'For Dalton's Penis.'"

"What-the-fuck-ever, right?!"

"Awww…are you getting angwy, widdew piggy? If I pulled down your pants and looked for myself would you cwyyyy?"

Dalton wanted so badly to smash her face in with the broken Betty Boop alarm clock and smother her to death with hot-pink, heart-shaped throw pillows.

He opted not to.

Nicole lay back down again and rolled to her right side, facing Dalton. She pulled her knees up under her chin. They stared at one another for days, not knowing what comes next.

Finally…

"I don't really…*sniff*..blame you, Dalton," she said softly. "Website. I don't blame you for that either. He broke your heart, didn't he? That's why you did it. He broke your heart. I know just how you feel."

"Actually—"

"Shhhhhhh. You don't have to say anything. I know. I know. Trust me. We should…*sniff*…be friends, Dalton. Lie down next to me. Just as friends. I promise I won't…you know…do anything."

Something told him to run run run run run…yet he stood perfectly still.

"Please, Dalton?" Nicole pleaded. "I want you to be my friend. *I need a friend.* Please?"

A voice in his head hollered, "Don't do it, faggot!" but Dalton ignored it, and lay on the bed next to her. Why? Guilt? Morbid curiosity? She rested her head on his chest, a few straggling tears dripping onto his shirt.

"We can be *girl friends*," Nicole giggled. "We can do each other's hair and dish about dudes." Dalton chuckled. Nicole smiled and nuzzled closer to him. Just as he was about to ask her to not be so in his mix, she rolled onto her back. He sighed in relief.

"I got an idea," she said. "Wanna play a game? I played this with my friend Brittany one time. It's fun. You owe me this much at least, Dalton."

"What's the game?"

"Close your eyes and think of the one person in the world you most want to sleep with. Could be anybody. Living, dead, famous, the mailman, Donald Rumsfeld, anybody…"

"No. Nicole, I know this game, right?" Dalton choked. "Please don't—"

"You *owe me this*, Dalton."

"NO!" he sat up. She pushed him down again.

"It's just fantasy. You owe me. Now shut your eyes."

Without another word, Nicole hopped on top of Dalton, and mashed her lips against his. He shut his eyes tightly, and tried not to get sick.

Oh god…throw her off! Throw the fucking cunt off! Uh…Tobey Maguire, oh…don't puke goddamntastepinkfuckingbubblegum Don't puke…Jude Law, Ed Norton…

Dalton kept his eyes shut tight and tried to ignore the vibrations of the girl's lips against his. Humming. Moaning. She moaned softly. Her moans intensified as he felt her hand moving against his thigh. Rubbing her fingers inside her ivory silk panties.

You don't have to do this! George Clooney, Jet Li, Push her away! Matt Damon, Carson Daly, Ben Affleck. Don't puke! Jared Leto. Don't fucking puke!

He could feel Nicole gyrating on top of him as her fingers flicked and rubbed and danced inside her underwear. He felt her breaths getting harder and faster against his cheeks, pushing out of the sides of her mouth. Teeth pressing hard against the back of her lips as she came closer and closer to—

Don Cheadle, FUCKING DON JOHNSON FUCKING DON KNOTTS WHY!?!?! God NO!!! John Goodman, Make it stop!

Nicole bucked and moaned and squealed, biting Dalton's lower lip. Spasm and spit. Taste of hot sweat.

She rolled off. Gasping. Whimpering. She turned her back to him, pulling her knees under her chin again.

"Mmmm…that felt soooo good. That was num num yummy." She reached over, grabbed a Nicorette from her night stand, and popped it into her mouth. Dalton wiped his lips furiously against his sleeve. He stood over her, glaring razor sharp sabers. She did not feel them.

"You should come back tomorrow, buddy. Goin' to sleep now. Bye bye."

"Whatever! How am I gonna get home?!"

"Feet. Metro. Bye bye, sweetie."

Dalton balled his hands into fists and raised them over his head in impotent rage. He dropped his arms, sighed, walked toward the door. Stopped short. Turned back one last time to get the final word.

"Just cuz I gave him what you couldn't…"

But she was already fast asleep.

click

AS SHERIFF LESTER SIMMONS leafed through Jeff Mican's 'zine, he absently fingered his .357. This was his *personal* firearm, kept only for target practice and home protection.

Sheriff Simmons had no interest in art or *trash culture*. He had no personal stake in pornography or First Amendment issues. His only concern was his *job*. His duty. To protect his community and uphold its standards. Community. Standards. Yes, sometimes that involved raiding theaters and art galleries. Sometimes that involved locking up curators and "artists" and smut peddlers. But that was such a *small* portion of his work. So much attention for so much nothing.

Whiny liberals and outside agitators liked to paint him as some sort of bigoted, reactionary, nazi, Neanderthal. Some sort of power-mad *moral crusader*. They loved to scream and wail whenever he was called to rein in the insanity, and profanity, and vulgarity, and obscenity. *As if this were up to him.* As if he could pick and choose what laws he was to enforce. Thinking about these whiny liberals and outside agitators, he absently fingered his .357. This was his *personal* firearm, kept only for target practice and home protection.

The libber *cause du jour* was this Mican punk. Filthy, nasty, perverted, violent, psychotic, idiotic…certainly not an *artist*. Sheriff Simmons knew that these latte slurping do-gooders would not have given two hoots about this rotten sicko if he hadn't busted him. "Asshole better give me a percentage," Sheriff Simmons grumbled to himself.

Simmons tried to keep down his lunch as he paged through the 'zine for a third time. Had the weepy lefties even *seen* this thing? How could any *decent* human being call this monstrosity "free speech?" Did Thomas Jefferson ever envision *Raped with a Crowbar* or *Virgin Mary, Whore of Jerusalem*? Would the Founding Fathers have given the thumbs-up to crude images of President George W. Bush hacking up black children with a machete? Or a giant, headless, massively endowed child molester? Or an AIDS infected junkie painting his apartment with his own blood, luring police to their deaths…*somethin' familiar about that one…*

Perhaps it's supposed to be funny. Satire or something. *Familiar…*

The good sheriff was not laughing, and he knew that most of Cincinnati was not laughing either. Simmons had support. His name was good here. And Jeff Mican had a rap down the block. Distribution and solicitation of obscene materials. Solicitation of child pornography. Solicitation without a permit. Any number of zoning-law violations. Contributing to the delinquency of a minor (probably). The only thing that would sweeten this pot would be if Mican made a break for it. *Or maybe got caught with an underage whore*, Sheriff Simmons thought, chuckling darkly and inspecting the chambers of his gun. *Hell, throw some kidnapping on top of there too.*

Sheriff Simmons tossed the 'zine into a wastebasket. Slid his .357 into its holster. This was his *personal* firearm, kept only for target practice and home protection. *She could use a bit of target,* he thought, patting the gun at his side supportively. *Squeeze off a coupla rounds. She gonna need a cleaning first.*

click

DAWN STRAPPED ON HER BACKPACK and climbed out the window. She had four changes of clothes, $20 in "mall money" her mother had given her for her birthday, toothpaste, toothbrush, extra toothbrush (because you never know), her sketch pad, four paint markers, a charcoal set, two number 4 pencils, and Flemming Brackage's Platinum Card. No plan. No set destination. Just "away." She was running away. Away. Wherever that is.

Late. It was late. Later than Dawn had ever been out by herself. It became apparent to her quickly that wandering through random Cincinnati neighborhoods in the middle of the night with nowhere to go and no way to get there was not, perhaps, the swiftest bit of thinking in which she had ever engaged. Time ticked by. She followed familiar marks to be on the safe side. But how long would that last? *I recognize this*, she thought, *I still recognize all of this.*

She recognized Delta Ave. Columbia-Tusculum area. Alms Park was nearby! Dawn and Jeff visited Alms Park nearly every weekend that they were together. She could hang out there until morning. Surely by then she would have a plan.

She thought about hitchhiking. What would that be like? Scary. Scary. But probably the only way to get away. Wherever that is. Then she thought about all *those men* who wanted to do things to her. Things. Do things. To her. It said so on the Internet. And they called her grandma's house. Would they be out driving around? Looking for her?! *No, of course not*, Dawn thought. *How would they know where to find me?* But what if one of them happened to be driving around and spotted her? *Well, I don't talk to strangers, duuuh…Of course that is going to make hitchhiking kinda hard…*

Tusculum. *Jeez La-weez, this is a big hill.* Now would be a good time for catching a ride. But no, Dawn didn't talk to strangers.

Practically no cars on Columbia Parkway this night. *Here comes one. Do I hide, or stick out my thumb?* She decided to do neither. The car stopped anyway and pulled up beside her. Down came the window.

"Hullo there, little girl. Can I give you a ride?"

Dawn peeked into the driver-side window and smiled her prettiest smile.

"Love you, Daddy."

"Love you too, sugargirl."

click

JOEY SPITFIRE'S GRAVE was a popular spot. Almost always somebody just hanging about. Emo kids. Rockabilly throwbacks. 'Zine geeks. The disgruntled and disaffected flocked to Joey Spitfire's grave like burn victims to a porno shop. That said, Caroline Powell was relieved to find herself the only visitor. She sipped happily at her mochaccino. *Thank God for styrofoam*, she thought. She would be littering today. She had already decided. *And screw the Sierra Club.* No checks. No balance.

"So how they treating you in here, Joey?" Caroline asked out loud. *Like a fucking prince, Caroline,* she thought to herself and chuckled. She chuckled again when she thought of something Joey once said to her. "Caroline," he said, "Regicide is a victimless crime."

"Blew the proverbial whistle on that junkie guard Kridell," Caroline continued aloud. "Wouldn't it be something if they sent him to Chillicothe? Chilly Cothy?"

Caroline looked about at all of the gifts people had left. Packs of Marlboro cigarettes. Unopened cans of Pabst Blue Ribbon. Shrink-wrap sealed copies of *Psychobilly Freakout!* with personal notes attached. One simply said, "You built this prison on rock 'n roll." Another said, "Vicious and Malicious but oh so Delicious" in blue lipstick. Same color as Clover Honey's suicide "note." *Tasteful.*

"Well, Joey-boy, I thought you should be the first to know," Caroline sighed, "I'm dropping out of the game. It's just not fun any more. And it's not necessary. Glok *unt* Spiel have become a rave act with no American distribution. I'm giving away my share of *PF!* Jeff causes so much trouble, *the actual press* writes his press—makes *you* look like Mister Rogers. He's going down in flames anyway. And there are other…complications I don't really feel like discussing with you at present. I've got more than enough money to live out the rest of what some charitable person might call 'a life.' Chet's still earning a decent wage. We're never gonna have kids, thank sweet Jesus and baby Jesus. Moving out of Landthattimeforgot, Ohio and back to LA—no imagination required. I plan to spend the rest of my days healing facelifts on the beach and drinking overpriced cocktails. All in favor of this plan? Aye. All opposed, speak now or forever lie rotting in the dirt. The 'ayes' have it."

Ring Ring

"Hold on a sec, Joey, that's my cell. I'll just be a moment." *beep*

"Caroline Powell."

"Caroline!"

"What's up, Bishop."

Caroline placed her hand over the mouthpiece and whispered,
"It's Bishop."

"Caroline, I've got some balls-out, crazy ass news! God, this is
gonna cost us a freakin' fuckin' fortune! Jeff Mican just broke bail
and took off for parts unknown and he kidnapped his daughter
and the fuckin' police are goin' apeshit!"

"Good. Best of luck to him."

click

SO I'M JUST SMOKING SOME OPIUM, can
you dig it? It's outta sight. Opium. I only smoke opium on really
special occasions—like I'm celebrating, right? Yeah. I'm celebrating. Schmokin' and celebratin'. Making a toast to Dad and his future. Best of luck to him. Oh, and I'm toasting Mom and *her* new
life. She met a guy. Guess it was touch-and-go there for a while
which team ole Mom was gonna pitch fer, but I suppose she got
all traditional at the zero hour. His name's Eliot. A Hamilton cop.
Now ain't that about a bitch? Mom's a …aw, I ain't gonna say it.
It's too obvious…Mom's a P-I-G-F-U-C-K-E-R! Sorry. Hey, it's
the opium, right? Blame it on the drugs. Guess this whole, new-
found, "rugged-guy, manly-man" sex appeal business that's sweep-
ing the nation caught up to her. Firefighters. Police. Brick layers.
Defense secretary. I'm not shitting you. Women are getting leaky
over these guys. Okay, everybody sing along—"He's got to be
tough/ and he's got to be strong/ and he's got to be fresh from the
fight/ I NEEEED A HEROOO!"

Now, all right, I can see *firemen*. Oh yes. I've always had a
thing for firemen—way before it was chic, can you dig that? It's
obvious. Black rubber uniforms. Huge, faceless figures spurting,

blasting, gushing, power hoses. They've *always* been heroes, yo. But cops? The attack dogs for the racist, sexist, classist, homophobic, status quo? Busting hookers, beating bums, killing blacks, rounding up dopers and sodomites and shipping us off to Hell…I don't care if we are at war, right? *They are the enemy.* Well, maybe not all of them, but this chowderhead Mom's fucking…Christ. Struts around the house in his uniform, which is waaay too tight. Always sporting those mirrored sunglasses, porn-fag mustache, Knight Rider haircut, forfucksake!

I wonder if he uses his nightstick on Mom when they're in bed. Making her beg for that spring-loaded corkscrew cock—*Oh, BUST me, officer! Book me, Dan-o!* Grunting like a farm animal, slapping her in handcuffs. Hey, that shit's popular again. Real men are back, dig? I read it in Vanity Fair.

But you know what? I can't even really feel the hate, cuz right now I am wrapped in a warm and fuzzy blanket, and the blanket can talk, and it's telling me that everything *issss outta sight!* I can't even remember why I was mad in the first place. Opium. Almost makes me believe in a god. You take that first big drag, and it fills you with warm lavender heaven, and you realize for the first time how much you dig the taste of *lavender.* Every time is the very first time. You never get used to it. You never get used up. It never degrades you. It just makes everything *clean again.* And it lies lies lies lies lies. Lies about everything. *Everything isss outta sight*, it tells you, and it wraps you up in a warm and fuzzy blanket. The world is burning and choking and dying— *But…not right now.* Little children far, far away are being cluster bombed and blown to pieces by our government in a war against "evil"—*But not really.* It's not really happening. The blanket told me so. See, there's no such thing as an opium *addict*, dig? There never was and there never will be. Anyone who ever thought he was addicted to opium was a yutz. He…she…they all were addicted to *the lie.* Can you dig that? The lie. And different folks find the lie in different places. Neither opium nor any other narcotic has cornered that market. Hell no. Get the lie wherever you can. Get it in family, get it in church, get it from tv, get it in art, get it from the government, get it from sex, just get the lie and wrap yourself in it and *believe in it*. Believe in it, yo. The lie doesn't lie. I only get the lie on special occasions—like I'm celebrating, right?

I've got a crazy theory about opium. Wanna hear it? It's like this: when you're smoking up, you connect to an invisible opiate network, right? You bond on an astral plane with everybody else who's smoking up (or popping or shooting up), and you all collectively share your thoughts and feelings—at that moment. It's the ultimate intergalactic high, can you fuckin' dig that, yo? It's not really that far out, since you're all feeling the exact same anyway, and thinking the same thing too, which is pretty much nothing but, "whoa, this isssss all right…" But still, you're all connected and you're not alone. That's pretty hip. Not alone at all. That's pretty damn hip.

I'm glad I decided to *celebrate* tonight, because something happened…something really bad and awful happened to me. I guess maybe I deserved it, and I asked for it, and I brought it on myself. But that doesn't make it any easier to deal with, right? Some might say that I probably secretly wanted it, but they are wrong. Horribly wrong. But it doesn't matter now. Nothing matters now. I am *untouched*.

I'm really enjoying this writing thing. I think I'd like to make a serious go of it. I honestly feel like I have something worthwhile and unique to say, right? I mean; I'm into drugs, I'm out cast at school, I hate my parents, I'm against society, I've got issues with my sexuality…how many teenagers can say that?

I'm out of this place. As soon as I sober up, I'm gone. Taking a notebook and a coupla bucks and I'm hitting the road, ya dig? Nobody's gonna care. Nobody's gonna miss me, right? I'm going to *experience*. If the world wants to fuck me over? Bring it on, man. The world wants to hold me down against my will and molest me? It's all just grist for the mill, motherfucker. And I'll *take* it all. Bring it on, yo.

Whoa. Shit's starting to wear off. Time to take another hit, and nod for the night.

One last thing: my soon-to-be little sister is out there somewhere. If you see her, tell her to be careful and tell her that I love her. I love you, Dawn. Wherever you are. Big sis loves you, yo. Be careful out there, baby.

click

Nine Millimeter in the Diaper Bag (and Daddy's on the Lam Again) —1992 BY D'ANTRE PHILIPS

Held the gorgeous little bundle in my arms.
No crying or fussing made the gorgeous little bundle.
Just a little sneeze or two and a curious inspection from
    round little black eyes.
I smoothed her little black tufts and tickled her little
    brown chin and wiped her little brown nose and nuz-
    zled her little brown cheeks and kissed her little brown
    forehead and whispered in her little brown ear—

"You don't have a chance in the world."

click

"I'M LEAVING, MOM."
Dalton stood before his mother defiantly. Head held high. Backpack packed to capacity—clothes, notebooks, pens, marijuana, opium, *The Free Jeff Mican! Issue*, *The Joey Spitfire Tribute*. His mother remained sitting on the living room couch. Eyed him through a vague, martini glaze. Disinterested. Next to her sat Sergeant Eliot the Hamilton cop. Sexy and ridiculous in his tight, county issued threads. Smirking and sneering as if Elvis and Billy Idol were playing tug-o-war with his top lip.

"I'm leaving. Today. I'm not going to school. I'm taking off.
I'm gonna be a writer."

Silence. Dalton continued, "So, you gonna sic your cop on me
or what?"

Sergeant Eliot scoffed out loud. Dalton's mother simply continued to sit in silence. She took a long, thoughtful sip from her
martini. Finally...

"So, Dalton," his mother sighed flatly, "My sweet treasure.
You're leaving me. Oh, dreadful, dreadful day. Whatever shall I do
without you, my darling son? My only?"

Dalton's faced burned with humiliation. Sergeant Eliot guf-
fawed, still smirking.

"I'm...serious, right?" Dalton said through clenched teeth.
"I'm hitting the, y'know, open road. I'm gonna be a writer."

His mother nodded. Sergeant Eliot rubbed the inside of her
thigh with his right hand. She locked her thighs around his fingers.

"I'm gonna...be a writer."

"Well, honeybuns, I've got the perfect opening line for your
first best seller—

'My mommy didn't love me.'"

click

"**PSSST! MOLOTOV!** Hey, yo, D!"

"Wuzzup, dawg?"

"Hey, I got that shit for ya."

"Word? You got it? You sure it's *opium*?"

"Goddamn, nigga! Keep yo' damn voice down! I'm for real,
you get caught with this shit, *you don't know me.*"

"Man, I ain't tryin' to get caught with nuthin', dawg! I'm out
in three days! You ain't even got to worry, ya heard?"

"So why you playin' with this ching-chong Chinese shit,
anyway?"

"Cuz I am *celebratin'.* Imma see my little girl, I'm gettin' my freedom, I'm pursuin' my writing. That's what we call sunshine and lollipops. Happily ever after is how I'm livin'."

"Man, you trippin', D. I'll holla."

"Aw'ight. Much love."

"Much love."

click

Weighing Me Down BY DALTON
I'm walking the wrong way down a one-way dead-end street
and I'm smoking out everybody that I meet.
I got keys with no locks
Clocks that tell me what time it used to be
Directions to nowhere
And a ticket to ride with no destination
I got a satchel on my back packed to the brim
With nothing, it seems, but my dreams

And it's weighing me down…as it's lifting me up.

click

RING RING
"Caroline Powell throwing in the towel."

"Caroline. We need to talk."

"Hoooly shit! If it isn't The Brackster himself!"

"Yes indeed. How have you been? Listen, Caroline, let me get right—"

"It's been a hundred thousand years!"

"Have you been drinking, Caroline?"

"Hell no! Of course not! Or, to put it another way…yes. Quite a bit."

"Uh huh, at any rate—"

"Wine coolers. I'm not a big drinker."

"I see."

"Hey! Brackage! Mr. Flemming Brackage. Have you heard the latest? I quit. Dropped out of the bizzz. Over. *Finito.* No more. *No mas.*"

"Well, it was a long time coming. Glad you finally came to your senses."

"Fuuuuh…cue…"

"Okay. Listen, Caroline, let me get right to it. My ex-wife-to-be is—"

"Ex-wife-to-be-is…" Caroline mumbled. Hint of melancholy.

"Right. She's telling me—"

"How *is she?*" Melancholy. Just a hint.

"—Telling me that my son has run off. My bride-to-be is in hysterics because her daughter has gone missing. And, what's this? Your degenerate client is on the lam. Now, I want you to tell me everything you know. I'm sure Jeff has the kids. Dawn at least. Where is he? When did you last hear from him? What is he up to? What the hell is going on?"

"I'd looove to help you, Flemming. I really would. Sincerely. Cross my heart and hope to die. But I'm telling you, I don't know—"

At this, Caroline dropped the receiver. It landed on her wine glass, shattering it. Shooting tiny shards all over the floor around her. Ignoring the broken glass, she picked up the receiver again.

"Shit. Sorry."

"Don't play dumb, Caroline. This is not a game. You know *something.* So just tell me, okay? Tell me everything you *do* know."

"All *I know* is…I'm just a princess, kissing frogs, and hoping for the best."

"Uh…huh…Yes. Very poetic—"

"But YOU'RE the *fairest in all the land*. Aren't ya, Flemming?"

"For godsake, Caroline—"

"Guess I *jusss* have a taste for poison apples."

"Caroline, please! I need—"

"Slay the damsels! Rescue the dragon!"

Aggravated silence. She continued,

"And...Brackage? We all lived happily ever after."

"Good bye, Caroline. I'm hanging up now."

"I'm just Cinderella, Brackage, slipping my feet into glass."

click

THE SPITFIRE GRILL

by Joey Spitfire

Howdy, kids! So, how are y'all enjoying the 1990s so far? I, for one, could not possibly be any happier. For starters; we got a bimbo gropin', no-daddy-havin', Arkansas good ole boy on Pennsylvania Avenue. White trash have officially taken over! Yee-haw! Next; thanks in part to the untimely passing of Kurdt *Go-bang*, boring, insipid *grunge culture* is breathing its last breath. Make way for the glorious return of surf rock! Or David Allen Coe. Or Johnny Cash.

Any of those would be fine wif' me.

Speaking of our boy Kurdt, am I the only mofo around here who noticed that his suicide note was written in *two different handwritings?* Just seems odd to me, cherubs. Check it out. Especially those of you considering suicide in a show of solidarity with homeboy. Not that I'm trying to discourage such activity. Lord knows, I fully support anyone's decision to off himself. Whatever gets you by. I understand his tombstone is a popular hangout. The disgruntled and disaffected have been flocking to Cobain's grave like burn victims to a porno shop. Like I said, whatever gets you by. And congratulations to Courtney Love, whose career has really gone gangbusters since her husband's (cough) *suicide.* I'm sure it's just a coincidence.

Okay...Fat Boy in The White house...death of grunge...I guess that's all I had to say. Gabba gabba HEY, WAIT A SEC! I almost forgot the reason for this column! My recent nuptials! Many thanks to all of you who sent messages of well-wishing. And for those of you who actually mind your own damn business and weren't aware...I was married last week in Cancun, Mexico to the hottest, finest, juiciest—er—loveliest, most intelligent, most wonderful gal in the whole golldern universe. What can I say, gents, *somebody* had to hit the jackpot. That somebody was yours truly.

Needless to say, I will be taking a brief (six week) hiatus from *PF!* Until I return, I'm sure you will all re-enjoy the classic reprints of *The Spitfire Grill* from issues past. If not, these pages make surprisingly good rolling papers.

Clover and I are planning to hook up with some freaky friends of ours in No Cal. I had best stock up on vitamin E. If you've never ridden the beast with two (or more) backs at sunset in Big Sur...then your life sucks. Of course, judging by the amount of letters I receive from Iowa, Minnesota, and Ohio, most of your lives suck already. I swear, if any of you ever catch me in such a state, feel free to execute me on the spot. See ya when I see ya. Hey ho, let's go!

And we all lived happily ever after,
JS

click

LIGHTS OUT. Lock down. Hamilton County. Shrouded within his flimsy jailhouse bed cover, D'antre Philips carefully placed the small crimson pebble onto a square of foil. It glowed bright orange as he placed it against the flame of his lighter. Lavender heaven filled D'antre's body as he sucked every bit of smoke into his lungs. Celebrate. Celebration. Freedom. Freedom. Wrapped in warm, fuzzy joy. He lit the chunk and hit the smoke one last time. Glowed, burning bright orange. He then wrapped it back in the foil.

Emerging from within his flimsy jailhouse bed cover, feeling connected to the universe, he squinted against the darkness. Retrieved his notebook. Put pen to paper. *Happily. Happily ever... ever...*

click

DARK. Ohio sky. Cincinnati night. East-side. Desolate. It became apparent to Dalton quickly that wandering through random Cincinnati neighborhoods in the middle of the night with nowhere to go and no way to get there was not, perhaps, the swiftest bit of thinking in which he had ever engaged. Time ticked by. Followed familiar marks to be on the safe side. But how long would that last? *Hopefully not much longer. Otherwise, what's the point of getting away?*

Ducked down an alley, over a jagged, rusted fence, to a bus depot cul-de-sac. Up a small hill to a train trestle. *This will work until sunrise.* Nestle in. Sweet view of the valley. Dark Ohio sky.

Shrouded within his flimsy denim jacket, Dalton carefully placed the small crimson pebble into his glass pipe. It glowed bright orange within the shredded green as he placed it against the flame of his lighter. Lavender heaven filled Dalton's body as he sucked every bit of smoke into his lungs. Celebrate. Celebration. Freedom. Freedom. Wrapped in warm, fuzzy joy. He lit the chunk and hit the pipe one last time. Glowed, burning bright orange. Burned until ash. Dust.

Emerging from within his flimsy denim jacket, feeling connected to the universe, he squinted against the darkness. Retrieved his notebook. Put pen to paper. *Happily. Happily ever...ever...Happily happily...*

SECTION TWO

My Prayer for Y'all BY D'ANTRE PHILIPS

Here I am. I'm inside my head. I don't want to be here any-more. It is too crowded and too chaotic and too dangerous in here. A nigga's liable to get buckshot...

I'm not really up for confession today. But you know, Abraham's God told my daddy to sacrifice his first born son. Lucky for me he ain't got around to it yet.

'Do you believe in God, the father almighty, creator of heaven and earth?' Well, do I have an option? In my neigh-borhood, God is just another basehead. Wasted and face-dead. I told him I was god now. He said, "Aw'ight, build your own prison." So I built this prison...

click

Dwelling Outside Possibility BY DALTON

I built this prison on rock and roll. Say "yeah." Put it on paper. I did! I stalked the perimeter. I mapped it all out. Planned my escape route. So what's it all about? Gotta capture a moment, ya dig? Steal it. Trap it. Trap yourself inside it. I suppose it really is all about being a prisoner. Is it really? Yep. Is it really about being a prisoner? Yes! Is it ever not about being a prisoner? NO! There is nothing else. It is the only story. Everybody. Prisoner. Visit from prison to prison...

click

My Prayer for Y'all (CONT'D)

Ever visit an inmate? Kind of like being a prisoner yourself. Visiting an inmate is a bit like being a prisoner yourself...

Shut-up-get-in-line-take-a-number-sit-down-shut-up-waitwaitwaitwaitwaitwaitwait. Wait in the waiting room with no room to wait. Waiting four thousand years for some bored, crackly, disembodied voice to finally call your name. And every waiting room's the same, come on now! Nothing but teenage white trash bimbos and their babies. Babies wandering around in nothing but soggy diapers. Screaming. Caterwauling. Sucking on bottles with RC Cola in them. Babies. Little coffee-colored babies...not that that matters, of course. The world ain't nothing but churches and liquor stores. And your heaven ain't nothing to me but one more prison...

click

Dwelling Outside Possibility (CONT'D)

We're nothing but fertilizer waiting to happen, can you dig it? Everybody's mother's gone shopping for body bags. I got nothing to lose. Plant me in the soil and I'll poison the earth. Prove your worth. Prove you're worth it!

click

I put the chrome to they dome and then send 'em on home, TAGOW! I got nothin' to lose. Say, boy, what's your cell number?

click

Clock me at 187 FM. I'm on the radiation station. The Caucasian Appalachian slave's vacation! Shooting off a midnight toy for the joy of one less colorless boy. And we're all just....fertilizer. And we got nothing to lose. But now we've been laid to waste. 30 spot pre-fab apocalypse in a silicon horror show. Suck and beg to be replaced. Like...so...not even... whatever...going there...commercial revolution in your face. There's a throbbing in my Temple 'cuz God is a traffic jam and I'm running in place. Give me death like it's a fashion accessory and I'm ironic in the back alley and I'm suitably debased. Lick me seven ways from Sunday and then you can judge my taste. Keep it Prozac monotone rave to the techno drone cuz we dry fuck in cyber space. But it don't keep me down. I got a smile under my frown, 'cuz at least my ganja's laced…

click

Just cuz some lucky motherfucker's hung…do we all gotta hang for the top forty song he sang? Or can we go our own way? And can we climb the walls, and tear down the walls, and dance on the walls, and escape from the…ohhhhh… Escape from the…Have we captured a moment? No. It's more than just "moments." It's gotta be. It's escape from the…moment…But we are imprisoned in the moment! If life is prison, then the point is to escape!

click

If life is prison…then the point is to escape! The struggle for freedom is not revolution, it's evolution! Freedom itself is stagnation…or death. But so is withdrawing from the struggle! You are face to face with your creator in a quagmire. We're stuck here cuz the traffic jam is God. The DMV is God. Ever see a five-year-old boy in a bank line? The struggle continues! When I was liberated from their schools…

click

From their churches…

click

From their society…

click

From their prisons? I built my own. I'm keeping you prisoner? Then I AM GOD.

click

Forgive me, Father, for I'm about to sin and I'm not one bit sorry about it.

click

God told my father to…

click

God told *my* father too. "Sacrifice your only begotten son," she said…

click

When I was in their prison, they asked me, 'Do you reject Satan and all his empty promises?' And I said, Well, that's certainly a loaded question. What exactly are these promises? But I couldn't be held cuz I'm a burnt-cork-black, Ubangi lipped, spear chucker—

click

Cock bobbin' fairy faggot pinko freak—

click

> *Powerhouse gorilla terrorist—*

click

Thrashing white trash super-colossal hard-core bad ass!!!

click

> *But I'm just waiting…to imprison myself somewhere else.*
> *I made my own satanic promise. Call it a compromise. I'm*
> *as holy as I need to be. So worship me with a beating heart.*
> *There is a throbbing in MY temple. Oh yes. Put it on paper.*
> *I made a beast of myself to avoid the pain of being a*
> *man…*

click

I made a man of myself to avoid the pain of being a
boy. I made a child of myself to avoid the pain of being a
fascist. I made a fascist of myself to avoid the pain of being
an animal. When Aristotle told me to my face, "If you are
not a citizen, you are either a beast or a god," I said, Bitch!
I'm all three! I made a god of myself to avoid your tedious
company…

click

> *In my neighborhood, God is just another basehead.*
> *Wasted and face-dead…*

click

Some nights I nod off with God in our wrought-iron holocaust. Paying the hollow cost. Down with a callow Faust. But I stalked the perimeter. Mapped it all out. Planned my escape route. Then I burned the map, cuz I still got everything to lose. I still got everything to lose—

click

I STILL GOT EVERYTHING TO LOSE!
I STILL GOT EVERYTHING TO LOSE!

click

LATE SHIFT. Another late shift, and Lindsey had a trig test in the morning. Lindsey Buckingham. (And yes her parents did deliberately, and with malice aforethought, name her after that guy from Fleetwood Mac). **YOU ARE BEING VIDEOTAPED FOR YOUR OWN SAFETY** read the sticker on the door. **CLERK DOES NOT HAVE KEYS TO THE SAFE** read another at the counter. The latter was a lie.

Except for *Maxim* and *Field and Stream,* Lindsey had already paged through every magazine on the rack. Luckily she found an old issue of *Glamour* from January 2001 wedged under the counter. "Body Hang-ups Buh-Bye!" was printed over the perfectly toned mid-section of the airbrushed brunette waif on the cover. "Special style section—are you a do or a don't?" "60 Sins You and He Should Commit By Feb. 14 nudge, nudge, wink, wink." "1. 'Date Me' 2. 'Love Me' 3.'Marry Me'—how to make all three happen in this lifetime." Lindsey wished she had a gun.

"Beat me, kill me, drill me," Lindsey said aloud to the airbrushed cover waif in the sequined butterfly halter-top. "In that order."

With no particular urgency, she flipped through the noxiously perfume-scented rag. Page 21 was a full-page "got milk?" ad featuring a quasi-bearded Noah Wyle with a milk mustache. *I'd fuck Noah Wyle*, Lindsey thought to herself, but couldn't muster the energy to continue that line of thought any further.

Hey, a customer. In walked a young black man, whistling, with a jaunty spring in his step. Whistling. "Zippity-do-dah." He was *actually whistling* "Zippity-do-dah." Lindsey wished she had a gun.

"And how you doin' this fiiiiine ev'nin', young lady?" asked the man with a broad, tooth packed grin. *Kinda cute.*

"Okay." Lindsey tried her best to smile.

"Imma just get me a forty, ya heard?"

"Okay."

Another customer. Disheveled, chubby, freckle-faced boy. *Aw, shit! It's that Dalton kid!* Lindsey's high-school had been thrown topsy-turvy when a website appeared containing photos of the football team's first stringers having an all-sausage suck-a-thon with some soft-bellied drag queen. Turns out it was that Dalton kid, who had not been to school in three days. Lindsey wasn't sure if she should acknowledge him or not. They were by no means friends. Of course the kid didn't have any friends at all, and had been on the ass-end of quite a few nasty jokes in his two years of high school. Lindsey often felt sorry for him, but then would quickly decide that he deserved it. Whatever *it* was. He was a rich kid after all, and they deserve any and all ill fortune.

The kid went straight to the snack isle. Focused hard and deep on the butter twist pretzels. As if they contained *The Answer*.

The black guy returned to the counter with two bottles of OE.

"Ain't actually allowed to have this shit," he said. "So don't you be tellin' my probation officer, now! Ha ha ha."

"Okay."

The man was just about to leave when his eyes caught the eyes of the freckled-faced boy. Turn and about-face. The two stared at each other. Completely still. Staring. Wide-eyed and petrified. Lindsey stared at them staring at each other. *What the hell?* For what may have been five full minutes, the two stood there beside the snack isle. Staring at one another. Finally, the black man asked softly…

"Say boy, what's your cell number?"

The kid did not answer. Pause, and then….the man walked slowly out the door. Disappeared. Melted into the black of the night.

"Clock me at 187 FM…" the kid muttered to himself.

Curiosity got the best of Lindsey.

"Did that guy just ask for your cell phone number?"

"No…" the kid answered absently. "Number on my cell…My own personal frequency…"

"You know that guy, Dalton?"

He turned to face her, and smiled.

"Lindsey Buckingham," he said, and walked back down the snack isle toward the freezer. At least he had the decency to not follow it up with a bar or two of "Gold Dust Woman." The typical follow-it-up.

Suddenly, out of the black, a robin's egg-blue VW bus screeched into the parking lot. Pulled in diagonally across two handicapped spaces, headlights blasting right into the store. The side-door of the van slid open, releasing four human shaped figures, and a white, *chose-the-pope* sized smoke cloud. The bus vibrated with thick, sludgy, ear-shattering, feedback-drenched stoner metal. The headlights switched off; the music did not. Lindsey could see the driver—a white knuckled mullet-head with *raw-eggs-and-ketchup* eyes that hung from his face, kept in place only by thin, sunken, ash colored lids. The smoke finally dissipated, revealing two young men and two young women. The first man was a tall, shirtless Indian (feathers not dots) with hair to his knees and "AIM" tatted crudely across his stomach. He swigged lime green liquor from a clear, diamond shaped bottle, and handed it to the second man—a black leathered Beowulf in bell-bottoms and stack heeled boots.

Attached to the Indian's hip was a round and rosy Janis Joplin-type in wood beads and a burgundy dress. About the three of them danced a tiny, barefoot dirty blonde wearing an *Orange Goblin* tee shirt, flittering like a wigged pixie. Lindsey gritted her teeth as she saw the *Goblin* girl staggering toward the door.

"Hey, Blondie!" Lindsey said as the girl stumbled in. "No bare feet in the store. Company policy." Lindsey hated herself for saying that. Policy. Company. The dirty blonde just giggled and lifted her left foot off the floor.

"Howz'bout jus' one foot at a time?" the girl slurred. "What if just my toes?" she continued, trying in vain to stand on tip-toes, and laughing at her own failure. Lindsey sighed, and returned to her magazine, keeping one watchful eye on business.

"Okay. I don't really care anyhow."

"Cooool. Yer all right, girlfriennn," sang the girl as she sauntered past the Moon Pies and Little Debbie's. Lindsey saw her grab Dalton's collar, and they ducked down behind the end display of two-liters. Lindsey strained to hear the girl whisper to him...but "Pssst! Hey Freckles! Wanna buy some..." was all that she could decipher. The two muttered back and forth incoherently. A few minutes later, Dalton and *Orange Goblin* walked past Lindsey on their way out the door, arms filled to capacity with cases of Milwaukee's Best.

"Just stealin' some beer," the blonde announced. "Hope that's cool."

"Okay."

They exited the store, climbed into the van with the *Goblin's* friends, and screeched away, leaving a cocktail of smoke and fading metal in their wake. *Why me...why me...Gonna get in trouble...*

Lindsey chucked the *Glamour* into the wastebasket and sipped a bit of lukewarm Yoo-hoo. She still had an hour and some before she was off. Free. Liberated. And she'd probably have to wait even longer, because Carlos was always late. Too busy banging his old lady. Or somebody else's old lady. Or somebody else's old lady's old lady.

Well, here's a familiar sight.

"How you doin' there, Lindsey?"

"Good evening, Sheriff. Or good morning. Whichever it is."

Sheriff Lester Simmons swaggered into the store with an air that said, "There's a new sheriff in town,"—even though he'd been sheriff since as long as anyone could remember and always ran unopposed. Sheriff Simmons stopped in most nights Lindsey worked late. Probably stopped in most nights period, but Lindsey could not prove that directly.

"Anything funny tonight, Lindsey? Anything, you know, *suspect*?"

Why yes, Sheriff Simmons, Lindsey thought to herself. *I'm glad you asked. Now I don't know for certain, but I'm pretty sure that I, an underage female, am not supposed to be made to work this shift all by myself. Isn't that a violation of state law?*

"Nope," Lindsey said. "Nothing too suspect tonight."

Lindsey always waited for that fantasy conversation to take place, but it never did. The Sheriff simply did not seem concerned with the legality of Lindsey working late shift alone. On a school night no less. Perhaps he had more important things on his mind. *Or perhaps he, like everyone else in Cincinnati, is stuffed into the front pocket of the corporate hog who owns this chain of convenience stores.* Even still, Lindsey was glad it was the good Sheriff stopping by every night, and not some patrolling beat cop. She'd heard stories of other girls who'd worked here in the past spending their shifts in the back room—on their knees, or bent over the slop sink, or bouncing in the lap of one of Cincinnati's finest. Say what you will about the Sheriff, he wasn't into *that*.

"So, Sheriff, what's the juice over the squawk-box?"

Sheriff Simmons wandered to the far corner of the store to obtain a refrigerated chocolate-oriented beverage. He bent over to grab a bag of butter twist pretzels, and was momentarily spellbound. He quickly shook it off and was back on task.

"Nothin' too outrageous tonight, hon. Got a runaway. Boy from yer high school, if I'm not mistaken! Seems he took off some three days ago, but his mother didn't think to notify us until to-night. Big money family...," The Sheriff turned toward Lindsey and winked conspiratorially. "You know how *they* are."

Lindsey smiled and nodded.

"Brackage is the name," he continued. "Mother called us all devastated. After three days, you understand. Three days. Oh, god, what's the kid? 'Darrell' I think. Darrell Brackage. Jah know'm?"

"Please?"

"Do you know him?" he enunciated.

"Nope. Sure don't. So Sheriff, did y'all ever catch that runaway cow up in Mount Storm?"

"Got a chopper on her as we speak, Lindsey," the Sheriff responded in all sobriety.

"What about that runaway pedophile artist who kidnapped his daughter?"

Lindsey was really pushing her luck now, and she knew it. Still, the Sheriff remained perfectly cool.

"Now, I'd reserve judging him a *pedophile* until all the facts are in. Personally, I don't even think he is. Really, just another talentless loser strutting around calling himself an *artiste*. Peddling his nasty wares on the streets of *my town*. No sir, buddy. This ain't your day. We got good people here..." Sheriff Simmons trailed off. He plopped the bag of pretzels and two bottles of Yoo-hoo onto the counter. Lindsey rung them up with a wry smirk.

"Good-bye, Blue Monday," she said.

"Please?"

"Nothin'. Have a good one, Sheriff."

"Ohh, I already *have* a good one, Lindsey..." Simmons began. *Holy shit! Is he actually gonna tell me a dirty joke!?* But the Sheriff just smiled and patted the gun at his hip. Lindsey nodded and grinned.

"Take care, Lindsey. Don't work too hard now." And he left.

Lindsey wished *she* had a gun. Late shift. Another late shift and Lindsey Buckingham had a trig test in five hours. A tabloid from across the counter glared back at her. It featured a picture of some candy-nosed Hollow-wood couple with a photoshopped "split" between them.

"Beat me, kill me, drill me," Lindsey said aloud to the two of them. "In that order."

click

RING RING

"Yeah. It's your quarter."

"Mommy?"

"DAWN?!?!?! OH MY GOD!!! Oh baby, oh sweetheart, where are you!? Are you all right?! Where ARE you?!"

"Shhh Mommy, it's okay. Don't cry. Don't cry, Mommy. I'm fine. I'm just fine. I just—"

"Where's your *father*?"

"He's putting gas in the tank. Mommy—"

"Tell me where you are and I'll come get you right this instant!"

"You don't need to do that, Mommy. I just need to ask you about the bleeding—"

"BLEEDING!?!?! What *bleeding*?! What happened? What's going on?! Oh god oh god oh god!!!"

"Okay, Mommy. I'll just call you back later when you've simmered down some. Bye bye. Love you."

"DAWN! NO! Don't you dare hang up on me, girl!!! NOOOOOOOOOOOO!!!!"

click

RING RING

"Pit-Stop Lodge."

"Yes. Is this Lewis Runlin?"

"Who wants to know?"

"Were you working two evenings ago? Did you see—"

"I said, who wants to know? Listen up, lady, I already told what

I'm *gonna* tell to the cops. You a cop?"

"No, sir. I'm a publicist. Actually, an ex-publicist. I'm looking for a former client."

"Well, listen, Ms. Ex-Publicist, I got nothing to say about nothing. Good day."

"Wait! I'm not looking for trouble! I swear, this won't involve you in any way. I just want to know if—"

"Look...I see a lot of shit float through this lobby. And I ain't here to make no *moral judgements* on nobody's character." Pause. "You wanna know about the young guy what came through here with the two young girls, right? That's what the cops was after."

"Two? Did you say 'two young girls?'"

"Did I stutter, utter, or mutter? Two young girls."

Another pause. A sigh. Then he continued...

"The one, I recognized. Been through a few times. Colored whore from around the way. Poor little thing. Can't be but fourteen if she's a day. But like I said. I ain't here to judge. She buttered her bread, she can sleep in it."

"Go on, please, Mr. Runlin."

"So yeah. The other girl, she was *real* young. White. She had a backpack. The guy had a big, like, drawing book I guess. And a coupla video tapes. Our rooms gots VCRs. Very popular."

"A little girl, an underage hooker, a sketchbook, videos."

"Like I said, lady. None of my business."

click

HEY. HOW'S IT goin', right? It's been a crazy night. I hooked up with these metalheads on the edge of Cincy and now we're camped out in this van on the OSU campus. I love these fucking people! They are *genuine* white trash, can you dig it? Well, except for that Indian. He's Navajo trash. Even cooler. I've always wanted to be white trash, but I was kinda born into the wrong tax bracket, right? But that's all behind me now. White by birth, Trash by choice, yo.

Apparently there's going to be some big, four-day, under-ground rock festival on a farm not far from Ohio State. *Doom Fest.* It was put to me like this—"Here we are. Out on the road. Good folks. Good music. A van load of quality pharmaceuticals. And no destination but *Doom itself*!!!" Can you fucking dig that! Love it. There's supposed to be an anti-war rally out on the main lawn in a couple of hours. That's why we're here. College protests are the per-fect place to unload a large quantity of Ecstasy. Or so I'm told. The money from the push is gonna get us into the festival, not to men-tion food and shelter and *whatnot* for a while. There's already been quite a bit of *whatnot* already. Believe that. Burgundy girl popped some pills a couple of hours ago. Turned her all Dionne Warwick. Swore she could see into the future. *My* future, dig? When I asked her what she saw, all she said was, "Giant exploding heads." We've been drinking absinthe. The bottle says—*Est. 1880 Absenta Des-tileria Y Fabrica de Licores* yadda yadda *Baleares España.* This stuff is no joke, man. Pure green evil. Like a licorice liquor lobotomy.

The X they've got is strictly for selling. Everything else is up for grabs. That's how I hooked up with this brood to begin with. *Orange Goblin* girl wanted to sell me some of that limp rave junk. I said no, but I'm looking for some opium, cuz everyday is a holiday. She laughed and invited me along. I was born to be a nomad, yo.

You know what's funny? I don't even know their names. Except the driver. His name is Poole. Here we are, the van is parked, every-body else is shagged out all over, dead to the galaxy, and Poole's still got his eyes bugged open and his hands wrapped around the steer-ing wheel like he's ripping a swath in the highway. Freaky.

This is what that big Visigoth-looking cat told me—

"Don't worry about Poole, man. He won't talk to you. He probably doesn't even know you're here. He probably doesn't even know *he's* here."

Turns out Poole drove a tank during Operation: Desert Storm. After the war, he came home and started getting headaches, and vertigo, and bad stomach ailments, ya dig? They'd come and go. He saw a few doctors, they couldn't find anything wrong. But when he and his new bride tried to have a baby, she miscarried. The fetus came out *gonzo deformed*. They tried again. Same thing. Fetus had no arms or eyes. And again! This one had a translucent skull and no brain. Actually lived for a few days, which is sad as hell. Finally, Mrs. Poole up and ran off. Said she couldn't stand having any more "mutants squirming around" in her womb. Had to be Desert Storm, right? Poole couldn't get a straight answer from The Brass. He and some fellow soldiers who had had a similar experience we're preparing to file a suit. They were all dishonorably discharged (and, it is assumed, threatened in some way. Poole's not too specific, right?). Everybody but Poole got cold on the suit and bailed.

That's when Ole Tight Knuckles up there snapped. Started plotting all these schemes, ya dig? Considered shooting a machine gun into the White House. Or mail-bombing some federal building. (Can't anybody ever get Asa Hutchinson in his cross hairs?) But his big plot was to fly a plane, kamikaze-style, into the Pentagon. Blaze of fury. When somebody beat him to the punch on Sept. 11th, and he saw all those innocent people get killed on tv, he just shut down. Stopped talking. It seems he's also stopped eating or sleeping. Now, all his does is drive this van. And pop trucker speed. And blast music non-stop. His world must be a hazy, vibrating hum.

Sun's coming up. Let's get this party started, ya dig?

click

"YOU HAVING FUN out here, sweetheart?"

"You know I am, Daddy."

The silver '89 Dodge Colt had been holding up, despite its oil leak and worthless shocks. And the brake pads had all but worn through. Otherwise, Jeff and Dawn had no cares, no destination, and no worries. (Except, of course, the endless warrants for Jeff's arrest and the faceless, leering freaks with a hunger for little girls—Dawn in particular.) It was all picnics and kicking around the soccer ball and hot chocolate and cottage cheese for every meal. Dawn's one additional request was cocoa with pink marshmallows. Done and done.

When they weren't driving, they were drawing. A "concept" a day. Like, "invent a character." Or "draw a smell." Their current game was to "draw your feelings." Jeff drew a 12 point buck leading a family of deer over a snow-capped mountain range. Dawn drew dolphins diving over the sunset. Both of them were lying.

"Did you talk to your mother?"

"Yeah, but she was all bawling and stuff. It was pretty wack."

"You seem edgy today, hon."

"My stomach just hurts a little. That's all."

"Yeah. We should start eating better."

"It's not that. It's cuz…never mind."

"What?"

"Never mind."

Of course she couldn't tell him. About the bleeding. He wouldn't understand. He'd panic. He wouldn't know what to do. But she needed to talk to *somebody. She* didn't know what to do.

"What do you want to do tonight, honeypie?"

"Let's rent some movies. Can we find a place with a VCR?"

Jeff, not known for being terribly observant, had noticed his daughter's *changes.* Started well before this excursion, but since the two of them had been on the road, they seemed to be happening *all at once. God, am I imagining this? It can't be…she's only nine! Way too young, right? Right?*

"Daddy? You're going to go back to jail, aren't you?"

"Well, I don't know. Maybe. I mean…"

"They're gonna find us."

"Don't worry."

Indeed The Powers were closing in. Word of the kidnapping was out. *FBI.* Precincts were looking for Jeff's Honda Civic. Thus the decrepit Dodge Colt. Jeff wondered daily if he had lost all sense. *FBI.* He'd never been one for rules per se, but *kidnapping?* He'd be the first to consider that *despicable.*

"Dawn, it's just that, they told me I wasn't allowed to see you, and then you ran away, and it was all I could—"

"I know, Daddy. It's cool. We're having fun, right?"

Jeff had been haunted by the thought of someone, some creep, some monster, or maybe just society in general, getting its claws all over his baby. Obsession. Since she was born. Obsessed. Thus the art. He saw "Dawn" everywhere. In the poor. The neglected. The sick. And to think that his very obsession may have caused...*NO!* And now here she was, *evolving* right before his eyes. *Less defenseless in some ways, maybe.* Stronger. *Maybe. Hopefully.*

"Are you having fun out here, Daddy?"

"You know I am, sugargirl."

She's a target. Jeff's baby, his one and only, was evolving into a very, *very* beautiful girl. Stunning. Gorgeous. A target. And Cecil would notice. *Cecil* was closing in.

"I'm thinking of starting a new piece tonight. I need some powerful images."

"Do you need me to model, Daddy?"

"Nah. Think about what movies you wanna watch."

"Daddy? You ever been in love with somebody and they didn't love you back?"

"Ask your mother."

"What was your first kiss like?"

"With your mother?"

"Just yours."

"Oh. Well, I guess I can sum up that experience in one word. 'Nosebleed.'"

Dawn held up her sketch pad. Jeff pulled his eyes away from the road long enough to see it. She had finally finished drawing a smell.

"Doctor's office," Jeff said. Dawn's eyes lit up.

"How'd you guess? It doesn't look anything like a doctor's office!"

"Nope. It looks like what a doctor's office *smells* like. You nailed it."

Dawn beamed. She looked out the window at the current little falling-down town. Same as every other little falling-down town they'd passed through. Someone, who looked like a pile of old laundry, stumbled along the sidewalk. In every shop window was an American Flag. "God Bless America," and "Let's Roll!" signs everywhere. A young black girl, all gussied up, no older than fourteen, stood on a corner. Shivering. Hooking? Shivering. Hooking. She was just what Jeff needed this evening. He pulled the Colt over to her and rolled down the window. She leaned in smiling brightly.

"Ev'nin', folks!"

"How much for the whole night?" Jeff asked.

click

INTERSTATE 75. South. 1:47am. Speed limit: 65. D'antre's speed: 97. The Roots blasting on his crackly, burnt out $50 stereo—

"Dat scat!/ I know you dig it when I kick it baby! Dat scat!/ I know you dig it when I kick it baby!"

D'antre's group Da Bomb Droppas had a few gigs lined up already. His first column for *Psychobilly Freakout!* was set to appear in the next issue. And yet, the giddy thrill of freedom had already begun to subside, as D'antre burned home from Penny Whistle's Showclub and Revue. This was his 16th strip club in two days, and he had yet to locate his daughter's mama—Tijuana Smalls. He'd called her house. He'd called her mother's house. He'd called all her friends that he knew. He'd stopped by over and over and over and over. Nothing. Nothing. He wanted to see his daughter. Dameka.

"Dat scat!/ I know you dig it when I kick it baby!"

No luck. No replies. Nothing. He'd tried all the juice bars. He was making his way through the topless joints. *She has to be working! She has to be someplace!* Frustration was his fuel, he stepped on the gas. One last joint to hit tonight. In Millville. Blasted off the exit ramp. Through West Chester. Through Fairfield. 103 mph as he burned through Hamilton. Through Hamilton. Hamilton. Red and blue rollers. Out of the phantom black. *Muthafucka…reeeeal swift thinking, D…*

The officer took his sweet time strolling up to D'antre's driver's side window. Oversized flashlight. He wrapped on the glass. D'antre lowered it.

"Evening."

"Ev'nin', Officer."

"Dat scat! I know you dig it when I kick it baby! Dat scat!"

"You wanna turn that off, please?"

"Sorry, sir."

"You know why I pulled you over?"

Well, I don't know…I was speeding, for one. Tags expire this month. I ran a red about 20 minutes ago. Failed to come to a complete stop at some point I'm sure. Bad alignment on this bitch—prob'ly wobbling some…

"No sir."

"You been drinking tonight?"

"No sir."

"Been smoking any reefer? You know, marijuana cigarettes?"

"Oh, *no* sir." Lie.

"It's forty-five through here, friend. What's the rush?"

"I'm trying to see my daughter, sir. But it's getting late and I'm tired. Gotta get home at a reasonable time, sir. I live in Downtown Cincinnati. OTR."

"License and registration."

Goddamn. D'antre managed to see the officer's badge as he handed over the pertinent information. *Muthafuckin' sergeant doin' a traffic stop?* The officer took his sweet time as he did whatever cops do when they've got you sweating on the side of the road while their fancy colored lights spin in your mirrors and all about your car, like a giant, flashing LEPER sign for other drivers to see for miles in either direction. *UNCLEAN! UNCLEAN! I WAS ONCE LIKE YOU!!!*

As D'antre watched the faceless figure of the cop emerge from his car and mosey back his way, he could swear the officer had a little swagger and skank to his step. *Guess I would too, if I was de big bawss may'n.*

"Well…D'antre…says you're on probation."

"Yes, sir."

"Not good."

"No, sir."

"Step out of the car, please."

D'antre exhaled deeply and exited his seat. Something deep in his head screamed *Run nigger nigger nigger nigger Run!!!!* He ignored it. No bullets tonight, if possible.

The cop blared his floodlight flashlight directly into D'antre's eyes.

"You got some pin eyes, boy."

"Zat right?"

"You been drinking?" he asked for the second time.

"Nuh."

"Smoking something you shouldn't?"

"Camel reds. They's killin' me."

"Funnyman. Lean your head back, extend your arms out flat with your shoulders. Now touch the tip of your nose with the tip of your right index finger. You got a big flat surface to aim at. Should be no trouble. All right, now your left. All right, relax. I'm gonna search your pockets. Anything in there I should know about?"

"Nuh."

"Pocket knife? Crack pipe? I'm not trying to insult you, but if I cut myself on something, you're eating this flashlight. You got me, boy?"

"Yup."

The officer pulled from D'antre's pockets, $2.73 in loose change and a few pieces of paper with phone numbers on them.

"Dealers?" The cop asked. D'antre could almost hear him smirking.

"Strippers. Keep 'em if you want 'em. I ain't got no use for 'em."

"Think you're something, don't you."

"Nuh."

"You like strippers?"

"Nuh."

"Come on, D'antre. Telling me you don't like *white* strippers?"

"Nuh."

The cop stood there for a second, letting the hideous silence swell. Finally…

"Well, you seem pretty clean. I'm letting you go with a ticket for speeding. This will be a mandatory court appearance due to the excessiveness of the speed. You're gonna want to contact your probation officer first thing in the morning. You still have outstanding warrants for parking and traffic violations."

"Warrants? And you *lettin' me go*?"

"Yer not my problem, fella. Just slow it down. I see you again, yer finished."

Don't say it, D! Don't say it!!!

"Traffic and parking violations," D'antre said in perfect clarity. "I thought that was an *executable* offense in these parts, Sergeant."

The officer smashed the butt-end of his flashlight into D'antre's jaw. He grabbed D'antre's neck and slammed his face into the hood of his car. D'antre could feel his mouth filling with blood, and his wrists clamping into cuffs behind his back.

"You dumb, sonuvabitch! I was letting you off! Couldn't not push it, could ya! This is not your day, boy. You just made it real hard on yourself. Boy."

D'antre felt the long handle of the flashlight whack into the backs of his knees. Already face down on the hood of the car, he almost slipped off onto the ground, as his knees buckled and his calves shot upward. He heard the cop stomp away. It was an early December morning, and the hood of the car nearly froze against his sweat-soaked cheek. The blood spilling from his gums onto the cold metal steamed before his eyes. Reds-and-blues still spinning. His backside pointed out toward Route 4. Bent over like a clothespin.

Before too long, a second squad car arrived. D'antre heard the voice of an additional man. The two cops mumbled somewhere in the distance. With D'antre still bent over the hood, the cops began to tear through his car. Searching. Pulling out the floor mats, pulling out the back seats. Popped the trunk, threw the spare tire out onto the ground. Finally, the second cop came around to D'antre.

"Rough night, hey young brother?"

Muthafuck... A black cop. By D'antre's figuring, there were two types of black cops. "Roundtrees" and "Tomboys." Roundtrees are Wyatt Earp, "elevating the race by eliminating the niggers." Tomboys, they just hate their own kind. Both of them are bad, but at least a Roundtree will *warn you* before he pumps you full of lead, or rams a baton so far up your ass it knocks your front teeth out. This painted pig here, definitely a Tomboy.

The black cop whispered to D'antre with a *faux* familiarity that was making him ill. And he was still handcuffed, face down on the hood of the car.

"Now, D'antre, I don't want you to worry too much about ole Eliot over there. He's a good guy, but I know he can get a little high strung. That's why, when he tells me that you've been combative and confrontational with him, I think, hmmm...I think I'm gonna go get D'antre's side of the story. It's definitely a thing that makes me say hmmm...ya know what I mean, brother? Ha ha ha. Now why don't *you* tell me what happened."

"Nuh'eh."

"Nothing? Well, *something* happened." The cop leaned in closer. "If Eliot did something out of line, you can tell me, D'antre. I will take care of it, I assure you."

"Nuh'eh."

"Still nothing. I suppose you cuffed yourself then, yes? Ha ha ha."

This scenario reminded D'antre of being upstate in the big clink. He'd be trying to sleep at night, and he'd hear some punk getting split in half somewhere. Usually the rapist would beat the kid, abuse and curse him. But sometimes, he'd coo in the boy's ear. Call him a woman's name and give him the Barry White treatment. The latter situation always made D'antre shudder. Although he never wanted either to happen, if it had to, he'd rather be beaten to hell and gone before being taken. Getting took. Right now, ass up, spread across the hood of his car with Uncle Remus singing him a happy tune, D'antre felt like a block wench getting seduced by force. The Tomboy's jabbering eventually just became more background noise, blending with the sound of traffic, the wind, and the buzzing over the two officers' shoulder boxes.

Finally bored with their game, the cops uncuffed D'antre and pulled him upright. He looked around at all of his possessions strewn about, including his back seats. The black officer smiled to D'antre before walking back to his car.

"We shall overcome," the Tomboy said with a wink.

"Eliot" stuffed the speeding ticket into D'antre's shirt-collar and smirked. D'antre was a statue as the white cop got inside his squad car as well. He did not move until the rollers stopped and both squad cars pulled away. He crumbled up the ticket and chucked it off into the grass. He then proceeded to gather up his belongings.

"Dat scat!/ I know you dig it when I kick it, baby..." he began to sing to himself. Then he stopped. He couldn't remember why the caged bird sings.

click

BURGUNDY GIRL awoke with a start. She bolted upright gasping, and stared at Dalton for a moment or two as she slowly remembered who he was. She looked around at her friends still sleeping soundly. A deep breath and she calmed down.

"Morning, Freckles," she yawned.

"Morning yourself," Dalton replied with a smile.

"So…" she continued casually, "You wanna screw?"

"Um, uh, well…uh, I…er, no…not really…"

"Yeah…me neither," she yawned again. "Just thought I'd offer."

She leaned back against the door of the van, pulled two cans of Milwaukee's Best from the case, handed one to Dalton, and popped the other. She gulped the entire can in two drinks. Dalton popped his and took a large swig. Warm and flat. Burgundy girl crumpled the empty can in her left fist and tossed it into a corner behind the shotgun seat where many dead soldiers lay. She grabbed a magazine and began to page through with total focus. *Psychobilly Freakout!*

"Any activity outside?" she asked.

Dalton leaned over to look out the window. A small group of people had gathered, and a few more were slowly filtering onto the main lawn.

"A couple of picket signs. Nothing about the war, though."

"What do they say?"

"Let's see…'Free Peltier'…'Free Mumia'…'Free The MOVE 9'…"

Burgundy girl giggled.

"There's more," Dalton continued, "One says, 'Free The West Memphis 3.' I don't even know who that is."

"Do any of them say, 'Free Johnny Taliban?'" she asked.

"Not yet."

"That's too bad. He's hot."

Dalton eyed the back cover of the *PF!* in Burgundy girl's hands. It was a full-color ad for the pornographic film *Honey Sssuckle.* The ad was *in French.*

"Decouvrez l'essence," Dalton read.

"Huh?"

"*Chevrefeuille.* Ad for Clover Honey's last flick. I guess they put the ad in French to make the picture sound *classy.* Heh heh. Yeah, I'll take that bet, ya dig?"

Burgundy girl licked her lips.

"Mmmm…Clover Honey makes me runny."

"*Made,* you mean," Dalton corrected. "She's dead, right?"

"Not to me," Burgundy girl answered matter-of-fact.

"What do you mean?"

"Never knew her outside of video or photographs. As far as *I'm* concerned, she didn't have no life outside of that. Seen more of her since she offed herself than when she was livin'. Same with Joey Spitfire. Never even knew what he looked like until after he was killed. Dying made him *more alive.* Guess that's how it is when yer famous. Or kinda-sorta famous."

"I can dig that."

Burgundy girl nodded and winked at Dalton. Suddenly, she hollered at the top of her lungs.

"ALL RIGHT YOU LAZY FUCKS, WAKE THE HELL UP!"

The three carcasses came to life with a collective groan.

"Come on, y'all! Let's make some money. *Doom's a-waiting!*"

Dalton became separated from his new crew within seconds of exiting the van. The small group of students on the main lawn quickly morphed into a shoulder-to-shoulder mob. Shouting. Chanting. Some were dancing. Banging pots and drums. A girl on a wooden platform shouted into a screeching microphone, "It's time to send the message to Bush and his cronies that we reject ALL terrorism—be it from Al Qaeda, or the Taliban, or THE UNITED STATES MILITARY!!!" The crowd roared in affirmation. A few white-ballcapped fratboys booed and heckled, throwing angry elbows and barking "USA! USA!" A sobbing young man held up a sign that read—"Lost My Brother 9/11—Our Tears of Grief are Not a Cry for War!"

Dalton tried his best to be a cool and casual observer. Stood back leaning against a tree.

But the energy was getting to him. Getting to him. Energy. Getting to him. The energy was getting to him.

A pocket of kids (five or six), who looked no older than Dalton, decked out in Chuck Taylors and ironic cardigans, waved him over. He looked behind himself to see if they were waving to someone else. "Join us! Join us!" he heard them shout. He didn't know what to do. *Probably trying to trick me with something, right? Fucking jerks.* He stayed leaning awkwardly against the tree. "Join us! Join us!" they persisted. Finally,—*They're gonna fuck you over! They're gonna fuck you over!*—he strolled across the lawn toward the pocket of kids. *Big mistake, yo.* They cheered when he joined them, slapping him on the back and offering clumsy high-fives. Chanting. Louder and louder. Almost in spite of himself, Dalton began chanting with them. Chanting. Whatever they were chanting. Some garbled gibberish about "blood and oil." It meant everything.

"Say, brother," a small but determined voice said to Dalton. He turned around to put a face to the voice. There stood a young Chinese fellow, a mere whisper of a guy, wearing ridiculously thick glasses with pine-green frames.

"Yeah?"

"Say, brother," the boy repeated, a shade louder to compete with the crowd, "Free Mumia." He handed Dalton a flyer containing a list of "facts" and a Xeroxed photo of a black man with long dreadlocks. "Cop Killer?" "Victim of a frame-up." "Voice of the Voiceless." Dalton took the flyer and gave it a once-over.

"Yeah, okay. I'll see what I can do, right?"

The Chinese boy laughed and extended his hand. Dalton shook it.

"What's your name?"

"Dalton. Just Dalton."

"Good to meet you, Just Dalton. I'm just Chen."

Charlie Chen, actually, but wisely he went by family name only (how *any* Asian parents, Chinese or otherwise, could name their son "Charlie" was the great mystery of young Chen's life). Chen's parents were immigrants, born and raised in Guangzhou. Fiercely pro-America. Profoundly right-wing. Chen's father owned a *Mail Boxes Etc.* franchise. A glorious manifestation of the American entrepreneurial spirit.

By the afternoon of the attacks on Sept.11th, Chen's father's main storefront was so covered with American flags and 'United We Stands' that it was next to impossible to see through the glass (but of course, that didn't stop neighborhood folks from opening up the front windows with flaming garbage cans, or spray painting 'DIECHINKS' on his Ford Mustang).

It was around the time of the attacks that Chen made the decision to break his parents' hearts.

He was their eldest child and had been their greatest pride. High school test scores indicated a near-genius IQ. Skipped ahead a grade, and at the tender age of 17 began his freshman year at Ohio State University on a full academic scholarship. It was around this time that Chen made the decision to break his parents' hearts. He just couldn't live the lie any longer. Had to come clean. He had to *come out*.

"Mama? Papa? I've got something to tell you. I'm…I'm a…I'm an…an…"

Anarchist. Without further consideration, Chen launched into his much-rehearsed diatribe against governmental tyranny.

At first his parents hoped for the best as they sat at the breakfast table mouths agape. Hoped. For the best. Chen began by lashing out at China. Lashing out. Against China's murderous oppression and hideous human rights violations. Mr. and Mrs. Chen nodded agreement—they despised the Chinese government. However, their hopes were dashed as their son, once favored above all, proceeded to call *The United States of America* "the most vicious, corrupt, monolithic Empire in all of recorded history."

"Shame! Shame!" screamed Mrs. Chen and burst into tears.

"I used to have son!" hollered Mr. Chen. "No more! No more! You out now! YOU OUT NOW!"

And he was *out*. Now.

As Chen and his group of fellow young radicals walked across the soccer field drinking cappuccinos the size of *Big Gulps*, he told his coming out story to Dalton. The protest rally had not so much ended as it had petered out over the course of a few hours, and everyone now had heads full of righteous energy. Needed to burn it off.

"So…" Chen concluded, "in a matter of ten minutes, I went from being their greatest pride to their second worst shame. Pretty remarkable really, if you think about it." A girl with dime store toe rings and fire-engine-red *Manic Panic* hair gave Chen a supportive hug.

"What's their *totally worst* shame?" Dalton asked.

"My uncle. Papa's brother. Doing time in Chillicothe for Assault and Battery. Blinded in his left eye a couple of months ago by some redneck with a razor blade. I hate to say this, cuz I'm against the prison-industrial complex and all, but I bet Uncle Ping probably *deserved it*."

"You don't say…" said Dalton.

"Hey, Dalton-dude," the *Manic Panic* girl chimed in. Her eyeballs vibrating with caffeine and ADD. "What's *your* story?"

"Aw, I…uh, I don't have a story, yo."

"Come on," exclaimed another boy. "Everybody has a story."

"Not me."

"Maybe you just don't have a story *yet*," said Chen with an awkward smile. "Maybe you're writing your story right now."

Dalton chuckled and nodded. *Say something cool! Say something funny and smart and witty and cool!* He couldn't.

"Well, Dalton, man," the other boy continued barely containing his excitement, "We're all going to a party tonight. You should like totally go with us and shit. We're not exactly, you know, *invited,* but these shindigs around here are so huge, it's not like we'll get

thrown out or any…well…anyway, I scored an assload of X at the
rally off this big Erik the Red-looking headbanger, so…that should
put us in some good graces."

Everybody laughed.

"So what do you say, Dalton?" Chen asked, a touch more insis-
tent than he had intended. Looked up at Dalton then quickly away.
Dalton tried to justify his flushed cheeks with a fake sneeze. He'd
never been invited to a party before, even by people not invited
themselves. And now two in a day and a half!

"Hey, yeah, you know," Dalton stuttered, affectedly aloof. "I
mean I *am* supposed to go to *Doom Fest*—"

Collective gasp. A pall washed over their pasty faces.

"—But…" he recovered, "Whatever, right? Yeah. I'm all about
it. Partyin'. So you know. Thanks and shit. Or whatever. Sounds
cool. I'm in."

And so Dalton found himself staying at Ohio State. Hanging
out with a group of nerdy (albeit progressive) college freshmen was
not tremendously cooler than chilling with high school kids, but
it was a far stretch more hip than hanging with *no one at all*…as
per his usual custom. Although his deepest desire just a night prior
was to rage himself into oblivion with a field full of degenerate
metalheads, suddenly that notion seemed frightening and hopeless. Frightening and hopeless. *What a change can come with the rising sun, grasshopper.* And this geeked out, freaked out, punked out,
collective of wide-eyed chess club anarchists was closer to Dalton's
page than anyone he'd met in his short life thus far. If Dalton was,
in fact, on any page at all. (Besides the novelty of peer companion-
ship, certain *other factors* were indeed at play. Factors. Other. None
the least of which maybe—this perplexing little Oriental enigma
in pine green Coke-bottle glasses who hated his first name like
Dalton hated his last. This Chen. Who was he? Shrouded invisible.
Like me, yo. Burning familial bridges. *Like me, right?* Clutching
nouveau radicalism in two desperate fists. *Maybe a world of hurt*

too. Maybe he'll understand me—NO! NO!!! Fucking idiot! Be cool for once! Be cool! This is why you don't have any friends!!!...)

"Hey, guys. What's going on, right?"

Dalton walked up to the robin's egg-blue VW. The tall, shirt-less Navajo leaned against the side of the bus next to the driver's side window. The girls and the Viking nowhere in sight. Poole continued to burn two holes in the windshield with his blood-shot laser vision.

"What do you say, little bro?" The Indian replied, offering his left hand. Dalton shook it.

"Hey, hey. Probably gonna skip the festival after all, yo. I'm thinkin' about stickin', ya dig?"

"Your loss, kid. It's gonna *raaaaage!*" the Indian bellowed, shaking his fist over his head.

"No doubt. No doubt. But hey, man, thanks for everything, still. Sincerely. I hope we can hook up again somewhere down the line."

The Indian chuckled and gave Dalton the sign of the devil. "Sure thing, bro." Dalton returned the gesture and turned to walk away.

"Hey, kid!" said a voice Dalton had never heard. Like loose gravel. And a hearty dose of Tennessee twang. He turned back quickly.

"Hey, kid," Poole repeated, "You know we ain't comin' back, right?"

Dalton blinked in surprise.

"You mean to pick me up? I, I figured that much, Poole."

"No. I mean *we ain't comin' back.* From *Doom.* That's where *we* get off at."

Dalton looked to the Indian for translation. For clarification. Indian bugged out his eyes and lolled his tongue, shaking like a hanging man. He gripped his AIM tatted stomach, doubling over with rasping laughter.

"America is *over,* kid," Poole continued. "It's been a hella-*sick* ride, but it's over. The fascists done gone and won. The pigs done gone and won. So we're jumpin' ship. *Doom's* the final stop."

Dalton didn't know what to say. He didn't fully *get it.* Looked to one then the other. At a loss. Completely. Lost. They looked back at him, matter-of-fact. He didn't get it. These two men, with their filthy hair, and their filthy denim, and their faded blue jailhouse tattoos…were the picture of serenity. Filthy. Blue. Serenity.

"Well…shit…" Dalton stammered, "I mean, I guess, I don't know…catch ya on the flip side maybe…"

"Ain't no flip side, little brother," the Indian said shaking his head and smiling wide. "Ain't no flip side."

Dalton nodded, shrugged, and turned again to walk away.

"Hey, kid!" Poole hollered out. "You know what they're gonna write on my tombstone? They're gonna write, *Here lies Poole. This muthafucka died FREE, bitch!*"

click

YOU ARE BEING VIDEOTAPED FOR YOUR OWN SAFETY

click

KNOCK KNOCK KNOCK

"Who is it?"

"Hello? Ma'am? Caroline Powell? I'd like to talk to you for just a second, Ms. Powell. I'm a friend of Jeff Mican's. Name's D'antre Philips."

Caroline swung open the door with great drama and leaned against the frame, blocking D'antre's entrance. In her left hand: an off-white folded envelope. In her right hand: a wine cooler.

"Sooo…Daddy Molotov I presume. Just got finished reading your first column this morning. Not bad. Not bad. You definitely have *flavor.* That issue comes out tomorrow I believe. Are you nervous? I was a close friend of Joey Spitfire's, you know…"

A pause. A drink. Then—

"Come on in, Daddy Molotov. Sorry for the boxes. I'm in the process of packing."

"Thank you, ma'am. So where ya movin' to?"

"Back to LA. Can't wait."

D'antre took a seat on a white leather sofa next to a large cardboard box that read: **miscellaneous.** Across his lap he held an 8 ½ by 14 manila envelope. Caroline sat Indian-style on an opposing sofa. She picked up a cordless phone and started to dial. She quickly hung up and turned to D'antre apologetically.

"I gotta make a quick call."

"'Scool. Iss yo' house, ya heard?"

Caroline smiled and dialed. *Love that good, earthy, black-talk…*

"Brackage? Yeah, it's me. Yeah, I got it. Thank you for the invite. RSVP. So what's the occasion? Ahh…Well, good for you. Going away party too, huh? For me? You're a weasel, you know it? Ha ha. Uh huh. Uh huh. Well, I might be solo. What's that? Right. 'Solo, but I'm not *so low.*' Ha ha. That's clever. No…I don't know where—I mean, I don't know if Chet'll be able to make it. Uh huh. Uh huh. Well, I'll scrounge up somebody."

Caroline cupped her hand over the receiver and mouthed, *'Just be a minute.'* D'antre nodded silently.

"Uh huh. Uh huh. Okay. Well, I gotta ask you. No…I gotta ask you…Is *she* gonna be there? Don't play dumb. You know who. Is she? She did? Well, maybe I don't want to talk to *her.* Maybe I don't want to *see* her. Okay. Okay. No. No, I'll be there. I said I'll be there. See ya then." And she hung up. "So, Mr. Philips—"

"D'antre."

"D'antre. You can call me Caroline. So, what can I do for you?"

"I need to find Jeff."

"Ha!" Caroline exclaimed in disbelief. "Ha ha ha ha ha! You and *everybody,* my friend. You and everybody. You. Me. FBI. Everybody."

D'antre sighed and removed a pack of cigarettes from his breast pocket. He pointed to the pack to ask *Is this cool?* Caroline nodded and leaned in toward him.

"You mind if I bum one of those? I've decided to start smoking again, and I'm also eating red meat again, and I have no idea why I just told you that."

They laughed.

"Well, Caroline, if I'da known that I'da picked up some Whitey's. Here, have a Red instead."

He lit both of their cigarettes and leaned back. Caroline took a deep drag and coughed harshly. Her eyes watered and her cheeks burned scarlet.

"Mmmm *cough hack*...satis—*cough*—satisfying...So whatcha got there?"

D'antre handed her the manila envelope. Inside it she found a letter and several Jeff Mican original sketches. Sketches she had never seen. *Oh my god*...they were all of a young black girl in various poses. Historic. Fantastic. Poses. Sitting in Huey Newton's chair. Looking out the window with an Uzi, *a la* Malcolm X. Charging into battle, sword aloft. Riding atop a giant eagle. *Breathtaking. Goddamn, Jeff.* Caroline looked at the letter enclosed. It said:

> *D'antre,*
>
> *Hey, bud! I hope this package finds you well and breathing the sweet air of freedom. I'm out here on the road with my baby girl, and every-thing's awesome. I've been thinking a lot about that project we had talked about in County, and I hope you're still interested. I certainly am.*
>
> *I've enclosed a few roughs of the images you had said you wanted. Hope they're acceptable (Ob-viously, I don't know what your daughter looks like, but you get the idea). Did you ever hear from Psychobilly Freakout!? I've been checking the indie news stands, but I haven't seen your stuff yet. I'll keep looking. When you get this, it might be a good*

*idea for you to try to get a hold of Caroline Powell.
I told you about her. If she hasn't completely washed
her hands of me, she might have some good ideas/
suggestions. Well, I gotta keep moving. I'm getting a
cell phone soon, so I'll try to call you. Take care,*

Jeff

"That no-good bastard," Caroline muttered bitterly. "So what's this *project?*"

"Well, you see...it's like this, Caroline," D'antre answered, slipping into preacher mode. "About a year ago, I got a funny idea. What was this idea you ask? Well, I'll tell you. I had just gotten out of jail, you see, up at Warren, and I was regretting *everything.* *Everything.* I was regretting my <u>whole</u> <u>rotten</u> <u>life</u>. My writing was shit. My music career was shit. My daughter...well anyway. My daughter...I wanted to do *something* for my daughter. So I got this funny idea. I wrote a story, knahme—I mean, do you-know-what-I-mean? Of course you do. Anyway, I wrote this story. Just a few pages. But very quickly, the story evolved. Into a book. A short, but substa—"

"What's it called?"

"What's it called? It's called *Princess Africa Jones.* About this little girl, knamsayin', *damn...*this little girl trying to get by in the projects. Living inside her own head. Something that a poor young girl of color can relate to."

"Cool. Okay."

"So I sent it out to a few places. Small press, you know. Willing to read unsolicited work. Basically. Never heard noth—didn't hear from anybody. At all. Then, before you know it and sure as hell, I'm back in lock down. Hamilton County. But there's a flip! I meet Jeff there, I'm already a fan of course, and we start to talking about our kids and work and shit, and I tell him about *Princess Africa Jones.* Showed him a few chapters, and he gets real excited and starts sketching, and we get the idea—Bam! To be a team! I get the damn thing published, and he'll illustrate!"

"Waitaminute, waitaminute, waitaminute...you want Jeff, *Jeff Mican*—multiple felon, escaped convict, kidnapper, and alleged child-pornographer Jeff Mican, to illustrate your *children's book*?"

"Juvenile fiction, actually."

"Philips, you're even crazier than he is."

"He ain't exactly an 'escaped convict' *per se*—"

"Thick as thieves..."

"Caroline, I just got out of County a couple weeks ago. Things have been pretty—pardon my language—fucked-up, since I got out. But yesterday, *I got a letter*. From Hedgehog Press, a subsidiary of—"

"Ah hah! Gotcha...And they liked *Princess Africa Jones*. Cool! That's cool! But did you tell them about *Jeff*?"

"Sorta...I sent them copies of the samples. Chatted with some-body or other. They seemed open. Figger'd they don't need to know *who* he is. Really." Caroline took another healthy drag from her rapidly burning out Camel Red. She suppressed the urge to cough and spit. *Progress.*

"Word," she said nodding. Then...silence. Excruciating. They both sat frozen in horror trying to pretend that she hadn't said it.

"I *do* know people, D'antre," Caroline recovered. "I do know people. People who know people."

"The luckiest people of all."

"Are you...by any chance...free this Saturday?"

"I could be..."

"You want to go to a dinner party? I need a date. You could use the connection. He's an agent. Flemming Brackage. Real chame-leon. Bet he knows some lit agents or people who could help you. And he also has a vested interest in finding Jeff..."

Caroline's eyes suddenly became cloudy and distant. She low-ered her head and stared absently at her feet. Held the wine cooler to her brow. D'antre looked about the room nervously. *What is this broad's trip?*

"Laina…" she whispered to herself.

"I'm sorry?"

"Nothing. Nothing. Should be interesting," Caroline said, lifting her head. Snapping out of it. "Should be an interesting night. I *know* these people."

"You got history, huh?"

"You could say that. You could say I got history with them. Yeah, I got history all right. With his…with her…Should be interesting…"

The ash from Caroline's cigarette fell to the floor. She rubbed it into the carpet with her bare heel. Finished off her lukewarm wine cooler and smiled to D'antre.

"*Princess Africa Jones.* Has your daughter read it?"

"Not yet. Not yet. Her mama's being difficult. And anyway, I want her to read it once it's published. So she can be proud, ya heard?"

"I understand. Can you give me a little taste of it? How about just the opening line."

"Opening line. Okay. It goes, 'Princess Africa Jones got no daddy.'"

click

DALTON STEPPED OUT into the cool December air. He hadn't fully realized how stifling hot it had been inside the house until the perspiration froze to his cheeks. *Ahh…yes…*

As the night had carried on, Dalton debated with himself as to whether or not he had made the right decision. To stay here at OSU. Sure, the people he had originally planned to spend the weekend with were preparing to commit ritual suicide, but *I'm not sure that would be any worse than this preppy-ass house party, right?* Dalton spent a good deal of time early on hanging with the kids he'd met at the rally. But before too long, the majority of them had dropped the Ecstasy that Dalton's star-crossed metalhead friends had sold them, and they ended up sitting in a corner for the remainder of the evening giving circle back rubs and brushing each others' hair languorously.

"You gonna drop some X, Chen?" Dalton asked.

"Uh uh. I don't do drugs. I drink a little, and I smoke a goodly amount of weed, and I'll pop Vicodins every now and then, but no drugs for me. What about you, Dalton?"

"Oh, I dig drugs, can ya dig that? But I don't have much use for a chemical that's gonna make me crave pacifiers or dance to the sound of a dialing fax machine."

Dalton indicated with a waving hand the loud, throbbing Euro-trash techno blasting from the house stereo.

"You're crazy, Dalton," the *Manic Panic* girl said in half-speed. "Do you even know who this music even is even? This is *Glok N Spiel*! Fucking German rave kings! True artists in the truest sense of the word 'artists.' *You* can't get hip to techno, cuz you just don't have the sooooooul to underst…" and she trailed off, delighted with the sensation of her teeth rubbing against her bottom lip. Dalton turned to Chen to say something, when Chen was lead away by the hand of a girl in a Tommy Hilfiger baby shirt. With no one to talk to, Dalton waded through the packed house back and forth. Squeezing by as best he could. Knowing no one. Pretending to be trying to go somewhere specific, to see someone who didn't exist. He caught bad jokes and bone-headed banter and bits and pieces of a thousand conversations, not a one he'd want to be a part of. *Graduate school. Football. Hockey. Sex. Osama Bin Laden. The Cincinnati "race riots." Mid-terms.* He was briefly happy when he realized he had to go to the bathroom, as it gave him a genuine place to go. But upon reaching his destination, the rather pained sounds of sexual congress coming from within said bathroom (and the disturbing hushed mutter of multiple voices), turned him around and sent him heading back away. The whole atmosphere reeked of conformity and fake smiles and yuppie beer and date rape. *Or maybe I'm just a prick, right?*

As Dalton stepped out into the night, he breathed in great gulps of frosty December air.

*Ahh...yes...*Savor the moment away. *Surrounded by people, always alone*, he thought, then chastised himself for being a sorry, melodramatic cocksucker. Cocksucker. He thought about Dawn. How she was. Where she was. Assured himself that she was perfectly okay, and she's probably back home now anyway and totally safe, *Right? Right?* Dalton reached into his backpack and retrieved his notebook and a pen. Put pen to page and let it burn:

December 2001 BY DALTON

I was tired of being the only young person around
so I went to where the other young people are
There was techno and keg stands and Rolling Rock
and some girl got gang-raped while she puked
and told me I'm too fat.

I was tired of being the only artist around
so I went to where the other artists are
We questioned each other's integrity
then begged for work at
Hallmark and Dreamworks and Elektra
I offered to sleep my way to the top
but was respectfully declined.

I was tired of being the only outraged person around
so I went to where the other outraged people are
but the outrages were all different and some outrages
out raged other outrages and the out raged were outraged
Then somebody told me a "pickaninny" joke
the one about Velcro on the ceiling.

I was tired of the fakers and phonies
and hypocrites and liars and poseurs

and sell-outs
but everywhere I ran there was always one there
and I finally realized there was no point in trying
to run away from me any longer.

No point in trying to run away from me any longer.
He heard light footsteps creeping behind him.
"Hey, Dalton."
"What's up, Chen."
"Fuckin' claustrophobic in there."
"For real."
"So how you like this Rolling Rock?"
"Funny you should ask. I don't. Fucking mook beer. But hey,
beggars can't."
Chen laughed and nodded. Dalton coughed needlessly. Chen
removed from his pocket a stick of *Vegan Hemp Lip Balm* ("A Hip
Trip for Lips!") and applied a quick slather. He offered it to Dal-
ton. Accepted. More fidgety silence.
"Hey, Chen. Your crew. Your little circle of friends. They're...they
seem really cool."
"Yeah, they're the best. My first couple weeks on campus, I felt sick
I was so lost. Hookin' up with them. Made things muuuch easier."
"So how are they all doing in there?"
"Man, those Shaking Head Pills didn't miss them."
"The who-what?"
"*Shaking Head Pills.* That's what the Chinese call Ecstasy."
"Dig it."
"They're all still doing a big marathon group massage."
"So...which of those girls is yours?"
"Oh, none of them. We're all just friends. The rest of the guys,
they're all pining for the chicks, but they gotta keep it on the down
low. It's crazy. They're all so libber sensitive they feel ashamed for
wanting the girls. They all wish they were queer. Cracks me up."
"Do you wish you were queer?"

"I don't wish anything. I just do *my* thing. Biggest laugh of all is, I'm closer to the girls than the other guys are. And I know that after spending all day lambasting their already emasculated comrades for being 'too macho,' every single one of them goes out and picks up the biggest, dumbest, most knuckle-dragging Neanderthal frat-cat she can find and rides his pole 'til sunrise. Of course they'll all be dykes in a year. And soccer moms come graduation. *Ahh sol,* the great circle continues."

Laughter.

"I can dig that," Dalton chuckled.

"I can *accept* it. Don't have an opinion one way or the other. So then...what about you, Dalton? What *is* your deal, Mister Mystery? Where did you come from?"

"Mars. It's like you said. I'm writing my story right now."

"What's your character like?"

"Full-on White Trash Superstar."

"Right on," Chen said grinning. "How's that working out for ya?"

"So far, loving it. I'm just like you, ya dig? Riding my own wave-length. Catching my own frequency. Totally free, right? I'm on the liberation station like an Appalachian straight off the plantation."

Chen burst out laughing, snorting and spraying beer from his nostrils.

"Man, that musta hurt, yo," Dalton observed.

"HAHAHAHAHA! You're all right, Dalton! Shit, man, if you've really got no plans anyway, you should road trip with us to Philly. We're leaving tomorrow afternoon. Once everybody sleeps it off. You can crash in my dorm room if you want. Haven't seen my roommate in weeks."

"Philly?"

"Mumia rally. Gonna be a big'un."

Dalton poured the rest of his beer onto the grass. It hissed and steamed.

"So y'all really think that cat is innocent, huh?"

"Not necessarily." Chen's eyes flashed. Shining bright behind his goggle-like spectacles. "Maybe he *is* a cop killer. Maybe he isn't.

I don't really care either way. Issue is: the system's corrupt, and he's right, and he's brilliant, and he's Galileo."

"I'm sorry?"

Chen stepped closer to Dalton, practically shuddering with intensity.

"The innocent get gassed every day, Dalton. Murderers go free everyday. Especially those acting on behalf of the ruling power. 'Justice' is meaningless. *Mean-ing-less.* I just hate seeing Galileo die all the time."

"I think I see what you mean, yo! Galileo! Or Socrates, right?"

"Exactly! Exactly! They don't give you the hemlock cuz you're *wrong.*"

click

VICTIMLESS CRIME? Jeff sighed as he read yet another newspaper editorial about himself. Actually it wasn't about *him* specifically. None of them were. The debate? Whether "virtual child porn" is, or should be considered, protected free speech. Oddly enough, not a single columnist writing on this topic could resist mentioning Jeff Mican by name. Relevant or not. Jeff Mican. Jeff Mican, Virtual Pornographer, who had never successfully operated a computer in his entire life. *I suppose that's beside the point.* Jeff's ever-growing legion of fans grasped the form sufficiently enough, and had uploaded everything Jeff had ever drawn that had ever left his hands. Spread all over the web. And in the process added another charge to Jeff's rap. Infamy.

Column after column after column—**HOW FAR IS TOO FAR? ARE YOU READY FOR 21ST CENTURY PERVERSION? ART, OR ABUSE?** And Jeff's personal favorite, **WHO WILL PROTECT THESE VIRTUAL CHILDREN?** Jeff shrugged and put the paper down. Thought about his work. What people had to say about him. Pro and con. "Renegade First Amendment Hero." "Deranged." "Visionary." "Visual Rapist."

"Brilliant Satirist." "Psychopath." "The Millennium's First True Genius." (*Doesn't take much to be a genius in some circles.*) "Pornographer." *Pornographer?* So many perspectives. So many labels. So many. Labels. *All I ever wanted to be was a cult figure.* Mission accomplished.

Pit-Stop Lodge. Sound of the television buzzing and mumbling in the background. Sound of giggling. VCR played some flick about an awkward girl who receives a magical makeover and wins the heart of the cutest boy in school. In the end, she realizes that being herself is the strongest magic of all. Giggling. And more giggling.

"Hey. What are you little hens clucking about over there?"

"Nothing, Daddy."

Jeff had solicited the services of a young black whore for the evening. Underage. Fourteen. *What the heck were you thinking?!?!* He was thinking that he needed an African American female between the ages of seven and fifteen to model for his new work. Not many other options available for an artist on the run. So he solicited the services of a young black whore with the look he needed. And in the process added another charge to his rap. Infamy.

The prostitute's name? MeShayle. Made fast friends with Dawn. With Dawn. As Jeff sat in the closet of the ratty motel room sketching backgrounds, Dawn and MeShayle talked and laughed and watched videos and did each other's hair and nails. Jeff smiled as he heard the girls whispering and laughing. And he realized that this was the happiest Dawn had ever been.

click

THE SPITFIRE GRILL

by Joey Spitfire

Howdy, kids! So what in Sam Hill am I doing in *Cincinnati, Ohio!?!* What can I say, cherubs, I've always savored life's absurd little ironies. When my better half Clover Honey (yes, THAT Clover Honey,

for those of you who haven't been paying attention)
told me that she was flying to pornophobic Cincinnati
to do a picture called (*Shoot It*) *All Over the Girl*, I
found the notion just too simply-delightful to pass
up. However, thanks to a tip off that fascist Hamilton
County Prosecutor Albert *Whatshisface* was stickin'
his big ole Nazi snout into the program, we ended up
relocating across the river to Covington, Kentucky. It's
just as well. The producers needed extras, and it was
much easier to round up strippers in KY like so much
synthetically augmented cattle. It's actually been surprisingly cool out here in the boondocks. We've made
lots of friends, and the video turned out pretty golldern hot, *hewww-dawgies!* Clover has become quite
enamored of a local negress—I've seen neither hide
nor hair of my beloved or her chocolate handmaiden
in some days now. (I can only venture a guess as to
what's going on there. I've never known the touch of
a black woman...I have, however, stroked myself often
whilst watching *Gone With the Wind*. Any man with
a pulse tells you he ain't got a thing for Butterfly Mc-
Queen, he's either full of shit or a full-on faggot). In
fact, we both have grown to love the area so much,
we've decided to buy an additional house nearby. I
ain't saying where, for all you would-be stalkers out
there (and I AM *heavily* armed, motherfuckers). Suf-
fice it to say, the quality of White Trash in these parts
is of a calibre I've rarely seen in this day and age—almost brings a tear to my eye.

So anyway, the flick...Let me tell you, *hombres y
chiquitas*, this picture has it all. Adequate lighting,
digital video, something resembling a plot, a real band
performing the soundtrack—none of that hideous
Casio garbage, and an orgy scene at the end what
could knock the hump out of a camel's back (There's
your plug for the week, darlin'). And did I mention
that it stars *adult entertainment sensation* Clover
Honey? Good.

"Hey Joey, where'n hell's this column going?" Glad you asked, Gomer. Hanging out here in the Queen City (or Da 'Nati as the homies apparently call it) has made me rather reflective. As many of you know, I was raised Joiman-Catholic. Papist Krauts founded this town. It's funny to see what "my people" have done with the place. Did y'all know that there is an anti-pornography organization here started by an admitted former "porn addict" who has since found Jesus? Seems the Lord came to him, told him to quit doing the knuckle shuffle, and to do whatever it takes to stop everybody else in town from doing it as well. Gotta wonder how that's working out for him. I mean, he must fall off the wagon every now and again. We're only human after all. And you know every time he hears the line, "Ah don't know nuthin' 'bout birthin' no babies!" he's spanking away just like the rest of us. I have GOT to talk to this guy. Unfortunately, he won't return my calls, although I did receive a lovely form letter which included this personal note; "Mr. Hellfire (sic) I prey (sic) for your soul." I bet you do, Chuckles. I bet you do.

All I want to ask the man is this—trading pornography in for Christianity, whatsafuckin' difference? Both prey (yes they do) on the lonely, the desperate, and the unfulfilled. Both appeal to our basest instincts. Both offer a tantalizing glimpse into a fantasy world that does not exist (not even for me, boyos. Sorry to disappoint). Both hawk cheap masturbation material—one spiritual, one literal. And best of all, both have an ugly little baby skeleton in the closet called child molestation that they each pretend isn't there. The Catholic Church especially. Believe me. It's a not-so-well-kept family secret that our revered and holy priests have a sweet tooth for little chickens. This has been covered up for a long time, but it's bound to come out. And soon. Just you watch. The porn world is in a similar boat, but I can honestly say that most of

them folks are trying to root out what they can. Bad
for business, of course, and that's the bottom line. The
Pope would do well to take a lesson from Larry Flynt.
But hey, it's none of my business. Frankly, my dear
Scarlett, I don't give two bits of flying pig crap.

Howling At the Moon (Sha-La-La),
JS

INTERMISSION

SHAGGED OUT, red-eyed, buzzing on Yellow Jackets, ready and raring to demand some justice, the group of young, would-be revolutionaries pulled into downtown Philadelphia a bit after sunrise in somebody's mother's SUV. Borrowed for the weekend. Dalton had spent the last twelve hours reading up on the case, of this Abu-Jamal character, deciding on the road if he supported the cause to free him or not. He did. Or did he maybe just want to be a part of—*Naw! I'm down with the program, ya dig?*

"You know, you guys," said the *Manic Panic* girl, eyeballs vibrating with trucker speed and ADD, "This doesn't have anything to do with anything, but I think Mumia is *goooorgeous.*"

In the distance they could hear chanting. Muffled just yet. In the distance. Growing louder like a war cry.

"I dunno," said a guy. "This may sound stupid and stuff...but I kinda feel like, you know, Mumia...is all of us, you know? Like he's a part of us."

In the distance, a war cry.

The rally was in full gear by the time Dalton and Chen and the rest of them arrived. The crowd was set on hype. Collective brain. Set. Ultra-hype. Banging drums. Chanting. Something about "Brick by brick, wall by wall..." From the looks on the faces of the ever-growing crowd, it meant everything. Everything. It meant everything. This was not weekend warrior activism. This was full-on. Battle mode. This is where people die.

"13th and Locust, folks," somebody called out. "Here we are. This is where the officer was killed." Dalton couldn't see. "Murdered!" Someone shouted from far off. Shoulder to shoulder people here. 13th and Locust. This is where people die. Buzz surged through the crowd, and half the OSU crew was swept away. "Brick by brick, wall by wall..." A monitor set up. Someone would be showing taped footage. "This is it!" Some invisible person exclaimed. "This is the confession!" The confession. Of the 'real killer.' Dalton looked to Chen. They had become separated from the

rest. 'The real killer.' Chen looked to Dalton and shrugged. Hard
to know the truth. Truth. Hard to know. Does it exist?

A crowd outside the crowd began to grow. And grow louder.
Crowing. Hostile. Buzz surging from the outside crowd. "Cop
Killer!!!" They shouted. "FRY THE NIGGER!!!" "FRY HIM!!!"
Hard to know the truth.

Suddenly...*surrounded*. Bicycle cops. Surrounding. Bursting
through the protesters. Swinging batons. Spraying chemicals. And
the crowd? Hysterics. Screaming. Running. "PIGS!" Screaming.
"PIGS!" Screaming. "SHAAAME!!!" Screaming running falling
fingers snapping against asphalt. Dalton saw a white man in Bud-
dhist robes take a baton to the ribcage. "SHAAAAAME!" Dalton ducked a swinging billy-club, grabbed a woman by the waist,
pulled her out of the way of the surging crowd. Dalton looked
around. He lost Chen in the exploding melee. Lost everyone.
Alone in a frantic mob. Blood on the concrete. A waifish Korean
girl slammed to the street by an officer in biker shorts.

Dalton caught his breath on the sidewalk. Doubled over. Out
of shape. An older woman came up behind him. Grabbed him by
both shoulders. Yelled to a nearby cop "We got one over here!"
Dalton pulled away and ran. Saw a young black officer. Eyes burning madness. On Locust Street. Officer withdrew his pistol. On
Locust Street. Grabbed a young white man. Put the pistol to the
white boy's temple and screamed. Burning madness. People scat-
tered stumbling screaming "SHAAAAME!!!" Fingers snapping
against asphalt.

"Dalton!" Dalton turned toward the voice. Chen. They ran toward each other. Chen tripped through passing bodies, and stumbled into a patrolman. Officer pepper-sprayed Chen. Full-on face
full. Much of the spray deflected off of Chen's enormous glasses.
Much. Not all. The cop carried on about his way as Chen fell to
the ground choking, gagging, coughing, gasping, clawing at his
eyes. Dalton ran to him. Scooped him up and dragged him off the
street. Onto a stoop outside a small shop.

"Chen!?! Are you gonna be all right? Can you see me? What should I do?"

Chen choked, and gagged, and coughed, and gasped, clawing at his eyes. Dalton saw a portly hippie-chick in Caucasian dread-locks with a Red Cross fanny pouch. Dalton waved her over. She ran as fast as she could.

"Pepper spray, huh?" She said, bending over to help Chen. "Fucking drag, dude." She reached into her pouch and removed a small bottle of fluids and a canteen of water. She removed Chen's glasses from his face and wiped around his eyes with a small white handkerchief.

"What's yer name, dude?"

"Ch—*gag*—Ch—*ugh*...Chen."

"Chen, dude, I need you to open yer eyes for me, *eww-kay*? Come on now. There you go. Now I want you to look up. This is gonna tickle some, so why don't you grab yer homeboy's hand here? *Heh heh.* Don't worry I won't tell anybody."

Chuckles all around. Ease the tension. Dalton held Chen's hand tightly as the dread-girl flushed Chen's eyes with the bottled solution. Chen jerked and winced, squeezing Dalton's hand for life.

"Told ya it would tickle, *heh heh*," the girl said, pouring water onto Chen's burning cheeks. "But I think you'll live."

"Thank you."

"No prob, dude. You dudes take it easy, dude." And away she went.

"You gonna be okay, Chen?"

"Shit fucking hurts like a motherfucker."

The riot continued all around them, but Chen and Dalton's world suddenly became very small. Small. World. A passing police-man intruded into their world briefly. Looked down on them with irked indifference.

"Everything okay here?" he asked unconcerned.

"Yeah," mumbled Dalton.

"Fine. Good. Have a blessed day," and he continued on.

"Keep your fucking god off me, Pig!" Chen yelled. But the officer didn't hear. Dalton laughed.

"Worthless cockswab. Can you see anything, Chen?"

Chen focused his eyes as best he could. He looked right at Dalton. Dark black irises swimming in pools of red. He held his huge green glasses in his left hand.

"I can see a little. Getting clearer. A little bit. Blurry but…But all I really see…" Chen trailed off. Wailing and chaos falling deeper into the background. Chen smiled. Eyes hot and sore. Dalton gulped.

"All I really see…is you, Dalton."

Chen reached up and caressed Dalton's left cheek. Slid his hand around behind Dalton's neck. Leaned up. Pressed his soft, wet, pepper-burning lips against Dalton's. *Ohhh god…*Dalton shut his eyes tightly. He could feel the lingering pepper-spray slipping down his throat. Dripping. Gulped. But he would not choke. He would not stop this moment. For anything. *Not for anything.* The madness and the hollering and the chaos and the crowd, slipped further and further away. Away. This was Chen and Dalton's world. Brand new world. A world of two. The other world slipping away into nothing.

click

THERE GOES THE NEIGHBORHOOD. *Okay, so listen up all you crackers and crackettes. Us bone-dog shitkickers here at* **PSYCHOBILLY FREAKOUT!** *have decided to kowtow to the liberal establishment and engage in some shameless tokenism. What's that mean to all you monster truck lovin' trailer monkeys? It means we went and got ourselves a Negro. But y'all know we couldn't just go the easy route and pick one up from the local welfare line. No sir, we went deep into Ohio's filthiest, nastiest penitentiaries and picked out the angriest, ass-beatin'est, honky-killin'est Buck we could find. And now we's calling HIM "massa." Ladies and gentlemen, we give you* **Daddy Molotov.**

Welcome to Niggertown BY DADDY MOLOTOV

Aw'ight ch'all. Iss good ta be here an' alla dat. Welcome to the first Niggatown rant from yours truly, da big Daddy. My reason for steppin' to y'all today is to give a different perspective from the usual hill-jack jibba jabba you likely to come across within these pages, ya heard? Imma take y'all straight to the hood, and *beyond*. I thought ya knew but in case you ain't learned, my home turf be Cincinnati, Ohio's very own Over The Rhine. OTR. Tha'ss home to me. Where the pigs be straight illin', talkin' 'bout grab a young brutha and paint the sidewalk with his brains.

If y'all ever bother to pick up a newspaper, you'd know that some months ago my bruthas and sistas, taken to the edge after yet another blue cowboy had to *Roach* a young cat, straight-up said, "Iss on!!!" Imma tell ya like it is, if I hadn't have been locked up during that time, I'da *burned this muthafucka doooooown*.

But fuck fuckin' up MY hood, ya heard? I'da marched up to Mount Adams and leveled that bitch. You'da seen some cocktails then, *Ta Gow*! Bye-bye, Omni-Netherland! C-ya, City Hall! I still say we oughta raze this fuckin' city from the Earth. Split up, and all join other towns, knahmean? But who's listenin' to me? Word.

See, though, that ain't even what went down. A few innocent white folks took a ass-whoopin'. Some dumb jiggaboos burnt up they own homes. Then the Master of the House said, Knock it off, got his blue goons to blast some niggas with they ball-bearing bean bags, and then that was it. Tha'ss the problem. Black folks is just *too damn nice*. Too damn nice. These Cincinnati riots wasn't nothing. Even that Rodney King LA shit wasn't nothing but a panty raid. Wreck some shit, loot some shit, some poor Korean cat loses his joint, and all the while The

Devils on the hill still get to sit back, sippin' a cool one
and cluck they tongues talkin' 'bout "Look at those *animals* down there." The guilty go unpunished again and
again and again. And again.

But let's call a spade a Spade here. Black folks just
don't know how to riot. Know what I'm sayin'? You
look at history, every time blacks have initiated a so-
called 'race riot,' they end up gettin' killed most of all!
Y'all wanna know how to race riot, you gotta take a lesson from the Irish (the original white niggers). After the
Emancipation Proclamation was put into effect, poor
Irish factory workers in Boston and New York was so
bugged out over the notion of niggas takin' they jobs,
that they went on a fuckin' rampage, man! Killed well
over a thousand black men, women, and children. That's
a fuckin' race riot. And all the while The Devils on the
hill still got to sit back sippin' a cool one and cluck they
tongues talkin' 'bout "Look at those *animals* down there."
We just a bunch of game cocks rippin' each other apart
for they entertainment. Ya heard? But it's they game, so
fuck it. I guess Imma get *my* prize. Whatever bullshit
prize it may be. Call it a *lovely parting gift*.

Peace out, ch'all. Much love.

click

CAROLINE POWELL could only but sit and marvel.
If Flemming Brackage had deliberately set out to create the tens-
est dinner party in history, he would not have thought to invite
the guests who would soon be sitting around his table. Only the
wicked hand of the Almighty, or some other devious supernatural
power, could have assembled this ensemble. Caroline was glad she
had prepared her notes.

Tina Salk born 1973 Florida
Ex-wife of Jeff Mican (see "Jeff Mican"). Mother of Dawn Mican (Salk?).
Bride-to-be of Flemming Brackage (see "Flemming Brackage"). Tina is barely a
generation removed from trailer trash. She's playing her new role of High Society
Girl fairly well, but the teased up gutter rat lies not too far beneath the surface.
Best not to cross her. Don't bring up Dawn. Don't bring up Jeff. Don't offer
information about Jeff.

D'antre Philips aka "Daddy Molotov" born 1971 Ohio
Rapper, columnist, multiple felon, soon-to-be published children's author.
Mysterious. Appears to be close personal friend of Jeff Mican (see "Jeff Mican.").
Writes for PF! (see "magazine" file) Gifted writer, but "all over the place." Very
engaging. Seems bi-polar. May be "bad luck." May also be carrying a concealed
firearm.

Eliot Samuelson born 1969 Ohio
Sergeant on police force in Hamilton, Ohio. Current lover of Laina Brackage
(see "Laina Brackage")

Joley Bruton born 1977 California
Sister of Laina Brackage (see "Laina Brackage"). Graduate student at
Northwestern University—MBA. Joley is very involved in grassroots political
activism, especially feminist and environmental causes. She is also extremely
flaky, silly, and prone to temper tantrums.

Laina Brackage born 1966 California
Soon-to-be ex-wife of Flemming Brackage (see "Flemming Brackage"). Laina
and Flemming have one child together—a son named Dalton. Laina is a
pathetic mess of a human being who is incapable of knowing what she truly
wants. She is also a pathological masochist who thrives on humiliation and
emotional pain. Probably an alcoholic. Definitely a problem user—cocaine.
Raised in privilege and has lived her entire life in privilege, she has no
knowledge of any world beyond cocktail parties and bulimia. Besides her
despicable lack of self-esteem, she is needy, clingy, and desperate for attention.
Having no apparent talents of her own, she surrounds herself with talented
people and feeds off them like a lamprey. She is, however, very attractive.

Flemming Brackage born 1963 California
Powerhouse talent agent. Some of Flemming's more well-known clients past and
present include—

"Caroline?"

Flemming Brackage tapped Caroline on the shoulder. She quickly stuffed her notes into her purse and looked up smiling enthusiastically for whatever the question would be.

"Caroline? Can I interest you in a glass of Merlot?"

"Yes. Yes, that would be great. Thanks, Brackage."

Flemming turned toward Del the Housekeeper (serving multiple tasks this evening). Caroline tensed up at the sight of Del and turned away.

"Del, could you please get Mrs. Powell a—"

"Right away, Mr. Brackage."

Pre-dinner conversations were light to say the least. Everyone in attendance trying desperately to introduce topics that would not upset and/or enrage another guest. The men managed to discuss professional basketball in some limited capacity. All the while, Sergeant Eliot eyed D'antre with vague suspicion, like a dog with a grape in its mouth. *I know that guy from somewhere...*D'antre, however, remembered Eliot as clear as day. *But I'll be goddamned if I'm bringing it up.*

After several aborted attempts at casual chit-chat, the women were reduced to *ooohing and ahhhing* each others' outfits.

"Is that Pamela Dennis?"

"I would *kill* for Jean Paul Gaultier!"

"I just picked up the most incredible Helmut Lang..."

"I swear Barney's will be the death of me..."

"That is vintage Vivian Westwood..."

"Balenciaga."

"Marni."

"For me," said Tina proudly, "Nothing beats Versace."

An uncomfortable silence fell upon them.

"Well yes…" said Laina trying to be diplomatic, "Versace is certainly not without his charms."

Tina made a mental note to slap herself later, and quickly recovered, "So Joley, tell us all about this adorable handbag!"

"Well," Joley gushed, "This is a Birken bag. Named after actress, singer, and '60s wild girl Jane Birken! As the story goes, Hermes was flying somewhere for some reason, and he ended up sitting next to Jane on the airplane. And she was complaining that there were no handbags that would hold all of her necessities, so Hermes darted right back to his studio to design the perf…" *bleh bleh bleh bleh bleh bleh bleh bleh bleh bleh bleh bleh bleh bleh bleh bleh bleh bleh bleh.*

D'antre overheard the women's conversation and regretted not bringing his gun. (Tina held her own in the great fashion debate, but secretly wished she had a gun as well. *No no, girl,* Tina thought to herself, *Hang with it. It's called a 'meal ticket.'*)

Thunder crashed outside. Wind and chilled December rain slammed against the French Bay windows. D'antre stared at the "food" on his plate. *I have absolutely no idea what this is.* He noticed that the cop didn't seem to recognize dinner either. D'antre waved Del over.

"*What the fuck is this shit?*" D'antre whispered. Del whispered the answer back to him and walked away. He still didn't know. *Fuckin' rich people food,* he thought. He held his breath and shoveled in a fork load.

"Mmmm…delicious, Del," said Joley. Affirmations all around.

"You know this is *my* favorite recipe," said Caroline.

Class War, D'antre thought.

"So, D'antre," Flemming said turning to him. "Do you mind if I call you D'antre?"

"Of course not." D'antre chuckled.

"Right on, brother. Pretty much everybody and *their mother* calls me Brackster."

"Okie-dokey, Brackster," D'antre smiled shut-lipped.

"So I understand you're the new Joey Spitfire. That must be a weird gig, huh?"

"Well, Joey Spitfire's dead. But I suppose I *could* be him if I need to be."

"Oh, god!" Joley exclaimed, "D'antre, I just want to tell you that I *love* your column. It's so *raw*. So *real*. *Welcome to Niggertown*, god, it gives me chills. I used to hate *Psychobilly Freakout!* cuz like I didn't get it, you know? I thought it was just a bunch of insipid, asinine white-male-macho bullshit. But now I like totally get the joke! Awesome. Awesome work. I love it."

"Uh…thanks. It's a paycheck, knahmean? Well…sorta."

Laughter. Crash of thunder.

"So is it just me," Eliot announced, "Or is this not the perfect set up for a murder?"

More laughs.

"That's why I'm glad you're here, Eliot," said Flemming. "Figured we're gonna need someone to solve the mystery."

"He did it!" Eliot pointed at D'antre cartoonishly. Hearty laughter all about the table. D'antre opened his mouth in a wide (and silent) guffaw. Slapping his knee with great vigor.

"Oh Lawdy! That's a good one, Eliot!" D'antre exclaimed. *Class War, Pig,* D'antre thought to himself.

After they all settled some, Flemming turned to Caroline. *Don't do it, Brackage,* Caroline thought as she dabbed her lips with a napkin. *Have some class for once.*

"So…Caroline? D'antre? Are you two *together?* I mean…Caroline? Are you *back in the game?*"

"Nope. I'm out. I told you I'm out. And that's for good." Pause. "D'antre doesn't need my help anyway." She smiled to D'antre. He smiled back.

"But I understand…" Flemming began with a smirk. Well aware of the chaos he was about to provoke, "…that our beloved Jeff—"

"Braaack!" Tina whined. "Why'd you have to go and bring him up?!"

"Sorry, sweetheart. We're just talking shop—"

"I want Dawn back!!!" Tina shrieked, losing control. "Brack, what are you doing to get her home!"

"Darling, please—"

"While we're on the subject, Brack," Laina interjected, "I want Dalton back too."

Flemming looked at his wife with genuine surprise.

"Why?" he asked. Laina pouted and finished her glass of Merlot in a single gulp.

"This is not a suitable dinner wine," she complained softly. "Not for this dinner at any rate."

"Hey," Flemming answered grinning widely, "We're *casual* here."

Laughter. *Class War*, D'antre thought.

"Ha…" Laina scoffed bitterly, "So when are we breaking out the *White Zinfandel*?"

"Anyway, back on topic," Flemming said. "D'antre, I was curious about how you felt about Caroline's…well let's not mince words here… rather *spotty* record."

"You motherfucker!" Caroline shouted. Rest of the guests dropped silverware in shock.

"Come on, Caroline," Flemming said with a bright smile. "That's a legitimate question."

"I'm not sure I know what you mean," D'antre said.

"What this prick is getting at, D'antre," Caroline said tossing the kid gloves, "Is that in my career, I've had three clients commit suicide, two are in federal institutions, and one was raped to death in a penitentiary."

"And let's not forget the runaway-kidnapper-pornographer."

"Brack!!!" Tina cried again.

"Okay. That last comment will be stricken from the record. Hey, cheer up, Caroline. What was it that Benjamin Sonnenberg said?"

"He said, 'Flemming Brackage is a pompous gas-bag,'" Caroline snarled. Flemming threw back his head laughing wildly. He pounded the table with his fist, tears in his eyes.

"Woo hoo! I think you're right, Caroline! That IS what he said! HAHAHAHA!"

Caroline scowled. Flemming nudged her shoulder.

"Hey, I'm only joshing ya, kid. Heh heh heh. You know I love you."

"No, you're right, Brackage. You're right. Everything I touch turns to *shit*." Caroline turned her eyes on Laina. Laina looked away.

"I think both of you are forgetting," Joley interjected, swishing her wine glass smartly, "That you are both *reflectors*. You can sit way up here in Indian Hill, thinking you matter, all you like. But without 'the artists,' you would cease to exist. You would dry up and blow away."

Caroline and Flemming both nodded. Flemming turned to D'antre and winked, giving him the thumbs up. D'antre smiled awkwardly. Shut-lipped. *Devils on the Hill,* he thought. Joley raised her glass. Everyone else followed suit.

"To the artists!" she toasted.

"THE ARTISTS!" Everyone drank, including Del the Housekeeper. Tell-all exposé getting longer by the day. Grist for the mill.

"I'm curious, Mr. Philips," said Laina, "Sorry, *D'antre*...What exactly is *the role* of an artist in society anymore? I mean, our culture, our entire perspective, was altered forever by the events of September 11th. People are afraid. They crave strong authority. They are skittish about *dissent.* What purpose does the artist serve, especially the, quote unquote, cutting edge or *underground* artist such as yourself?"

"Well, ma'am, I haven't stopped being a *lyrical* terrorist."

Chuckles all around. D'antre continued,

"And anyway, I've always been hip to the concept of The Artist as *a burden* on society."

Following dinner, the party retired to the study for cocktails and...

Flemming dropped a vinyl LP onto an antique Gramophone. Needle on the record. Procol Harum. *A Whiter Shade of Pale* began to play. Everyone, save Laina, took seats on the rounded couches. Knowing what was coming next, Laina didn't bother sitting.

"Still Just Saying No, Laina?" Flemming asked removing a plastic bag filled with cocaine from a tin snuff box.

"No cola for me, Brack," she said. "But I don't want to get in your way. You all have fun."

"Will do." Flemming looked up at Eliot sheepishly with the bag of coke in his left hand. "Uh oh...Uh, officer, I swear this isn't what it looks like!" Laughs. Eliot snorted out a chuckle and pointed his finger like a pistol at Flemming.

"Stick 'em up!" he said smirking. More laughter. D'antre wished he had *his* gun. But he was looking forward to a little speed buzz. He'd been trying so hard to mellow out since being released, that he was worried about getting soft.

"So how is that shit, Brack?" Joley asked, eyes shining with anticipation.

"Best since Harlan," Flemming said laying the powder out on a large mirror, cutting fat lines.

"I miss Harlan," said Tina pouting. "They just don't grow dealers like him anymore."

Flemming, Joley, and Laina all nodded agreement.

"Yep. He's getting the worms high now," said Flemming. Laughter. Flemming leaned over to D'antre. Whispered in his ear, *"You see Del over there?"* D'antre looked and nodded.

"A mouth like you wouldn't believe," Flemming continued, *"Suck a golf ball through a garden hose."* Flemming winked and grinned. D'antre smiled shut-lipped.

Laina walked behind Caroline, bent down, and whispered in her ear, *"Do you want to walk with me?"*

No, Caroline thought.

"Sure," Caroline said.

click

"OH, DALTON! CHEN!" the *Manic Panic* girl exclaimed, "You two look *sooooo key-yooote* together!" Dalton and
Chen looked at each other smiling. Embarrassed. Unsure. Sharing a telepathic joke. For some women, queers are like spoken-for
puppies in a pet shop window. Cuddly. Non-threatening. Heart-
breakingly adorable. Completely unattainable. The girl couldn't
resist giving them each a noisy kiss on the cheek. *Forever on display
in the fag-hag petting zoo.*

The crew met back at the SUV. Long ride back to Ohio. Long
ride back. Long and tedious. Long and insufferable.

"What do y'all say we hang in Philly for a night or so?" someone suggested.

Agreed.

Not a one of them yet 21. The reality of that fact had not oc-
curred to anybody until they attempted admittance into a number
of drinking establishments. And ended up back on the sidewalk.
Again and again. And again.

"Dude, this is very rapidly becoming a colossal drag."

The only joint that didn't ask questions? This little hole on
the wall called *The Hole In The Wall.* Chen, Dalton, and the rest
of them took nervous seats at the bar. The barmaid was a fiftyish
old bat with a rattling smoker's hack, four missing teeth right up
front, and tattoos so worn and faded they looked like nothing but
shapeless blue stains. World-weary resignation hung about her like
a second layer of dead skin. She sighed in despair at the thought of
taking one more breath. Dalton loved her right away. *White Trash
in all its tar-ridden glory, yo.*

"Waddayaneed, hon?" the lady asked Chen.

"Um…two kamikazes please, ma'am."

The lady blinked twice. The second time, her left eyelid
seemed to stick for a second before separating properly.

"I got no idea what that is, hon. You wanna order something *normal* people drink?"

"Uh ma'am?" Dalton interjected. "We'll just have two gin and tonics."

"Now you're speaking English," she said coughing. Dalton looked at Chen with pseudo-disdain.

"What?" Chen asked.

"It's okay. I still dig you."

"Kiss me."

"We just got here. I don't wanna get beat up just yet."

The rest of their group began to titter and whisper amongst themselves. *Manic Panic* girl slid surreptitiously over to Dalton and Chen.

"Hey, you guys," she whispered, "We were just talking about how rad it would be to drop some peyote and wander around downtown Philly."

"Where you gonna score peyote, right?" Dalton asked.

The girl grinned and nodded casually over to a corner booth. There sat two of the most grizzled Indians any of them had ever seen. One of them: Face covered in knife scars. The other: Missing his right hand. In its place was a metal contraption that looked like the business end of a pair of barbecue tongs.

"You're out of your fucking mind, Janet," Chen said. "Those guys could, would, and *should* wreck all of our asses in seconds flat."

"Two gin and tonics," the barmaid coughed.

"Hey Tappy," some fat, Cat Diesel hat-wearing trucker called to the barmaid, "C'mere fer'minit." To which Lady Sisyphus sighed heavily and pushed her boulder down to the end of the bar. *Love her,* Dalton thought to himself.

"Don't be so paranoid, Chen," the girl continued. "I bet those guys are here for the rally. You know…Leonard Peltier supporters showing solidarity. They're our *comrades.* They'll hook us up."

To which the rest of the crew walked over to the corner booth and sat down with the two most grizzled Indians any of them had ever seen.

"Explain it to me, Dalton. What is it with you white people?"

"Huh?"

"I mean, even the most liberal and progressive among you hits the stupid wall when it comes to drugs. 'Every Mexican has weed.' 'Every Asian has opiates.' 'Every Indigenous American has herbal hallucinogens that will *alter your reality*.' It's like narco-racism."

Dalton leaned in close to Chen.

"*Ahem.* Excuse me, but I'm still right here, dig?"

Chen smiled. "*Ahh, so solly*," he replied. They laughed.

"Think about your little theory the next time you ask a toothless woman with blue tattoos on her forearms for a *kamikaze*."

Chen squeezed Dalton's thigh. "Touché," he said.

Suddenly, the sound of ugly, barking laughter began to echo off the front wall from the corner booth. Dalton and Chen looked around. The two Indians in the booth clearly delighted in watching the frightened young college fresh-persons squirm and jitter like a deranged puppet show. The Natives controlled the scene. Gurgling incoherent ridicule. Leering with grotesque intent, cackling ferociously. The kids got up and quickly scurried back over to Dalton and Chen.

"They don't have any peyote and they're insane and we're leaving. Come on."

"Okay," Chen sighed. "Let me just pay for these drinks."

"They already paid for your drinks. Good bye." And they ran out of the bar.

"What?!?!"

"Hey, China doll!" The scar faced Indian called out to Chen. "Come on over!"

Chen sat petrified. He looked to Dalton in terror.

"I paid for ya drinks, kid!" the other yelled. "Come on over! You don't wanna be rude, now!"

"What should we do, right?" Dalton asked. Chen shrugged. Sweat beads dividing and multiplying on his face. Dalton looked to Tappy the barmaid.

"I got .357 if you wanna use it, hon," she offered. "But I'm gonna need it back."

"China doll! We're waitin'!" they heckled. Without thinking, Dalton stood up and turned toward them, blood pounding in his cheeks. Jaw locked. Fists clenched.

"He's *my* China doll, can you fuckin' dig it?!"

Dig it they did. The two Indians howled and banged their hands (and what stood in for hands) against the table. "Then *you* come on over, son! Come on now!"

So…Chen and Dalton walked slowly over to the corner booth. The two Natives smiled wide as they approached. Teeth broken and dark. An air about them whispered *Death is of no concern.* The one-handed man had his shirt unbuttoned to the navel. Dalton noticed a crude jailhouse tattoo over his heart. It said: AIM.

"Sweet ink, man," Dalton said, masking as much fear as he could manage. "I had a friend in the American Indian Movement too."

The man raised a solitary eyebrow.

"Is that a fact? What ever happened to him?"

"Well, if all went according to plan, he's dead."

"Good for him."

"That's right," hissed the other. "Best an Injun can hope for." He offered a welcoming hand toward two empty chairs. Welcoming. Hand. *Death is of no concern.* Chen and Dalton sat. Stiff.

"Yer friends seem to have high-tailed it outta here. Where do you kids go to school at?"

"Ohio."

"Huh. Well, guess they didn't want no peyote afterall. Haha-haahahahhahaha!"

"They thought…you guys might, you know, be here for the rally."

"How's 'at?" Coughed and spat on the floor.

"The rally. Thought you might be…representing Peltier," Chen said trying to sound matter-of-fact. The two men grunted surprise. Taken aback. Leaned in. Attentive.

"What do you all know about Brother Leonard?"

"Everything." Chen said. "He's famous."

"Shut the fuck up." The scar faced man growled in disbelief.

"He is. There's a massive worldwide movement to free him. I'm sure you've heard of…" Chen trailed off. The one-handed man snorted derisively.

"Helluvalotta fuckin' good it's done. You don't know nothin', little laundry boy."

"It's the truth."

"Fuck off. Run on back to your little prissy, brainwash academy. Go on. I'm bored with you already."

Chen proceeded to tell them everything he knew about the Peltier case. The shoot out on the Pine Ridge Reservation. The two FBI agents who were killed. The illegal extradition of Peltier from Canada. The frame up. The intimidation of witnesses. The fabrication of evidence. Dick Wilson and his murderous GOON squad. By the time Chen had backtracked into the fine details of Wounded Knee II and the birth of the American Indian Movement, a second round of drinks had been ordered. And then a third. And a fourth.

"You know," the one-handed man said pointing to the tattoo with his barbecue tongs, "This *used* to stand for American Indian Movement. But it don't no more. Now it's just a target. Like ready, AIM, fire. Heh heh. By the way, I'm Larry Greyshadow. This here's Hides In The Wind. Most people call him Steve."

Drink after drink, hour after hour, Dalton listened to Chen wax revolution with the two most grizzled Indians anyone had ever seen. Wild Turkey. And more Wild Turkey. He tried to pace himself, but they kept coming faster than his fifteen-year-old body could process. The Wild Turkey had cut out his peripheral vision. He tried to focus on the conversation, but the Wild Turkey had muffled the sound. "Black Hills." "South Dakota." "Land of Our Elders." He was able to pick up pieces. Fragments. "White Man's Uraninum Mines." "Cancer," "Spontaneous Abortion." Larry

Greyshadow was on a rant of some sort. "Destroying our women with their poison." "Uranium." "Spontaneous Abortion." *Something about Uranium in the Black Hills, yo. Something...*He watched Chen closely. Chen was clearly wasted, bombed out of his gourd, but still he held his own. Wild Turkey. It seemed to push Chen out of his turtle shell.

"So what are you gonna do about it, Larry?!?" Chen shouted. "Steve?!? You gonna just roll over and let the Devil rape you again?!"

"I'll tell ya what I'm gonna do!!"

More muffled sound and fury. Loud and glorious madness. After losing his hearing completely, Dalton watched Chen with pinpoint attention. Passionate. Brilliant. *God, you're so cool, yo.* Ranting glorious madness. *Goddamn you're so hot, yo.* Madness. Ranting. Something about the Black Hills. South Dakota.

"The Whites put up their faces! Huge looming white faces staring down on my ancestors. My ancestors cannot rest! No, my ancestors cannot join the Sky World!"

"So what are you fuckin' gonna do about it, Steve!?" Dalton stood and yelled. Eyes rolling back in his head. Last thing heard before Dalton fell across the table—

"WE'RE TAKING OUT THE MOTHERFUCKING FACES!"

click

THEY DID NOT SPEAK at first. They just knew. They. Caroline and Laina. Knew. That they both wanted to walk in the cold December rain. Rain. Cold. Laina was avoiding the cocaine inside the house. Caroline was avoiding...Caroline was avoiding.

The rain had eased. Just a touch. Thunder still pounded in the distance. They walked across the back lawn of the Brackage estate. They. Laina and Caroline. Laina held her $780 Ferragamo pumps under her arm, keeping them safe from the mud. She walked wrapped in Caroline's ankle-length camel's hair coat.

"I'm not cold," said Caroline.

"I miss you," said Laina.

They continued to walk in silence, save the sound of the rain-drops plopping into the fishpond.

Finally.

"So...Eliot seems okay enough."

"Don't start, Caroline."

"I'm just saying. He seems fine."

"He *is* fine."

Pause. Listen to the rain.

"I just think...it's amusing, that's all. Sex. The female. All so...*fluid*."

"You're one to talk."

Caroline scoffed. "I never signed a contract saying 'I promise to be a *thoroughbred*.'"

"Neither did I." Pause. "I miss you, Caroline. It's been seven years since you last—"

"Are we really gonna talk about this?"

"No."

Why does it have to be so difficult? Caroline thought. *I don't care! About any of this! Why am I even here? Why have I spent most of my life asking that question?!*

"How's Chet?"

"Don't start, Laina."

"Just tell me what you remember," Laina insisted, trying not to be betrayed by the quiver in her voice. "What do you remember when we were—?"

"Nothing."

"Lie."

"Those were...*interesting* times."

"Nothing's interesting anymore."

Suddenly, Laina stopped walking and hurled her $780 Fer-ragamo pumps deep into the black. They squished into mud far out of sight. She gripped her hair with both hands and screamed. Did not take Caroline by surprise. She did not even blink.

"I *DIED* THAT DAY, CAROLINE!"

"Just…try to relax."

"I *DIED*!"

"It's been fifteen years, forfucksake. Either get over it or go ahead and…"

"You're so cruel to me! You've always been so mean and cruel."

"Just like everyone's always been to you?"

"Just like EVERYONE'S always been to me!"

"Now why do you suppose that is?"

It was about this time, cold and December, fifteen years ago, that Caroline and Chet were married. Dayton, Ohio. Catholic church. Packed house—family, friends, well-wishers. Flower girl and ring bearer and tradition with a capital T. Caroline Vance, 22 years old, blushing bride, a vision in white. Needed a moment to herself. Alone.

knock knock knock

"If that's Chet, you know the rules, sweetheart."

The door creaked open slowly. Caroline heard the sound of sniffling behind her. She didn't need to turn around to see. Unmistakable. *Laina.*

"Why?" she heard Laina whimper.

"I didn't think you were coming."

"Why?"

Caroline stood up and turned to face her. She quickly turned away again. *Never been able to watch her cry.* When Laina was sad, her lips actually turned downward. Like a cartoon frown. *Can't stand to see it. Can't stand it!*

"Why?! Why what?! Why am I with Chet? Why am I getting married? Why am I wearing a white gown? Why am I in a fucking *church* in Dayton fucking Ohio surrounded by people I can't stand?! Because that's the way the game is played, my love. That's the fucking game."

"Why don't you want to be with me instead?!" Laina sobbed. *Don't cry, Caroline.*

"Because I…because that's not the game. Okay? That's not the game. And I need to be a player. I need to *win*. I am going to win. And Chet's…just fine. He's just fine. And he's got all kinds of connec…I need a window. Just to get through."

"*I* need a window, Caroline! To jump out of!"

Caroline ran across the room and grabbed Laina's face with both hands. Pressed her forehead hard against Laina's. Both sobbing now.

"Don't do this to me goddamn it! Not now! Not today!"

"I need you," Laina cried.

"What do you want from me?! Why are you here? You wanna fuck me right now in my white goddamn wedding dress?"

"Don't say that! Don't say *anything* about fucking! We never *fucked*. So harsh and nasty and ugly. *We* don't do that. We *make love*, Caroline. We make love *together.*"

"Not anymore we don't."

knock knock knock

"Caroline, sweetheart?" Chet, Caroline's husband-to-be, asked from outside. "Caroline? Are you okay dear?"

"I'm just great Chet, honey! Just need a moment alone! Go on with ya. Love you! Love of my life!"

Caroline cupped her hand over Laina's mouth to muffle the wrenching sobs that ensued. Caroline could feel her own tear drenched cheeks sticky with mascara and foundation and blush.

"This is, *sob*, crazy! It's crazy! I mean…*huh huh*…who gets married in December anyway? Laina, listen *tuh*, listen to me. Maybe nothing really, *sob*, has to change. Maybe it doesn't, okay? Let's just get through this thing. Let's just get through today. All right?"

"I can't live without you, Caroline. I'll never need anyone the way I need you."

"Then don't."

Fifteen years later and it's December and Ohio again. Caroline angrily yanked her camel's hair coat away from Laina and threw it to the ground.

"Everything could have been fine," Caroline spat. "But *you* had to ruin it. Nothing had to change between us," Caroline pointed at the house, "But you had to go out and let bastard in there—"

"I was lonely! He was—"

"—and you had to go out and let that bastard in there *ejaculate inside you*! You *had* to do it. And then you had to go and have that...*boy.*"

"You leave Dalton out of this!" Laina ran away toward the circular driveway. Caroline chased after her.

"He *is* out of this! I don't see him anywhere! He's the only one smart enough to get away from you!"

"So fucking cruel to me all the time. Just like everybody."

"You don't know cruel. You don't know cruel!"

Cruel. What you crave. Caroline grabbed Laina by the arm and ripped her soaked, ruined Pamela Dennis blouse. It tore in half, leaving one sleeve. Laina screamed and wrapped her arms around Caroline's shoulders. *Don't make me do this, Laina! Please!* Caroline reached down and gripped the bottom of Laina's skirt. Jean Paul Gaultier. Ripped. Shredded to the waist. Laina cooed and bit her bottom lip. Caroline grabbed Laina's hair furiously and swung her around, sobbing, slamming her into Flemming's Bentley. *Don't make me do this!* Thunder crashed as the downpour began anew.

Caroline jumped back away from Laina. Covered her mouth in shock. Horrified with herself. Horrified. She looked at Laina. Somebody's mother. Standing naked in the cold December rain. Lust. Disgust. Pity. Anger. Contempt. She looked pathetic. Dalton's mother. And beautiful. Naked. But for the scratches and bruises on her shoulders. Caroline was horrified with herself. *You made me do it. You made me.* She had the urge to run and grab the camel's hair coat from the ground. Wrap it around her, Dalton's mother, and tell her how so terribly sorry she was. But she didn't. She didn't.

"I'm cold, Caroline. And the rain is hurting me. Rain looks like it would feel good on your bare skin, but it doesn't. It hurts. It's going to leave welts on me." Welts. "At least you could *try* to warm me up," Laina said softly. Defeated.

Caroline wrapped her arms around Laina. Caroline was not an experienced hugger. But she did her best. They held each other, desperate and lost. Ridiculous and foolish and desperate and lost. *I never want to feel anything again.* Pressed against Flemming's Bentley. Laina lifted her legs and slid onto the hood. Leaned back and pressed her cheek against the cold metal.

"Make love to me, Caroline."

"Yeah. Sure. Whatever you wanna call it."

click

DALTON AWOKE with a legendary hangover. In the back of a speeding, rickety, VW bus.

"Starting to think I won't be *able* to sleep in anything else, yo," he muttered.

Chen lay beside him. In a plaid sleeping bag. Awake. They kissed.

"Who's sleeping bag is that, Chen?"

"Don't know."

The van was full of Indian men and women. Many alseep. Dalton caught the eye of a thirtyish Indian woman bobbing her head, listening to a Discman. She smiled. He smiled back.

"Where are we going?" Dalton asked Chen.

"South Dakota. Remember?"

"Ohhh…right…"

They kissed again. Deeply.

"You were talking in your sleep, Dalton. Yelling at points, actually."

"What was I saying?"

"Something about 'Murdering pigs! I'll murder the pigs!' Then you said, I can't forget this, *'Fuggin'* pigs. I was *sick*. I needed help. And you *murdered me!* Come on through that door. You built the monster now face the monster. I'm a—'"

"—Walking living fucking *biohazard*." They said in unison.

"What is that, Dalton?"

Dalton's eyes became clouded and misty. Just a touch. Blinked it away.

"I was…channeling the junkie again, yo. Channeling the junkie. It happens sometimes. I see through his eyes…ya dig…" Dalton trailed off. Chen unzipped the plaid sleeping bag halfway.

"Are you cold, Dalton? You wanna get into the bed roll with me?"

"Yes. Yes indeed I do."

click

REPENT WALPURGIS. Procol Harum. D'antre wasn't familiar with this music, but he swore he had heard this same song three times in a row. Despite his elevated heart rate, D'antre did not feel particularly *motivated*. Back of his throat numb with chemical glaze. He looked over his shoulder at the Gramaphone to see if it had some sort of automatic flip device. Took another large swig of brandy. Looked intently at the marble coffee table, *I mean I guess it's a coffee table.* Studied the bazillion dollar rug as if it contained *The Answer.* Anything to keep his eyes off what was going on in the rest of the room. Surrounded on all sides by these corny, horny, coked-out honkies, he'd never felt so *black* in his life. *A Whiter Shade of Pale, knahmean?*

On the adjacent sofa sat Sergeant Eliot. Pants bunched at his ankles. Young Joley, naked and sweat-soaked, bounced vigorously in the cop's lap like a minimum-wage checkout girl. Del the Housekeeper slid up and down behind her, kissing her from shoulder to heel.

In a dark leather recliner, Flemming sat jittering, hand down the front of his pants, eyeing the action like an impotent emperor. Lips and lids flittering. Glistening wetness under each nostril. His bride-to-be, down to panties and engagement ring, shared couch and personal space with D'antre. Tina stirred cocaine into her brandy like sugar into iced-tea. *Brandy sure ain't missed this bitch.* Tina turned to D'antre and smiled. Hazed-out and near-gone. She tucked her feet under her and put her arms around D'antre's shoulders. He did not move. She kissed, licked, and nibbled his neck, where jaw meets ear. He did not respond. Sat perfectly still. She didn't seem to care.

"Y' knooow," she slurred drunkenly, "I've always liked you black dudesss. But sometimesss, y'all are tooooo rough. Don't be so rough with me."

"Aw'ight." *Get the fuck offa me, goddamn it.*

D'antre was surprised by his own behavior. Or lack there of. He decided, in a moment of clarity, that he didn't want this world. At all. And he didn't know why. *Devil is on the Hill.* It seemed like paradise. Paradise. Seemed like it. If someone had told him a year ago he'd find himself indifferent to super-sweet candy and rejecting hot tail, he'd have laughed in their face. Laughed.

"Hey Mandingo!" Flemming yelled to D'antre. D'antre looked over at Flemming. Right hand still inside his pants. Arm jerking fruitlessly. *Devil is on the Hill.* Flemming licked the tips of his left index and middle fingers and made the crooked finger beckoning gesture with both. "Hey Mandingo! Give her the 'g-spot come-hither!'"

"*Hey Mandingo,*" Tina whispered, "*I want you to give me...*" and she fell off the couch onto the floor. Unconscious. Naked but for panties and engagement ring. No one, save D'antre, noticed. At all. And no one noticed when he stood up. And no one noticed when he bent over and picked up the bag of cocaine. And no one noticed when he stuffed it in his pocket. And no one noticed when he walked out the door. Into the cold December drizzle.

"So long, folks," he said. "It's been a thin slice o' paradise."

No one noticed.

click

THEY SAT NAKED in the mud. Together. They. Caroline
and Laina. Wrapped in the camel's hair coat. Together. Shivering.
Staring blankly into the night. Indian Hill. Cincinnati's wealthi-
est suburb. And they sat naked in the mud. Freezing. Wrapped in
a camel's hair coat. Caroline wished she hadn't bought it. Wracked
with guilt. That camel needed its hair. She vowed to write a fat
donation check to the National Wildlife Foundation first thing in
the morning. Tax deductible…but of course, that's immaterial. In
her current state, Caroline couldn't remember if camels were native to Ohio.

"I'm sorry if I hurt you, Laina."

"Don't *apologize,*" Laina snipped. Curt. She rested her head on
Caroline's shoulder. Their clothing, some of it shredded and ruined, lay strewn about the lawn. Laina's $780 Ferragamo pumps,
gone forever perhaps. Gone forever. Perhaps.

They watched D'antre exit the house. He spotted them, offered a thin, pitying smile, and turned to leave.

"Hey, D'antre!" Caroline called out. "Where you going?"

"Yo, check it, I got people down in Mad-ville. I can hoof it
that way." Mad-ville. Madisonville. A small, predominantly black,
lower working-class neighborhood. At the bottom of Indian Hill.
"So, um, Caroline…I'll call you." And he melted into the black
of the night. *It's funny how everything goes wrong sometimes. Damn
funny.*

click

INSIDE THE HOUSE, Eliot suddenly stood up with
a start. Assed-out and still at attention. Joley fell off of him and
plummeted to the floor with a scream.

"Goddamn!" Eliot shouted. "I remember that black bastard
now!!!"

click back

OUTSIDE IN THE MUD, Laina nuzzled her lips against Caroline's neck. Caroline kissed her forehead.

"Stay with me."

"What?"

"Stay with me. Forever."

"Here in the mud?"

"Yes. Stay with me. Sinking in the mud. Forever. Until we disappear."

click

for Dameka
Daddy loves you, baby girl.

click

PIT-STOP LODGE. VCR played some flick about an awkward girl who receives a magical makeover and wins the heart of the cutest boy in school. In the end, she realizes that being herself is the strongest magic of all. Dawn and her new best friend MeShayle watched the movie, giggling, pretending to find it funny instead of captivating. They actually found it captivating. Giggling. And more giggling.

"Hey. What are you little hens clucking about over there?" Jeff teased. He sat inside the ratty motel room closet sketching backgrounds.

"Nothing, Daddy," Dawn giggled.

"Mr. Jeff, are you *sure* you don't need me for nothing else?"

"Actually, MeShayle," Jeff said, standing up. "I need one more pose. Then you're free and clear for the rest of the evening. Oh, and Dawn has an extra toothbrush if you need it. So anyway…the picture. Are you familiar with Huey Newton?"

"Uh uh."

"He was minister of defense for the Black Panther Party for Self Defense," Dawn whispered to MeShayle.

"The Black what?" MeShayle whispered back.

"My big sister told me about him. He was really cute I guess."

"MeShayle," Jeff said, "All I need you to do is sit in this chair and wrap your right hand around the stem of this lamp. We're gonna pretend it's a shotgun."

The girls laughed. Jeff had already used the TV's remote control for an Uzi in a sketch of MeShayle posing as Malcolm X.

"Come, on girls," Jeff laughed, "Use your imaginations."

"I have faith in you, Daddy," Dawn giggled.

"Mr. Jeff, do I gotta put my shoes on? Cuz if I do, we gotta wait a minute. I still got wet polish goin' on."

"That's okay," Jeff said chuckling. Dawn had painted MeShayle's nails sparkly blue.

Jeff studied the young black whore as she sat perfectly still in her Huey Newton pose. Taking the role seriously (although she didn't fully understand it). Approached the job like a sophisticated professional (although she didn't fully understand it). Jeff looked at her from all sides, studying the angles.

Dawn watched them both intently. She looked at MeShayle—a fourteen-year-old girl sitting in a ripped up easy chair in a rundown motel room. She then looked at Jeff's sketch as it progressed—the same young girl now a warrior in a black beret, sitting on a rounded wicker throne, right hand wrapped around a shotgun as tall as she.

After a while, Jeff thanked MeShayle again, and returned to the closet.

"Waitasecond. Mr. Jeff? Could I see them pictures once you done with them?"

"Here you go, hon. I'm finished with these two."

Jeff handed MeShayle two charcoal sketches. MeShayle sat on the bed. Dawn sat closely beside her. The first sketch featured MeShayle holding a large sword over her head. Leading a medieval looking army into battle. The other was of MeShayle riding a giant eagle over the ocean.

"Wow. Your daddy sure do draw good."

Dawn beamed with pride.

"Dawn, do you draw too?"

"A little, but—"

"Lemme see whatcha got!"

Dawn paused, shy hesitation, but then shrugged and handed MeShayle her sketchbook. MeShayle leafed through the pages with great enthusiasm, often whistling or "ooo"ing certain pieces.

"Now Dawn, I don't know why, but this picture here reminds me of the clinic downtown. Like how it *smells* or something. I don't know why, but it does. That's something else."

Continued paging through. With great enthusiasm.

"These faces here, these are the shit, girl. I'm feelin' these. It's like they ain't happy and they ain't sad. That's how I feel mosta time."

MeShayle finished the book, and looked to Dawn wide-eyed.

"Dawn, these drawings are off the hook!"

"Thank you so much. I like to draw, but…I'm thinking about maybe trying something else. Writing or something."

"I don't understand art at all. But I like it a real lot."

"That's good enough, I think."

Dawn and MeShayle talked and laughed and watched videos and drank rootbeer and ate cheese popcorn and did each other's hair and nails. MeShayle seemed rivetted by the mundane details of Dawn's (former) life. Going to school. Doing homework. Talking to the boys in her class. Talking about the boys in her class. Shuttling back and forth between her divorced parents.

"What is that you are singing, MeShayle?"

"Girl, this is *my song.*"

"You wrote it?"

"Not really. It's just my song. Everybody has they very own song that is completely special to them. My grammama told me that when she was still alive. And it's true."

"I can't sing."

"That don't matter. Now where you gonna go for junior high?"

MeShayle was less open about discussing *her* day-to-day routine, but Dawn didn't mind. MeShayle. Warm and funny and smart. More fun than anybody Dawn had ever met. And Dawn was happy. The happiest she had ever been. Ever. Happiest.

"How old is you, Dawn?"

"Nine. Why?"

"*Nine?* You don't look no nine to me, girl. You look twelve or thirteen at least."

"Thanks…I guess. This…" Dawned waved her hands in the air indicating her body, "Just kinda happened all at once. One morning a week or so ago I woke up, looked in the mirror, and I didn't recognize the girl looking back at me. Kinda scary. It just kinda happened all at once."

"Well, that's just how it is for some folk, Dawn. Ain't no thang really. I see ya sittin' there with your back all hunched tryin' to pretend like you ain't got no boobies. Well, you do, girl. You do. So what if other girls ain't got 'em yet? They will soon enough. Ain't no shame to your game."

"I'm not ashamed. I'm just a little…freaked out."

"Okay, so stop bein' freaked out. Cuz you ain't no freak." Pause. "You very pretty, Dawn."

Dawn blushed bright red. "Not as pretty as you."

MeShayle smiled and looked away. "You can stop that now, cuz you gonna give me a big ole head. And my head's too big already." She peered over toward the closet. "I think your daddy crashed out."

Dawn looked at Jeff, half sprawled in and out of the closet, large sketchbook spread over his face and chest. Dawn giggled.

"Yeah, that's how he does it. He'll go four or five days without sleeping, then it will land on him like a giant rock."

Laughter.

They talked and talked the night away. Away. The night. They. MeShayle and Dawn. Talked the night away.

"MeShayle? Can I ask you a question that's none of my beezwax?"

"I...guess so. What's up?"

"You ever loved somebody and they didn't love you back?"

"Aw, girl, I don't fall in love with *nobody*. You realize how fucked up my life would be if I did?"

"But it's not like you can control it."

"Yeah, you can. If you try real hard. I mean, I meet people all the time who I like a lot. Course I also meet a lot of..."

"Cocksuckers."

"That's what I'm screamin'."

"That's my favorite word. 'Cocksucker.' It's got nice *foh-en-ett-icks*. *Fun-ett-icks*. Something like that. I like the sound. 'Cocksucker.'"

"It's all in the technique."

"Please?"

"Nuthin'. The deal is, I meet a lot of people that I do like. Like you. We just met today and I feel like we already great friends—"

"We are."

"But it's important for me not to *need* nobody else. Nobody but me. I *like* people. But I don't *need* them." Pause. "So, Dawn, what's with the question anyway? You like somebody who don't feel the same?"

Dawn sighed, and double-checked to make sure Jeff was still asleep.

"It's so embarrassing. I just feel terrible all the time. All the time, cuz, well...see, back before Daddy and I became runaways, Daddy was in jail. And there were these people...men, uh...I don't want to talk about that...But anyway, Daddy was in jail, I was scared and lonely, and there was this somebody who I really liked a whole, whole bunch. And I went to this person's house, and...I kissed *this person*. Cuz I was lonely. And scared. But this person...

did not want to kiss *me,* I guess. And this person was really freaked out by what I did, and I felt so *ugly.*"

"Ohh…"

"Yeah…"

"But you *ain't even a bit* ugly, Dawn! You ain't. This somebody probably just had they own thing going on. That's all."

"The worst thing is, MeShayle…the worst thing is, I always wanted my first kiss to be super special! I'd been planning for it since as long as I could remember. I wanted it to be perfect, you know? I had passed up chances because I wasn't sure if they were gonna be right. And I wanted everything to be *just right.* And now…I . .blew it!" Dawn burst into tears. Put her face in her hands and cried deeply. "I ruined it. I ruined, *sob,* my first kiss. I wasted it! And I'll never ever, ever be able to…to get…*sob*…get it back!!!"

Dawn wiped her eyes on the sleeve of her shirt and sobbed. She clenched her teeth and pulled at her hair. MeShayle quickly wrapped her arms around Dawn. MeShayle was an experienced hugger. Smoothing Dawn's hair softly out of her tight fists. Calming. Soothing.

"Aw, come on, now, Dawn. Come on now. It ain't gotta be like this."

"MeShayle, I'm such a *fuck up!*" Dawn cried.

"You ain't no fuck up, girl. Believe me, I seen some fuck ups. You ain't it."

MeShayle held Dawn in her arms. Rubbing her hand in circles on Dawn's back. Letting her get all the cry out. Singing softly to her.

"Is that your song?" Dawn sniffled.

"Uh uh. That's Ella Fitzgerald."

"I'm never going to stop feeling sad."

"Now listen here, Dawn. Just listen. You got it all wrong, see? I don't think you ruined nothin'. You ain't wasted nothin'. You know how come? Cuz you gotta *share* a first kiss. That's the rule. And you ain't done that yet."

Dawn looked up at MeShayle with questioning eyes. Still sniffling.

MeShayle continued, "Come to think about it, I ain't never shared no kiss with nobody neither. Plenty a' fools got *they* thing on…but I ain't never shared nothing with none of them. None of them."

Dawn smiled and wiped the rest of the moisture from her cheeks.

"I really like you, MeShayle."

"I like you too. A real lot." Pause. Long pause. Forever pause. Then…"I'd like to share with *you*, Dawn…but only if you'll share back with me."

MeShayle leaned over and pressed her thick, soft lips against Dawn's. A rush of warmth flooded over Dawn's face and down her neck. Shiver in her shoulders shimmied down her spine, tingled in her special area, shot out the tips of her ruby-painted toes. *Nothing else to it.* The two of them sat perfectly still for a few seconds (*or maybe years*), lips pressed softly against the others'. Softly. Still. And then, they stopped. Looked at each other shyly. And looked away. Smiling.

"Dawn, that was *my* first kiss. Thank you for sharing it with me."

Dawn felt giddy and light-headed. She wasn't sure what came next after that.

"I don't know…I mean, do you want me to…kiss you…you know…*down there*?"

"Naaaw, girl…we just *friends*. If we did that then our first kiss wouldn't be special no more. And I want to be special to you. Cuz you special to me." Pause. "And besides, I got my period right now. I was kinda countin' on your daddy just wantin'—"

"You do?!" Dawn asked excited. "You're having your period?! Oh, you gotta help me then! I started mine for the first time a couple of days ago, and it's getting really bad now and I've been using bunched up t.p., and I've been too embarrassed to say anything to Daddy, cuz he's, well, you know, he's not exactly—"

"Okay okay!" MeShayle laughed. "Simmer yourself down already! I got you hooked up. Don't you worry about nothing. Don't worry. Every little thing is gonna be all right."

Dawn took a deep breath and smiled. Took MeShayle's hand in her's.

"So anyway…how you …feeling now, Dawn?"

"Like every little thing is gonna be all right."

click

"Like every little thing is gonna be all right."

click click

"Like every little thing is gonna—

click

ALL WAS STILL inside Larry Greyshadow's rickety VW bus. VW. Packed to capacity with sleeping Indians. All sleeping. All was still. Still. *Almost.* In the back of the van a large, plaid caterpillar squirmed. Two young boys became who they were inside it. Clumsy, silly, messy, gorgeous. Becoming. The sun rose over awkward orgasms in South Dakota.

"How do you like South Dakota, Dalton?"

"So far, love it!"

click

Welcome to Niggertown BY DADDY MOLOTOV

Awright ch'all. So the other day this hokie-pokie honky muthafucka comes up to me trippin', talkin' 'bout "So Daddy Molotov, what are your feelings regarding the death penalty?" To which I replied, "Oh, you mean

'Operation: Kill The Niggers?'" So then he's like, "Ah-
hah! I got you right there, cuz just last week in Cincinnati, they put a man to death, and he was *white.*" Yeah? So?
So they killed a *white nigger.* They do that from time to
time. But you see, there ain't *nobody* on Death Row but
niggers. As far as you can see in either direction, nigger
nigger nigger nigger nigger nigger nigger. I can't figure
why they don't just go ahead and name it Nigger Row.

Oh, but they got black niggers, and beige niggers, and
tan niggers, and red niggers, and white niggers, and light
brown niggers. All the flavors of the nigger rainbow. We
finally got everybody together! You'd think ole Jesse Jack-
son would be pleased as punch. Happy as a clam. Happy
as a lark. Happy as Sambo with a big ole plate of buttery
pancakes. But no, he don't like capital punishment (As
we used to say in the joint, "You ain't got the *capital,* then
you get the *punishment*). Nope, Jesse don't like Nigger
Row one bit, ya heard? Goddamn. Just no pleasin' some
people...

click

"PRINCESS AFRICA JONES *got no daddy," the
other girls liked to say when she walked by. But Princess Africa Jones
paid them no mind. Her momma had given her all three names, and
everybody called her by all three. "Princess," so everyone in the world
would have to address her with respect. "Africa," the Motherland,
where all of us came from. "Jones," her daddy's name, even though
she'd never met him, and probably never would.*

*"Princess Africa Jones got no daddy, and her momma got no
money," the other kids would taunt and laugh. But Princess Africa
Jones paid them no mind. She had a policy about dealing with mean
people. "I ignore them," she'd say. "It's really that simple." Princess Africa Jones could hold her head high, because she had a secret. She had
a secret that she would never tell.*

"Princess Africa Jones? Pull your head out of the clouds and join the real world!" her teacher Miss Laurie Pritchett would say. But Princess Africa Jones paid her no mind. She had a policy about dealing with mean people. And she would **not** *be pulling her head out of the clouds. "That's where my head is comfortable!" she'd say. "It's really that simple." And she would* **not** *be joining the real world. She had a policy about dealing with a world so nasty and mean.*

"I ignore it," she'd say. Princess Africa Jones held her head high, because she had a secret that she would never tell...

click back

Come on folks, step right up to Nigger Row! We got guilty niggers, innocent niggers, circumstancial evidence niggers, "self-defense" niggers, "He was dead when I got there" niggers, "God told me to" niggers, "I had no choice" niggers, "I am the Angel of Death" niggers, and my personal favorite—"I did it cuz I loved her" niggers. It's a grand nigger close-out! A nigger clearance! EVERY NIGGER MUST GO!

click

Princess Africa Jones seemed like a shy little girl. She lived on 6ᵗʰ Street with her momma and auntie Benita. She didn't make noise, and she didn't talk back, and she did her homework right after school, and she went to bed at 9:30 sharp. You probably wouldn't even notice Princess Africa Jones, unless you were looking for her. And if you were looking for her you'd probably wonder how she could walk right on by when the other girls laughed, and the other kids pointed, and the grown ups all clucked their tongues and shook their heads and said, "What is wrong with that Princess Africa Jones?"

Princess Africa Jones could tell you how she's able to ignore all the meanness, and meanosity, and meanitude. But she won't. It's her se-

cret. But it's not MY secret, so I will tell you. You see…it's like this. Princess Africa Jones isn't really from here.

She's not really from the "real" world. And she doesn't really live here either. She only visits for a short time each day, and then she goes back. She goes back to where she's from. Where she's from, she really IS a princess. But that's not all. Oh heavens no! That's not all at all. She's also a warrior and a sorceress and a great solver of mysteries. She cracks codes and frees slaves and defends the weak and battles evil tyrants all night long. She has important business in Nairobi, and on Jupiter, and a thousand wonderful places. No wonder she doesn't care about long division. She has her kingdom to defend! She doesn't need to play double dutch with a bunch of silly girls. Not when she could be riding her giant falcon over The Black Sea!

click back

But you see, y'all, Operation: Kill The Niggers really is quite the expansive undertaking, ya heard? I'm sayin' it's got more tentacles than Dr. fuckin' Octopus! Death penalty ain't nothing but a left-over antique from the gallows South back when bruthas was left *hangin'*.

As far as pure nigger-killin' genius is concerned, don't nothin' beat the War on Drugs. God-muthafuckin'-DAMN that's some evil brilliance at work. First, make the shit nice and illegal, thus creatin' a never-ending souce of non-taxable, multi-billion dollar revenue for those folks brutal and swift enough to get they cash on. Folks like, say, the CIA for instance. Cut and cut and cut and cut product stretched as thin as possible, with whatever poison available, thereby maximizing profits, knahmean? Then, force the poor into a straight-up desperate, hopeless spiral of pain and misery. F'real. Then when they self-medicate, they either **A**. Die from all the additives, or **B**. Get caught up in lockdown, making them forever unemployable, un-educated, undersocialized, and forever dependent on the

Devil for *everythaaang.* Fuckin' genius. Word. One thing I
love about the Drug War more than any other arm of Operation: Kill the Niggers be this—yo peep it: *Sometimes
the Devil's chilluns get caught up in the dragnet.* It don't happen all that often, ya heard, but from time to time you will
see some Suit's little precious in lockdown on a drug rap.
Oh, they'll get off for *murder.* But drugs? Sometimes *they*
go down too. What happens to the chillun? Where do the
chillun go? I guess there ain't no chillun no more. I seen a
JUDGE'S boy get dragged in cryin' one time, bawlin' all
up in this piece talkin' 'bout "Don't you know who I am?!"
Aw, I know who you is, brah. You's a nigger now, boy! Ya
Heard? Grab some burnt-up cork and paint that child's
face up, cuz we got usselves a nigger! Damn, y'all shoulda
seen what happened to *that kid.* I was in a catercornered
cell, and I still got splattered, knahmean? Hey! Mr. Judge-
man! Iss yo' system, ya heard? You don't like your baby
boy gettin' split in half like a punk? Well...iss yo' system,
boss. Iss yo' system. You hear what I'm sayin'? You spea-
kin' my language? You don't like it? Iss yo' system.

Peace out, ch'all. Much love.

click

"*Princess Africa Jones got no friends," the other girls would say.
"We all decided we don't like you, Princess Africa Jones." But Princess Africa Jones paid them no mind. She had no time for hopscotch or
make up. "It's really that simple." She had clouds to dance in. "That's
where I'm most comfortable." She had books to climb inside of. That's
where she belonged. In Books. In EVERY book. She lived inside every
book she could find. Everything from demons and dragons to The Underground Railroad. And she was a hero. She was ALWAYS the hero.
She was powerful. She belonged.*

Princess Africa Jones wished she could stay in her books. She wished she never had to come back to the boring, mean "real" world with its boring mean people, who spend all their boring meantime being boring and mean to her. She wished she could find a book from which she COULDN'T escape. And then one day, her wish came true...

click

DALTON AWOKE without realizing he'd been sleeping. Looked over at Chen. Fast asleep. Bundled in the plaid bedroll. Van empty. Dalton looked out the window at the vast green nothing. South Dakota? South Dakota. Van door slid open. Larry Greyshadow peaked his head in with a smile. Teeth broken and dark.

"How ya feeling, kid?"

"Better. A little. Man, we got here in no time, Larry!"

"Son, you been sleepin' for two days. We thought you was dead at one point. Sat you up and gave you some...well, you don't need to know what it was, but needless to say, you ain't dead, so you're welcome."

Laughter.

Larry Greyshadow continued,"Both you boys had a pretty severe case of alcohol poisoning. And it's all my fault. So we let ya sleep. But if you're feeling better, we could sure use an extra hand."

"Extra hand. Heh heh heh..."

"Shut up," Larry chuckled, shaking his barbeque tongs at Dalton.

"Where is everybody, Larry?"

"Tent village. About a half mile into the forest that way. Picked up another caravan of brothers and sisters just outside Pennsylvania."

"That's why you were in Philly..."

"Brothers and sisters..."

"I missed all of that, yo."

"You missed alla that. It's all my fault."

"What is it that you need?"

"Right now, I need somebody to help me haul some dynamite."

"So it's really happening?"

"That's right. We been planning this for a long, long time. De-cades. You boys was in the right place at the right time. I believe in destiny, kid. You might not, but I do."

"Chen?"

"We'll come back for him. Come on."

So Dalton followed blindly through the brush. Carrying a soap crate filled with explosives. Dalton shuddered as the contents of his crate shifted and rolled. Scared, thrilled, ready for the inevi-table. Whatever it was. *Born to be a nomad, yo. Born to be a...*Came into a clearing. Even before he saw it, Dalton felt the warmth of the campfire. A group of Indian men and women, 25 or 30 in all, sat around eating pancakes and drinking coffee. Straight from the fire. The woman who had smiled at him earlier smiled again and extended to him a ceramic mug. She indicated a safe spot for his crate, and handed him the cup of steaming black coffee. He gulped it, hot and burning and glorious. *Ahhh...yes...*his remaining hang-over melted away in a river of molten black. Several people studied maps. Some sat in a circle, eyes shut, nodding their heads rhythmi-cally. Dalton removed his glass pipe from the pocket of his denim jacket. Packed a pinch of shake around the tiny pebble of opium, and put a flame to it. Breathed in the smoke. Deep. Lavender heav-en...

"What you got there, Dalton?" asked Hides In The Wind. "Smells like a gift from Mama."

"Mama?" Dalton coughed.

"Mama. The mother of all of us. You're standing on her right now."

Dalton handed his pipe and bag of weed to Hides In The Wind.

"Please," said Dalton, "Pass it around, Steve. There's enough for everybody. Mama says to share, yo."

"That she does, kid. That she does." Hides In the Wind hit the pipe. Waved the smoke up to his face, passed it on. "You understand what's goin' on here, Dalton? You really want to be a part of this?"

"I'm here to help you in anyway you need, ya dig?" Pause. "I'm just wondering if anybody's gonna get hurt."

"We been planning this a long time. Long time. We got guards working for us. People on the inside we trust. We're gonna make sure that there ain't nobody near the bottom of the hill when it goes. Nobody near it no where. If anybody gets hurt, it'll be one of us. And I'm willing to go."

"But we gotta make sure that doesn't happen, right?"

"Listen, kid, you can't make no omelet without bashing a few people's heads in."

click

Hey. It's good to see you again. Daddy's asleep in the closet. Sort of. Kinda half in half out. But he's dead to the universe. Me-Shayle's asleep on the bed. Isn't she pretty? I'm watching her sleep. I like to watch people when they're sleeping. It's funny how her palms and the bottoms of her feet are a different color from the rest of her skin. It's funny. Funny. And if you look closely, her lips are two different colors. Dark brown on the outside, pink on the inside. Very pretty. Us white folks, our lips only got one color. Except sometimes they turn blue I guess. So never mind.

I'm glad to see you. Where are the rest of those people? Yeah, your audience. Where are they? Oh…All of them? There's no one left at all? Well…do you want to keep doing this? Okay. It's up to you. I'm going to just keep doing my thing. Whatever that is.

I miss Dalton so much. Is he okay? I miss him. If you see him, tell him I miss him and I love him. I love you, Dalton! Wherever you are.

Everybody's asleep. I've been watching TV a little. I was just watching this news thing and they were talking about this place. I can't remember what it's called, I didn't even think it was a real place, but you hear about it in Christmas songs. In this place, a bunch of people came and took the land away from the people who were living there already. Kind of like how the pilgrims did to the Native Americans I guess. Well, the people who lost their land, they've been living in like tents and stuff, and they're really upset and they feel hopeless. America has been helping the pilgrim people, the people who stole the land. And the other people feel hopeless. Cuz how can you fight against tanks and stuff when all you have is rocks? Hopeless. So some of the boys and even some of the girls have been putting homemade bombs on themselves and blowing themselves up, trying to kill the pilgrims. For some reason, I can't stop thinking about that Mr. Childress. Mr. Alain Childress. You've heard of him, right?

It's really hard to know what is right. What if nothing is?

Even some of the girls have been blowing themselves up. Blowing themselves up. So much for leaving a good-looking corpse. Is this what happens to the children? Are there even any children left?

What if *nothing* is right? I keep thinking about Mr. Alain Childress.

We all reflect on each other.

I'm looking at MeShayle sleeping. She's pretty, huh. She's my new best friend. I'm afraid to fall asleep, because I know she's gonna be gone when I wake up. Asleep. Gone. I made a list of all the reasons I can't wait to be grown up.

WHY I CAN'T WAIT TO BE A GROWNUP

1. I won't need anybody else but me.
2. I won't need anybody else but me.
3. I won't need anybody else but me.
4. I won't need anybody else but me.
5. I won't need anybody else but me.

I won't need anybody…but *you*. But you. I know who you are. I figured out who you are. Who you are. I. Know. Miss *Omniscient Narrator*. Narrator. Omniscient. I remembered the word. And I know. A week or so ago I woke up in the morning, looked in the mirror, and I didn't recognize the girl staring back at me. The girl. I didn't recognize her. But then, I started to. Recognize. She looked a little like an older version of me. She looked *a lot* like a younger version of you. Of you. The girl in my mirror. I don't want to sound like I got a big head, but…I think you're beautiful. And I'm happy to meet you, because I can see that everything must turn out okay. And every little thing is gonna be all right. Little thing. All right. Every little thing is gonna be all right.

click

CHEN AWOKE alone in the VW bus. Looked out the window at the vast green nothing. Still South Dakota. That's cool at least. Spotted Dalton's notebook. Opened it, and quickly shut it. Looked around, and opened it again:

Here in South Dakota BY DALTON

I avoid this sort of thing, normally.
Little did I know I'd end up this way.
Outside looking in, like a desperate specter, is how I used to be.
Very like a phantom indeed, and
Everything beyond my grasp.
You robbed me of my misery.
Or maybe did I rob you too?
Us. Will I ever get used to the sound of that?
Creeping slowly, you came up behind me. Surround me. Inside me.
Higher than Heaven in a wasteland we are perfect.
Earth and sky but pebbles and mist below us.
Normally, I'd avoid this sort of thing.

Chen chuckled to himself. *We're just such silly little kids.* Van door slid open. Dalton peaked his head inside. Chen looked up at him and smiled.

"I love you too, Dalton."

"Huh?"

"I said 'I love you too.'"

Dalton crawled inside the van.

"Oh…cool!"

They kissed and lay down side by side. Chen ran his fingers through Dalton's hair.

"You gonna grow it out?"

"Hell yes. Might cut it into a mullet."

"Hmmm…we'll talk…"

"It's really going down, Chen. It's really gonna happen. They… WE are gonna do it. We're taking out the big white faces."

"Dalton…what is *art,* do you think?"

"Art? I dunno…something *created* I guess. Anything created… with intent."

"Anything?"

"Sure. You can't put too much of a quality cap on the definition, cuz who sets the standard for quality, ya dig?"

"I hate living by another's standards. I hate ALL authority. Especially arbitrary authority. But I hate all of it."

"You ever hear of Thomas Hobbes? He didn't think most people could make any decisions on their own. No faith in free will, ya dig? He believed that you should follow whoever was in charge. Even if they're corrupt. Or incompetent. He'd fit right in these days, right?"

"Well, fuck him right in the ear," said Chen, "Ya dig?"

"I do."

"So what about *destruction,* Dalton? Can something be art if it's *destroyed with intent*?"

"Guess we'll find out, right? Gimme a day or two and ask me again." Pause. "Chen, did you know we were asleep for two days?"

Chen crawled on top of Dalton and rested his head against Dalton's neck. Kissed him lightly around the ear.

"Well, it's not like we *slept* the whole time."

"Knock it off," Dalton said grinning. "You're gettin' me all fired up again."

"Every time I woke up I'd see you thrashing around," Chen said, smoothing Dalton's hair. "Choking or shaking or mumbling to yourself. You've got an awful lot of noise going on up in there, baby." Chen tapped Dalton's forehead.

"Yeah, it's pretty crowded in here. Chaotic and dangerous. Loud and crowded. A dude's liable to get buckshot…I last dreamt I was visited by a thousand ghosts. Ghosts, ya dig? Ghosts of *dead boys*. They were angry spirits. Bitter against the living. They felt they'd been cheated out of a lifetime of orgasms. And they had come to collect their back pay. It was a pretty exhausting night."

"Wow."

"Hey. Nobody makes it through this unmolested."

"I feel like I'm a ghost sometimes. Like I'm not really here. I'm just kinda…haunting the place."

"That's how I feel too. It sort of makes me think that my actions have no consequences, ya dig? *Outside looking in, like a desperate specter, is how I used to be. Very like a phantom indeed, and everything beyond my grasp.*"

"That's why we're perfect for each other."

"Here we are, malevolent ghosts. Blowing up the heads of our benevolent hosts. Hey! I gotta use that somewhere." Pause. Rolled Chen off of him. Kiss. "Come on. We gotta get up. Imperialist art ain't gonna destroy itself, ya dig?"

click

"PSSST! MR. JEFF?"

Jeff Mican awoke in the ratty motel room closet. Sketchbook slid off his chest. Sketches completed. Vague recollection of finishing them. Young black whore knelt over him poking him in the shoulder, dressed and bundled as warmly as when he'd met her. Not very.

"What's goin' on, MeShayle?" Jeff yawned.

"I jus' wanted to say Bye, cuz I'm leavin'. And I wanted to give you this back."

MeShayle extended her hand holding a roll of bills. Jeff did not take it.

"You should take this back," she insisted, "I ain't done nothin' to deserve it. And I had a really good time last night. I ain't supposed to get paid for enjoyin' myself."

Jeff closed MeShayle's fingers around the money. He was startled by how small her hand felt inside his. She had seemed so much older than fourteen, but she felt like a little girl in his hand.

"Sweetheart, you know who I am, right?"

"Yessir."

"You know I'm famous, right?"

"Yessir. Well…yessir. I guess 'famous' is as good a word as any."

They chuckled.

"MeShayle, someday when you have a résumé, you can say you modeled for me."

She nodded. Stuffed the bills into her pocket. As she walked toward the door, Jeff could swear she had a little swagger and skank to her step.

"Take care of yourself, Mr. Jeff. And please take care of that one over there sleepin'. I ain't *never* gonna forget her."

"Yeah. She has that effect on people."

"She be like a…bright shining light."

Jeff nodded. And she was gone.

click

RING RING

"Mail *Bock-uh-sez*, Etcetera."

"Papa?"

"Ohhh…commie son calls. Oh what joy."

"Good to talk to you too, Pop."

"So? What you want?"

"Just calling to say 'hello.'"

"Aw. Yes. *Hallo*, then. You do well at big college? Spread liberal lies everywhere?"

"I met a boy, Papa. He's gorgeous. We're in love."

Chen's father sighed. Long and pained. Then, "Aw yes. Met a boy. In loooove. You make a *fathah* so proud, *Chah'lie*. So this boy...he *uh* commie too?"

"*Anarchist*, Pop. I'm an anarchist."

"So what next, huh, *Mistah I-Hate-America*? You plot to kill Vice President? You wipe ass on Old Glory?"

"Actually, Pop, I'm calling from South Dakota. Dalton and I...that's my lover's name—Dalton...we're helping some renegade Indians blow up Mount Rushmore. It will be the ultimate physical manifestation of our love for each other."

Long pause...Muffled chattering in the background. Then, "*Chah'lie, yoll sah'casm*. Not funny."

"Sorry, Pop. I'm trying my best over here."

Chen could hear his mother jabbering in the background. His father jabbered back at her. "Pop? Is that Mom? I couldn't hear her. What did she say?"

"*Yoll mothah* say South Dakota very cold. Wear warm sweater."

click

"DAWN? HONEY? It's time to wake up, sugargirl."

Dawn shot upright in bed with a start.

"Oh my god! Daddy! We gotta get out of here! We've been here way too long! They're gonna catch—"

"Shhhhhhh...It's okay. We'll be fine. But you're right. We do need to go."

Dawn looked back at the empty bed behind her. She looked up at Jeff. The look in her eye ripped Jeff's heart into seventeen separate pieces. And he didn't know why. Dawn sighed and looked at the floor. She walked over to the window and peered out.

"It's starting to flurry," she said. "Bet it's gonna get cold to-night."

Jeff stood silent. Not sure of what to say.

"Daddy?"

"Yeah, hon."

"Love sucks."

"I don't know what you mean, sweetheart."

"I love you, Daddy."

"I love you too, sugargirl."

"Daddy...sometimes...your world is choking me."

"It's not my world, baby."

"Daddy?"

"Yeah, hon."

"Cecil is closing in."

click

INTERSTATE 75. South. 10:47am. Speed limit: 65. D'antre's speed: 53. *All Things Considered* mumbling quietly on his burnt out $50 stereo. *Life ain't nothin' but churches and liquor stores,* D'antre thought to himself as he lit up a Camel. *Life ain't nothin' but one grand-ass disappointment.*

His ex-wife Tijuana Smalls was playing him. Once again. Again. *Finger my buttons, TJ. Play me like a goddamn accordion.* Promised him he could see their daughter. Dameka. "How's tommorow for ya, D?" TJ said. "You can pick up Boo-girl at my mama's." So first thing come sunrise, D'antre was off driving into Crackerville (West Chester) to his baby's grandmama's place. Crackerville. Surrounded on all sides...*Knock knock knock.* No answer. *Ring Ring Ring.* No answer. **KNOCK KNOCK KNOCK.** *Not again...*

Mommy's got the power.

He wanted to tell her. Dying to tell her. Her. Dameka. About his book. *Princess Africa Jones. It's gonna get published, baby!* He said inside his head. *I'm a f'real writer, ya heard? 'So proud of you, Daddy,'* she'd say inside his head. Inside his head. Inside. His head.

Here I am inside my head. I don't wanna be here anymore. It's too crowded, and too chaotic, and too dangerous in here. I wish I could just jump on my giant falcon and fly away. Fly away. Beyond the sunrise...

Took the next exit for supplies. Smokes, a lighter, a forty, and some sort of rapidly prepared egg-related breakfast item. Drove past a New Life Baptist church that used to be a bar and still looked like a bar, but now displayed a big, gaudy cross on the door. The sign out in front of the dive/house of God read—"A Man Can't Stumble When He's On His Knees." *Yeah, but he can choke...*

Pulled into the convenience store parking lot. Chuckled at the sign out front and walked in. *Good day for signs.* It should have read, "NOW HIRING CLOSERS." The 'C' had fallen off. *I should apply.*

"And how you doin' this fiiiiiiine morning, young lady?" D'antre asked the clerk as he set a forty and two lighters down on the counter.

"Okay."

"I seen you befo'."

"I'm always here."

"Ain't you s'posed to be at school right now?"

"Yep."

"Pack of Camels."

"So you just got outta jail, huh? That's so rad. What'd you get locked up for?"

"Bein' stupid."

"Ahh...so that's finally illegal, huh?"

They laughed.

"This store ever close, uh..." D'antre looked at the girl's name-tag, "...Lindsey?"

"Nope. 24/7."

"Then why they hirin'—"

"Check you out, looking for logic," the girl laughed, twirling a rope of hair around her index finger. "You gotta give that up right now. Logic. It's just like that sticker right over there—**YOU ARE BEING VIDEOTAPED FOR YOUR OWN SAFETY.** Wrong. You are being videotaped for THEIR safety."

"I feel you," D'antre said nodding.

"*I wish,*" the girl said under her breath.

"Please?"

"Nothing. Your change." The girl smiled and handed D'antre three bills and something else. He smiled back and walked out. Out to his car. Looked at what she'd slipped him. Piece of paper. Phone number. 'Call me,' with a little ☺ next to it. *Sorry, Lindsey,* D'antre thought as he crumbled up the paper and tossed it in a can. *I got too much freedom on my side this time, girl.*

D'antre's car moseyed on down I-75. Going home. OTR. No particular hurry. He reached under his seat and pulled out his foldable wooden pipe. Packed with sticky green. And one little chunk of red rock. *Ohhhh...yeah...*Fire to the goods, glowing orange.

A voice muttered inside his head. *Too crowded in here.* Not his own. Another voice. A boy. Familiar.

Getting Chinese, are ya?

"And you know this!" D'antre said aloud to nobody. Nobody.

Me too, yo. In more ways than one.

"Blazin' and hazin', cuz it's just so amazin'."

I can dig it. Where are you?

"Nowhere. Cincinnati."

I heard ya the first time, ya dig?

Laughs.

"Where are you?"

South Dakota. Falling in love and engaging in petty terrorism.

"That's a full bill, ya heard?"

Where are you now?

"I-75. Just over the Norwood Lateral. All sorts of industry and chemical plants. Quite a landscape, knahmean?"

What's killing us...

"There's a gigantic stone prick jizzing out black smoke right about a hundred yards from me. Underneath it is a sign that reads 'God Bless America.'"

There is not a single word in that sentence that means a thing to me, ya dig?

"True. True."

What's killing us....
"I got a little girl, y'know? Where do the children go?"
There are no children.
"Maybe so."
I gotta sober up. Destiny awaits, yo.
"I gotta sober up. Destiny awaits." Destiny. *Whatever.*

Ring Ring Ring. D'antre darted up the steps of his apartment building. He could hear his phone from the first floor. *Ring Ring Ring.* Eviction notice on the door. Changed locks. *Ring Ring Ring.* Kicked the rickety thing right off its hinges. Splintered. Smashed. Pushed through the broken wood and ran inside.

Ring Ring Ring.

"If this is TJ, you got some explainin'—"

"Hullo? D'antre?"

"JEFF! Where the fuck you been at, dawg?!"

"Ha ha. Where have I NOT been. Good to talk to you, bud."

"It's about to get even better. We did it, Jeff, ya heard? Somethin' called Hedgehog Press is gonna publish *Princess Africa Jones*!"

"Awesome!"

"Hell yeah it's awesome! And they want you too, dawg! I sent them samples you sent me and they fuckin' loved 'em! We's partners now, partner! So you gotta get your ass back home. Like yesterday."

"Well, I'm still pretty darn *wanted*, you know."

D'antre could barely hear Jeff, for the high-decibel caterwauling in the background.

"Jeff, what is going on over there?"

"I'm in the car. I bought a cellphone. That's my daughter Dawn, she's...uh...singing."

"Could you ask her to take it down a notch? I can't barely hear you."

"Nope. Sorry. I'm not doing that."

D'antre smiled. Thought about Dameka for a brief moment.

"I feel you, dawg. I feel you. Makin' a joyful noise, ya heard?"

"Exactly."

"Look, Jeff. I been in and out of correctional institutions since I was ten years old. If there's one thing I've learned, it's that high profile people don't catch the wrath. I bet this publishing house can get you off. Or maybe my agent knows somebody. I got a lit agent, ya heard? Some cat named Flemming Brackage hooked me up with a friend of his. Name of Sal Willis. You know this Brackage cat, yeah?"

"Heard of him. Have you talked to Caroline?"

"She's gone, man. Gone. I think she moved back to Neverland. Either that or she sank into the mud. One or the other."

"Okay. I'll see you in a couple of days, D. I'm coming home. We'll make this happen."

"We'll make it happen."

click

DALTON AND CHEN hauled crates and asked few questions. The vibe within the camp seemed to undulate. Ebb and flow. Tense and ease. Tense and ease. Finally, there was nothing left to do but wait and wait. Until sundown. Sundown. Nothing left to do but wait.

"You folks may not believe in destiny," Larry Greyshadow said, lighting a cigarette, "But I do."

"Larry?" a woman asked. "Is this really going to make any difference?"

"They've got to know, Willa," he answered. "They've got to know that we ain't going to just roll over for them no more. This is just the beginning. It ain't gonna stop with empty symbols and angry gestures. They *will* honor the treaties they signed, and they will cease in exploiting us. Or they will be forced to kill every last one of us fighting." Larry Greyshadow shut his eyes tightly. Shook his metal tongs over his head. "Where have all the warriors gone? *They* have warriors...but where did ours go? Are there none left?

Can we go on living like this forever? No. No more. No more compromise. They can call us 'terrorist' or whatever they want. Try to compare us to *whoever*. But *we* know who the true terrorists are. We *recognize* them. We can name them. And they will *recognize* us. We're making our stand."

Shouts of affirmation.

"It's going to be an interesting millennium," Chen said. Chuckles and nods all around. Hides In the Wind knelt down next to Chen. Handed him a set of keys.

"I'm giving you the van, Chen. Be careful driving it, cuz it's stolen. Feel free to ditch it wherever you like. But you young brothers should be taking off now. I'm glad to have met you both." Shaking hands. "Dalton, you're the first White I ever met that I didn't want to strangle with my bare hands."

"I take that as a high compliment, yo."

Dalton and Chen tore blindly through the brush as the circuit breakers responsible for lighting Rushmore all blew out at once. Urgent. Not knowing when it would happen. Would they have time to make it to the van before the area was covered in rubble? No idea where they were heading. Just black surrounded by black. Cold December. South Dakota. Nothing. Black. Nothing.

"We made it."

"Not yet."

Scurried blind like frantic rodents. Rodents. Frantic.

"I see it."

"Are you sure?"

"No. Just follow me."

Found themselves inside the van, not entirely sure how they got there.

"I don't believe in destiny."

"Neither do I."

"Let me drive."

"Aren't you *fifteen*?"

"I'll be sixteen in two weeks. And anyway, what difference does it make, right? It's a stolen vehicle anyway, yo."

Pulled out onto the barren highway. Smooth. Calm now. Silence for a bit. Smooth and calm. Waiting. And waiting.

"What have you left behind, Dalton?"

"Nothing."

"Any brothers or sisters?"

"No. I'm an only. Well…that's not entirely true. I have a little sister."

"Okay, so which is it? Are you an only or do you have a little sister?"

"I have a little sister."

"What's she like?"

Dalton turned to Chen quickly and smiled. Put his hand on Chen's thigh. Eyes back on the road.

"Only person I ever loved, 'til now."

Chen took Dalton's hand and kissed it. Rubbing his cheek over Dalton's fingers.

"Yeah," Dalton continued. "She's incredible. Beautiful. Strong. Powerful. Maybe *all* powerful, ya dig? She'll be around when the rest of us are long gone. She's a bright shining light." Pause. "So what are your sibs like?"

"Chinese."

"Hmmm…not everybody can say that."

"No, but *most* people can. Majority of the people in the world are Chinese."

"What do we do after this? Doesn't it seem like we're peaking kind of early?"

"I guess we just grow up and get boring. Provided we escape."

"There's a little place just outside of Napa Valley. Or maybe it's in Napa Valley. It's called *The Valley of the Moon*. Always wanted to go there."

"That sounds cool."

"It's probably just a stupid little town like every other stupid little town."

"Then let's never make it there. Let's always be *going* there."

"You know I'm in love with you, right?"

"Little did I know I'd end up this way."

"I avoid this sort of thing normally."

click

JEFF BOBBED HIS HEAD with no discernable rhythm as Dawn sang at full voice. Loud and boistrous. And utterly off key. At a stoplight, she rolled down her window and sang to a group of people waiting at the bus stop. Applause.

"You're sure in high spirits today, hon'."

"Sure am, Daddy o' mine!"

"Your moods are weird, Dawn. One day you're sad. The next day you're singing. Sad, singing. Sad, singing. Ever since...oh... Never mind."

"I'm a girl, Daddy."

"Well, duuuuuh."

They laughed. Jeff continued, "So what is that you've been singing the past week? I've never heard it before."

"Of course not, Daddy. It's my song. Everybody in the whole world has a song that is completely special and unique to them. You just gotta find your very own song. I think I've finally found mine."

"Is that a fact?"

"Yep."

"Awesome!"

"Yes. Yes it is, Jeff. It is awesome."

"I wonder what *my* very own song sounds like."

"It's probably gross."

"That goes without saying. You've been talking about giving up drawing for some other type of art. Are you thinking of becoming a musician?"

"Gosh no, Daddy! I'll never be *that* down and out!"

Laughter.

"Okay…what about sculpting?"

"Nah. I was thinking about being a writer."

"Oh honey…Writers are wretched, miserable people. Day and night hunched over a keyboard, not seeing other humans or the sunlight for weeks and months at a time, chain smoking, muttering insanely to themselves—"

"That sounds *kewel*."

"But you're a people-person!"

"It's just a phase." Pause. "I like people, Daddy. I don't *need* them."

They drove in silence for a while. Enjoying the sound of the tires against the highway. December wind slamming against the steel and glass. Asthmatic Dodge Colt engine wheezing—yet determined. **SERVICE ENGINE** light flashing on the board.

"I gotta get that light fixed."

"I can't believe you're gonna draw a *kids book*, Daddy."

"Juvenile fiction."

"I can't believe you're gonna draw—"

"Stranger things *have* happened, sweetheart."

"Nuh uh. No they haven't. I'm worried about driving through Cincinnati."

"Don't worry."

"You're not well liked there."

"True…"

"Besides Mr. Philips, did you make any other friends while you were in jail?"

"Well, I wasn't in jail all that long."

"You just weren't applying yourself."

"How's your stomach today?"

"I feel completely better. Today's just a good day. I don't know if I believe in God or anything, but I feel like *somebody's* watching over us right now."

click

"AIRTEL. THIS IS ALEX."

"Alex, this is Special Agent Hargroves. I have Robin Lewis from the DA's office on the line."

It had been a pretty slow day for AirTel Supervisor Alex Nabor up until that point. Double shift. Overtime. Time-and-a-half. More time for nothing. He'd spent most of the morning playing rounds of Internet "MASH" trivia. Listed "for experts only." Around about lunchtime he started six flame wars on random website message boards. Perused the art samples on freejeffmican.net (after which he opted to skip lunch), and was just about to download some choice images from cavernousasses.com, when he was suddenly called upon by the Federal Bureau of Investigation to step up and be the hero he had always secretly known he could be.

Mr. Robin Lewis explained to Alex that they had a court order giving them permission to track an AirTel cellular user. He then proceeded to prove said order by giving the passcode.

"Alex, you understand, of course, that we cannot give you too much information about the circumstances. I will tell you that this case concerns a kidnapping. The perpetrator is a young male in his late twenties/early thirties, and is considered to be unstable and possibly dangerous. We know that this individual kidnapped his daughter in the greater Cincinnati area, and we have reason to suspect that he may be heading back that way. Your help in this matter may very well save the life of a scared and defenseless little girl."

Mr. Lewis gave the kidnapper's mobile ID number. Alex scanned the central office computer, eyeing a multitude of little triangles on the monitor. Each representing a different cell tower.

"Gentlemen, I am triangulating the user's location based on his proximity to—okay, he is near two transmitters at the moment and I am getting a strong T1 from...ahh yeah...I see what he's doing. Yes he is moving, and yes he does appear to be near the Hamilton County area in Cincinnati, Ohio."

In the background, Alex could hear his information being re-layed to another man. Special Agent Hargroves informed him that this third party was Hamilton County Sheriff Lester Simmons, who was in contact with police precincts in the tri-state area. Alex tried to pick up as much info on the case as he could, but "No sir, buddy, this ain't your day," was the most he could decipher.

Once Alex pinpointed the exact road and approximate loca-tion of the individual, he was met with a curt "Thank you for your time." And then a whining dialtone.

What sort of evening could follow that? Alex attempted to re-turn to his routine. Needless to say, bringing down a wanted, and possibly dangerous, criminal rendered electronic nudity and *trivi-afun* rather trite and useless to say the very least. No matter how much "expert" knowledge was required. Alex Nabor spent the re-mainder of his work day entertaining notions of joining the FBI himself, or perhaps the CIA, or perhaps becoming a cyber-vigi-lante. Or maybe even using his skills to track and stalk past girl-friends. *No, no,* he thought himself, *I must use my powers for good instead of evil.* He clicked back to freejeffmican.net. Checked out the art samples. Felt quite ill. Wanted to look away. Could not. Captivated. And ill. *Enough computer.* Flipped on his radio. NPR news. Another terrorist attack. Rushmore. Mount Rushmore is no more. Rubble and dust. No confirmed casualties at this time. No suspects.

No hope...

click

ROOSEVELT was the first to go. Nestled in the corner, he brought most of Jefferson with him. A blast and orange flash and a crash and a rumble, like thunder with perpetual aftershock. The rumble hit them, Dalton and Chen, as they stood in a desolate field of nothing. Waves of energy rippled through their young bodies. Shuddered and flooded with shiver shocks and a warm glow cast about them. Jerked and spasm, holding each other close, in South Dakota in December. In a desolate field of nothing.

"We're definitely peaking too early."

From where they stood, they couldn't even see Rushmore. What was left of it. Four black smudges on a black canvas of tiny white specks over black evergreens. Four black smudges, and then two. Another orange flash and deep, hollow rumble. Hollow. And then none. But for Lincoln's brow. Rumble continued. Rolling boulders and debris. Crashing and rolling, thunder in the distance.

"Remember when there used to be Rushmore?"

"Nope."

"There's gonna be sirens soon."

"I hope no one was…you know…"

"Are you hoping, or *praying*?"

"I don't pray."

"Still, it's an interesting concept. Prayer. Especially praying for someone else. 'I shall talk to the sky on your behalf.' It's like, 'Yeah. Thanks.'"

"Can you hear the sirens?"

"Barely. But yeah."

"I love you."

"I love *you*."

"I could see praying to the sun. That makes a certain amount of sense. I'd pray to the sun and ask him never to rise again."

"So what comes next?"

"Maybe nothing."

click

"THIS IS IT, JEFF!" Sheriff Simmons called out through the megaphone. "This is where it ends, son. Come on out of the car. Easily. Quietly. For your daughter's sake."

For my daughter's sake. Jeff sat frozen to his seat inside the 1985 silver Dodge Colt. Surrounded. Every which way. Radio screaming

"Mount Rushmore is gone!" Dawn shut it off. Surrounded. Every which way. Rollers spinning wildly. Red and blue. Like a giant, flashing LEPER sign. *UNCLEAN! UNCLEAN!*

"Come on, Lester," said Sergeant Eliot of Hamilton, weapon drawn. "We can just take him."

Sheriff Simmons clicked off his megaphone and shook his head. "My jurisdiction, Eliot."

Jeff peered into his rear-view mirror at the mass of uniformed officers. Three separate precincts at least. Officers. Standing in empty Ohio farm land. Under the lifeless, hopeless haze. Standing ready in empty space. Ready to pounce.

Out of the corner of his eye, Jeff saw *him. Him.* Huge and headless. Rippling muscles. Engorged and throbbing, ready to burst. *Waiting for Dawn. Waiting for Dawn. Waiting...*

"Don't let HIM near my little girl!!!" Jeff screamed. The police did not know who *He* was. "I'm not getting out of this car until he's gone!!!" Gone. Until he's gone. Gone. Gone. Until *HE'S* gone. Huge and throbbing, ready to spill. *NO! Not inside my baby!*

"Daddy?"

"What is it, sweetheart?!"

"Please don't cry."

"I don't care for you, Jeff! You hear me?" Sheriff Simmons called out. Instantly filled with regret. Speaking without thinking. "But!" he tried to recover, "I promise you, your little girl will be safe. I promise, Jeff. I promise. Say what some will about me, but I'm a man of my word. Come on out of the car." Speaking without thinking. Thinking without cognition. Understanding without conflict. What is *right.* Without conflict.

"You see, Dawn," Jeff said desperately, turning toward his daughter, "They said I couldn't see you anymore, and then you ran away and—"

"I know, Daddy. It's cool. It's cool. Are we having fun out here?"

Cecil stood waiting in Jeff's rear-view mirror. Red and blues spinning wildly. *UNCLEAN! UNCLEAN! UNCLEAN!*

"Jeez, Daddy, you creative types sure are a not-stable bunch."

"He's everywhere," Jeff muttered.

"WE creative types I mean."

Red and blues spinning wildly.

"You're trying my patience, Jeff. Outta the car now!"

UNCLEAN! UNCLEAN!

"I see him everywhere, honey. Everywhere. Drawing him kept him out of my mind. But he's always there. I can't let anyone *hurt you.*"

"He's not there, Daddy."

"Jeff?! You hear me, boy?!"

"Yes he is! He's everywhere! And no one will ever stop him! He destroys the little things. The little things. He's everywhere. In the churches. In the schools. In the government. In the military. On the police force. On television. In our homes. Watching. Always. Ready to…I kept him out of my mind by drawing him, but he's everywhere. He destroys the little things."

Destroy.

Huge massive solid rippled swollen thick pulsating rough bulging popping throbbing spilling gushing raping bashing cutting crushing ripping slitting splitting tearing spindling mutilating destroying the little things.

"Daddy? Every little thing is going to be all right."

Driver side window smashed in. Black clad arm penetrating the space. Door swung open and Jeff was dragged out into the cool December evening. Dawn jumped out on her side.

"Someone wanna grab the kid?" Eliot grunted.

"Daddy! Don't worry! It's all okay! It's all okay!"

Cuffed behind his back. Jeff was led to a squad car. Cops every which way grunting and barking and informing him of his rights.

"Someone wanna grab the kid?" Some Roundtree bellowed.

"It's all okay, Daddy! It's all gonna be all right!"

Jeff was pushed head-first into the back of the squad car. Engines fired. Jeff pressed his forehead against the glass. Looked out the back window as it drove away.

"*Love you,*" he mouthed. And then gone.

"Love you!" she shouted.

"Someone wanna grab the kid?"

Officers every which way hopped back into cars. Engines firing. And away. Away...

Away.

"Someone wanna grab the kid?!" Dawn asked aloud. To no one.

They all sped away. And gone. No one left to protect her. None left to brutalize her. Gone. Gone. Alone.

Dawn stood in the empty Ohio farm land alone. Under the lifeless, hopeless haze. Alone.

Alone...But for *me*...

Dawn? Dawn, can you hear me? Dawn...

...*That's where I saw her.* Standing alone in the nothing. Looking every bit the little girl. But even now *evolving*. Beautiful. Stunning. A target? Powerful. And alone.

"I know you're there," she said to me. She did not turn. Faced instead into the nothing. "I don't want to sound like I have a big head or anything, but I think you're beautiful."

Beautiful.

"Are you remembering?" She asked. "Or am I really here?"

Are you projecting? I asked. *Or am I really here?*

"What's it like?"

I don't need anyone.

"Who hurts you? Who hurts us?"
    No one. Ever.

"I'm glad to have met you. Because now I know that everything will be all right."
    When will I see you again?
"Never. But I'll see *you*. Staring back in my mirror."
    I'll see you when you are me.

"I won't be me then."
    I won't be you.

"What happens to the children?"
    There are no children.

"I won't need anyone."
"Do you miss…"
    I don't need anyone. I don't often

"Is it just…"
    recognize the woman staring back in my mirror. I reach inside and pull her out and throw her to the floor and…don't need anyone…

Dawn turned to face me. Walked with feather footsteps. Beckoned me near her. I bent down. She stretched up. Licked her lips and sighed and shuddered and closed her eyes and cocked her head and pressed her lips against mine…

I don't often recognize the woman staring back in my mirror. I reach inside and pull her out and throw her to the floor and…she ravages me. I don't need anyone but her. I don't need anyone else. I don't need anyone…There's no one left at all…

Dawn licked her lips and sighed and shuddered and closed her eyes and cocked her head and pressed her lips against mine… And then she disappeared…Disappeared. Gone. *It's a glorious age.*

Skipped ahead? *It's all but a click away.* Disappeared. Became one with me? Gone. *So click away.* Disappear. *There are no children.* Jumped on a giant falcon and flew beyond the sunrise. Disappeared. *Or maybe she just clicked.* Clicked.

Maybe she just clicked it.

Maybe she just clicked it all away.

goodbye

Acknowledgments:

Thank you:

To everybody at Bleak House Books/Diversity Incorporated, especially Ben LeRoy for his tireless work and dedication to this book. It wouldn't have happened without you. Thank you for taking a chance on an unknown from nowhere. Also thanks to Blake Stewart, Alison Janssen, Julie Kuczynski, and Kate Fletcher.

To Roxy Erickson and Peter Streicher for their beautiful and distressing cover art. I can think of no better image to accompany this novel.

To Carol Fass and Courtney Camp at Carol Fass Publicity. Thank you for getting it. You're true professionals.

To Dr. Jon Saari and everyone at Antioch for giving me the freedom, support, and guidance to create what I needed to create.

To Andrew Miller whose encouragement and guidance has always kept me on tract when I'm just about to derail. Thank you to Mark Mills, Jim Saul, and Blaise Weller for being the perfect sounding board throughout the entire development of this piece. The world needs your work, brothers, whether it's ready for it or not.

To all my family and friends for tolerating the psychosis that fueled, and was caused by, the writing of this novel. I guess it paid off.

To Mom, Dad, and Matt for being there when things fall apart.

To Kurt Brueggemann and Aaron and Brian Tyree for supporting me on stage and off. Hope y'all aren't busy, we've got minds to blow. Thanks also to Kurt for the photo.

To the whole Performance Gallery crew. You're all brilliant.

To everybody who has ever seen me perform. Outraged walk-outs and all. Thank you especially to the angry policemen who opted to not get violent (yet). That ol' First Amendment's a bitch, ain't it.

And of course, all the thanks in the world to Julie, my light in the fog. I love you.

See you all on the road.